Author, artist, and filmmaker, Aaron Dries was born and raised in New South Wales, Australia. His novels include the award-winning *House of Sighs*, *The Fallen Boys*, *A Place for Sinners*, *Where the Dead Go to Die* (with Mark Allan Gunnells), and the novellas *The Sound of his Bones Breaking*, *And the Night Growled Back*, and the highly acclaimed *Dirty Heads*. *Cut to Care*, released in 2022, is his first collection of short stories. Aaron Dries is one host of the popular podcast, *Let the Cat In*, also co-founded *Elsewhere Productions*, and is a member of both the Australasian Horror Writers Association and the Horror Writers Association. His fiction, art, and films have been celebrated domestically and abroad.

Aaron Dries currently lives in Canberra. He is busy working on his next novel and a number of screenplays. Feel free to drop him a line at: aarondries.com, Twitter @aarondries_writer or, on Instagram at aarondries.

CUT TO CARE

A Collection of Little Hurts

By Aaron Dries

Cut to Care: A Collection of Little Hurts

All Rights Reserved

ISBN-13: 978-1-922556-80-6

Copyright ©2022 Aaron Dries

V1.0

Stories first publishing history at the end of this book.

Printed in Palatino Linotype and Signo.

IFWG Publishing International
Gold Coast

www.ifwgpublishing.com

Dedication

In memory of Everett De Roche and Dallas Mayr.

Acknowledgements

I'd like to take a moment to thank the following people for their support.

Alpha Cheng. My co-hosts and friends on the *Let the Cat in Podcast*, Kaaron Warren and J Ashley-Smith. Adam Cesare, Matt Serafini, Scott Cole, and Patrick Lacey—AKA The Black T-Shirt boys. John Boden. Cat Sparks. Robert Hood. Alan Baxter. Silvia Cantón Rondoni, who was instrumental in helping this collection see the light of day. Paul Mannering. My editor, Maria Kelly, and proofreader Stephen McCracken. Gerry Huntman at IFWG (your faith means the world). Don Noble, the artist behind the striking cover. The wonderful guys at *Elsewhere Here Productions*, Joshua Koske and Shane Walsh-Smith. Tony D'Aquino. Lee Gambin. Jamie Blanks. Jonathan Lees. Brennan Klein. Bee McKenzie. Ryan Larson. David Demchuk. Damien Angelica Walters. My family, Anne, Warwick, Brent, and Kyle. And heartfelt thanks to filmmaker/writer/friend, Mick Garris. FUZZBUCKET forever.

"Here is where all the lies end and everything else begins."

-     DAMIEN ANGELICA WALTERS, S is for Soliloquy

Table of Contents

Horror Hurts:
An Introduction By Mick Garris

Because I work almost exclusively in the horror genre, the question I get asked most by interviewers is, "What scares you?"

Well, latex monsters and CGI aliens don't scare me, nor do ghosts or vampires or possessed children. Even the more earthbound serial killers and their bloodthirsty kin don't keep me awake or invade my dreams. They are great times at the movies, but you don't really carry the fear home with you from the cinema after the credits roll.

For me, horror is a deeper and more personal thing than that. Perhaps it is because I have experienced the loss of so many friends and family members. The agony of withering disease, the sudden loss and deteriorating health of those close to me. I have played tag with death and loss. And it isn't much fun.

It doesn't make for the most entertaining interview answer, but what scares me is the delicate balance between life and death for those I care for most. Not for my own life, necessarily, as I don't fear death so much as I do the pain and suffering attendant to it.

The horror that sticks with me is personal, deeply rooted, when an author or a filmmaker touches a place that feels like my own heart. I love a good old blood feast as much as the next gorehound, but those aren't the ones that are going to haunt me. The ones that make me *feel*, that touch a nerve inside me, that remind me of losses I have or might suffer; to me, *that* is fear. That is the essence of horror.

I'll be openly confessional here.

My first professional directing job was a little TV movie that I wrote and directed for Disney called FUZZBUCKET. It's about a child who has an imaginary friend who turns out to not be a figment of his imagination, but rather a creature who is invisible to others. After being away on his adventure for a couple days, he is reunited in what was intended to be an emotional reunion. When my wife, Cynthia, saw it in the first screening, she asked me why nobody was hugging and sobbing when they are brought together again, and my mouth went agape. She was so right. Of course, it would be so heavy with relief and joy and love that you wouldn't be able to pry them apart.

Well, my family wasn't like that. We weren't huggy and loving toward one another, despite the fact that we did love one another. It's just that it wasn't expressed so physically. The FUZZBUCKET experience has never left me to this day. It wasn't just a little TV movie that gave me working knowledge about how to construct a film but served to be a life lesson as well.

From my youth and inexperience as a director, the passage of time has led to a deepening of practical and emotional experience, and has opened the door to deeper, more resonant fears. And now, a subgenre I like to call Emo Horror, is where I most often find myself working and playing.

Horror that hurts is horror that stays with you. It can have a sense of humour, it can be playful, but it needs to hit you in the heart. Richard Matheson's STIR OF ECHOES does it, as do Stephen King's THE SHINING and Clive Barker's SACRA-MENT. They tell of ghosts and terrors familiar to readers of horror fiction, but they are personal, painful, experiential.

Aaron Dries has written novels that delve into that Emo Horror world, perhaps most notably with HOUSE OF SIGHS and THE FALLEN BOYS. And this collection is specifically devoted to terrors that live in the heart and fill the soul.

This volume is filled with feeling and personal dread and pain and loss, the true horrors of real lives lived. They are effective because we, too, have felt the pain and loss that Aaron's characters have, or at least as he relates them to us in ways that feel so genuine to us that they must surely be real.

Consider these: a caregiver who takes on the persona of dead loved ones, so their survivors might cope with their deaths better; the nursing home of the future where our need to assuage guilt-abandonment comes with a hellish cost; a woman who chooses to experience the grief of suffering others, to dire consequences; and characters who discover the depth of responsibility when you save a life. All this, and more.

Yes, they are characters, but they are identifiably human, much more than ink on a page. The stories—be they psychological or supernatural, weird or terribly sad—are all poetic and beautiful. And so fucking operatically sanguinary.

Aaron works from the inside out and has great skill at making us feel and share the horrors of others. It makes these tales resonate with the frisson of touching death.

Because he knows that horror hurts.

Damage, Inc.

1

I'm not her mother, yet I'm paid to love her like a mother.

She leans into me, touching my back. I can't remember the last time a client held me this way and I felt something. They've whittled me down one by one, and sometimes I worry about what will be left behind, the residue of who I used to be.

I'm thirty-four in August, too young to be this numb.

"We're sorry about what we did," Monique says, sniffling. "Jenny loved me, is all. I can't help being this way, you know. I—*we* couldn't help it."

My fingers run through this young woman's hair, combing it, parting it, toying with it the way my mother used to when I was a kid. Details seal the deal. I can't be soft with my clients, let alone fake. They sniff inauthenticity at fifty yards. Be concrete. Let them beat their grief against me, a literal wailing wall. Nobody said this job was easy.

I invite the numbness. It used to be a self-defence mechanism, but the scales tipped long ago. That might be why, during sessions such as this, thoughts drift to Mum.

Don't go there, Kaylee. You're on the clock.

Easier said than done.

(Memories of her busted face and the dirty spoons and the belt about her upper arm and the bitter stink of our old flat.)

All it would take is a single spark for my anger to ignite. So, I push the past back as far as it'll go. If I can't control it, I can't be trusted to run my fingers through Monique's hair without flinching, raking gouges along her scalp.

I pitch my voice down a notch to sound older. The brief said Monique's mother was in her forties when she died. "Do you want to tell me anything else, sweetheart?" I ask.

"Jesus, god. I don't know if I can. It's hard for me, Mum."

"Shhh. It's alright. This is tough on you."

"I want to tell you everything. But—"

"I know. Gosh, I hate seeing you struggle like this, Mon'."

Mon'. The abbreviation is a risk, one that has backfired in the past, resulting in ruptures that needed instantaneous repair. But Mon' melts, evidence that gambles can pay off if you're ballsy enough to roll the dice. Sometimes. We sigh together. Hers is a sigh of comfort. Mine rings with relief.

"Oh, Mum," she says. "Jenny and I. We. We—"

"Sweetie, it *sounds* like you've had such a hard time keeping all this in."

Monique nods. My job isn't to cure or erase what's happened. My job is to let her be heard. "It must've been hard," I say again.

Her perfume is cloying, sad, and reminds me of the lavender I harvested a few years ago when I was between jobs and had nothing to do. The plant grew rampant on the Yarralumla property, which I still rent, a shitty house wedged between McMansions in Canberra's most expensive suburb. You would find me hunched on a stool with scissors, cutting back the flowers, a wide-brimmed hat pooling shadows over my knees. Petals stripped from their stems, filtering dust and dead baby spiders through a sieve. Bundled the lavender in muslin sacks tied with twine. Deposited them around a house I worried I'd have to surrender should employment evade me much longer. Little did I know a life-changing job lurked around the corner. This job.

Go home, Kaylee, shrieks this memory. *Do something for yourself. Get the scissors out again. If you keep working this hard without rest, you'll burn out. And burning out puts you at the risk of hurting yourself. Or someone else.*

"You fought to keep it together," I say to my client.

"Uh-huh."

"I can't imagine how difficult that must've been, Mon'."

We sit in a knot of limbs, surrounded by tissues. My eyes wander as we wait for the right moment to untangle ourselves. Monique's apartment overlooks Garema Place where the trees are dead, where public servants power-walk from meeting to meeting. Floor-to-ceiling windows separate the cold from the artificial warmth making me sweat.

No shadows. Light and dark merge as one.

The apartment must have been bought with Monique's inheritance. I don't begrudge her this, even if denying my jealousy is harder than I'd like it to be. After all, what did my mother leave me? Hurdles, that's what. And a breed of empathy that makes me perfect for a job like this, but if not reigned in, not monitored, just might destroy me. How lovely.

Photographs on the walls. A television. Ladles hang from the kitchen backboard. None of this fits with the young woman—a girl, really—in my arms. Then I notice breadcrumbs on the counter, a knife smeared with Vegemite, and see a child in want of a mother who would never breathe again, regardless of my efforts today.

"Mon', I knew about the two of you," I say. "I knew and couldn't say. And I regret not speaking up. I guess I was afraid."

"Afraid of what?"

"That you'd run. I figured you'd come to me when you were ready. It's okay to not be ready, no matter what anyone else says."

"You knew?" she says.

"A'course I did, sweetie." I rock her. "I'm a mum. Mothers know everything."

Monique laughs, as they often do in the end. She sits up to touch my cheek, smiling the kind of smile that makes all this worth it. The magic fades though, a spell un-weaving now that this stranger has obtained what she requires from me, what she's paid for.

Monique fingers my wig.

Suds pool between my toes as I scrub the client out of my hair. This routine is an essential part of my work wind-down. Soap. Jasmine. Herbal oils. Evening sprawls on the other side, indefinite and often purposeless.

Wind makes branches scratch at the bathroom window. Once I've blow-dried my hair, the ends frayed and split from over-caring, I climb into pyjamas and exhale until I'm empty. The shell of me flicks on *Family Feud*, whips up a stir-fry, pours a glass of wine I know won't just be a glass. Then, cued up and predictable, comes the anxiety.

The weekend is still one day away.

Just because you love your job doesn't mean you don't dread it.

Pranav texts to see if I've got anything on tonight. That last word, *tonight*, punctuated by a question mark like one of his curly pubic hairs, locks in his intent. He's a nice guy, and were I in a better place, I might let this be more than it is. My fingers dance across the screen. The delightful BING of my reply is thrilling — and thrills are rare these days.

Maybe one more glass won't hurt.

The bed isn't made. Dirty washing in the basket in the corner of the room. I can't muster enough fucks to worry. Not that my lack of self-consciousness is without limits. I tug off my pyjama bottoms to change undies.

A lavender bundle sits in the lingerie drawer. I pick it up, the bag crunching, no scent unleashed. This, more than anything else today — hell, the whole week — I *do* care about. It signifies something I'd rather not admit: like that smell, the woman who harvested these flowers isn't here anymore.

We kiss too hard, teeth touching. Pranav has accountant's hands, soft though precise, punching my buttons as he does numbers. I like predictability, the anchor of his charms.

He tries to roll me so he's on top, but I fight him, pushing back, our thin bodies slick. Reflections in the window like swishes of neon calligraphy on a dark board. My bedroom overlooks Lake

Burly Griffin. No moon.

"Will you put one on for me?" he asks, coy.

Panting, I tilt my head. "What?"

"You know." Pranav nods to my wardrobe, that glimmer in his eyes. He wiggles, brown hips pushing me this way and that. I'm not sure I want this. Yet I'm pulling him out of me, wiping my hands on his legs, swishing across the room. Lamplight touches the wardrobe's interior, the place I locked myself in last year before admitting myself to the psych' ward at Canberra Hospital. I was there for three days so I didn't have to feel. Now, I don't feel enough. I know my wigs by touch and draw out today's bob. It's silver, as the brief said it should be.

"Who are you?" Pranav asks as I fit the net over my brow. It sits right, a dull thud in my chest where my racing heartbeat had been.

I go to him, bending to lick his nose, inhaling his scent as I lower myself onto his long but slender cock. "I'm Monique's mother." Despite myself, nerves riot. The moan is genuine.

Pranav, the Tinder fuck-buddy I never wanted to leave, offers a thrust I move with, not giving him what he wants. Not yet.

"Tell me, Monique's mother," he says. "Tell me everything."

"I died three years ago."

Pranav leaves at two in the morning, as he always does. I see him off, as I always do, watching him run to his Prius at the end of the driveway, arms wrapped about himself to keep the winter cold away. Rain spits. Trees clatter, bone-like in the dark. Headlights swirl the shadows we share, and they reach out for me. I lock up. Check the windows. Check them twice. Sweat-stained sheets call, but I need to wash my hair again. I didn't cum.

2

"**G**ot a curly one for you, Kaylee."

Sakura towers over me, profile in hand, the epitome of Friday. The week has scrubbed her down, as it has me. Monday Sakura is a sculpture.

"Gulp," I say.

My boss hands it over, bangles clattering.

The manila folder is beige, as though this were any other old thing in any other old workplace. I cradle it, leaning back in my chair. In another life, I'm stronger than I think I am and tell my boss of three years I'm not up to this, that maybe George should outsource it or reallocate the job to Cynthia. I guess I'm a lot of things in that alternate reality, but none of those things define me here. George might as well be a million miles away, not across the demountable picking his nose. I open the folder, revealing faces I'd rather not see yet am paid to see.

Sakura leans against a bookshelf of psychology volumes. "Take the day to digest it," she says, rubbing her neck. "The service isn't until next Friday."

"If it's a biggie, can we make it earlier in the week? Not Monday, of course. Maybe Wednesday or something?"

"I tried to negotiate but the couple—they're married, a twosome here—are busy. Also, they're a bit nervy. Understandable. The extra couple of days'll give you the legroom to prepare. Knock off early on Thursday, give yourself a bit of respite. On the Wednesday, book yourself in with Lynn."

"Lynn?"

"She's taken over from David at Clinical Psychology. Go see her, charge everything to our account. I think it'll do you good to clear your head so you're fighting-fit for Friday."

"Will do."

"If you need anything, let me know."

"How about a drink?" I say.

"Seven hours to go and then freedom, Kaylee. Fridays, huh?"

"Fridays, indeed."

Sakura leaves, the closing door shaking the demountable walls. One of these days a storm is going to blow through Canberra and whisk this building off to Oz. There had been talks of the Grief Exploration and Recovery Team—ridiculously referred to as GERT—relocating into the main building. That won't happen, not with funding as fickle as it is. Maybe next year, if we're lucky and Sakura works wonders with our numbers. She's good to us, and that goodness keeps me here.

George comes over, brandishing a coffee mug with the words I LOVE MY DADDY on the side. It's so cute it's maddening.

"What's on the slab, Ms K?"

"Not sure yet. I'm to brace myself for a curly one, by all accounts."

"Yikes. What's your caseload like? Want me to talk to Sakura about taking one for the team? Cynthia's back next week. I don't mind."

"It'll be fine." I drop the file on my desk next to my notes, the training package for next Monday and the book I've been trying—and failing—to read on my breaks. "How's Michelle and the kids?"

"Kicking on. Michelle got a promotion, which is a relief."

"Way to go, lovely lady." We high-five. George is a good guy, albeit a bludge. That happens when you're in this industry too long. You shuffle workloads to spend time staring at your computer bidding on eBay shit you don't need instead of going into the community to pretend being someone's dead or eloped loved one so they can stumble across relief

"We'll have to have you over for dinner again soon, Kaylee."

We nod at each other. I take my folder into the day.

Canberra winters threaten snow but rarely deliver, the days constipated with cold they want to shit out. Leaves crunch as I take my work along the street, cutting through a park by the closed swimming pool to a café where the staff know me by name and give me what I need without asking. I don't wear a name-badge or lanyard like government workers in the neighbourhood. It's important I keep my identity under wraps. Canberra is a small city, and it's not uncommon to cross paths with former clients. The last thing I want is for one of them to find out who I am and add me on Facebook.

The café is crowded. My favourite barista hands me a long black. Warm air, almost wet. Fogged windows with kids drawing faces in the condensation, eyes that drip and smiles that bleed the outside world in. I take a seat and slurp, opening Sakura's folder. Parents with prams glide by, workers in need of a Friday fix. Some stay, some go.

I look like one of them but I'm not of them. Not with the story of Richard and Bernadette Braintree in front of me.

And the photograph of their dead daughter.

Coffee finished, I head for the office again and try to push the dead woman from my mind. Plumes burst from my mouth as I walk, scrolling my phone for distraction. A notification beeps across the screen I cracked a month ago.

The email is draining.

I told her not to contact me again—and to her credit, she held out two years. But I can't budge, even though I hate myself for setting the ultimatum in the first place. Mum wants to meet. Her correspondence overspills with apologies. We've done this dance before, and I'm so fucking tired.

The face from the manila folder blooms out of the sky like unfolding origami. As I knew it would. As it was always going to.

Emma.

She was thirty-seven when she died, twelve years ago. The daughter of a rich government official and his partner, a former nurse turned trophy wife. Emma's resemblance to me doesn't go unnoticed, and I wonder if that's why Sakura shot the file my way in the first place. Similar looks make the job easier. You don't have to work so hard to embody the character, easily drawn dots for the desperate to draw conclusions between.

Come next Friday, I'll be Emma's ghost.

Damn it. This is Mum's fault. I bet she needs money for—

A bluebird lies on the ground by the demountable steps, flapping its one functional wing. "Poor, darlin'." I scoop it up, the cheep-cheeps Disney-delightful, though I know these sounds are its agony. How awful that they appear the same. The bluebird dies in my hands.

3

Today's the day.

From the bathroom window, I see leafless trees like Franken-stein's Monster stiches on a wound separating wet sky from wet ground. The concept of going out there is awful. Bed, blankets, and that book I've been trying to crack are more attractive offers.

I adjust the wig, which is a similar shade to my own hair and only a few inches longer. Purple shirt, jeans with thermals underneath. Purple was Emma Braintree's favourite colour. A heavy coat on top. Buttons slip through slit eyes, cool to the touch. My lipstick is conservative, natural. I've painted my nails a glittery purple, too. Smells funny. I don't often wear nail polish.

An emergency call pager—flat as a Fit-Bit—is strapped to my inner thigh. It doesn't bulge through my jeans. Good. The mobile phone is charged, outgoing calls set to private. One of our white work sedans waits for me outside, the kind of nondescript car you wouldn't think of looking at twice, and that's the point. Discretion. Workers aren't allowed to use their own vehicles to get to and from consultations, either—not because Sakura won't reimburse the mileage, but to avoid chances of clients taking down our number plates.

There are gatekeepers to pass through on the way to the GERT team, starting with a referral from an in-territory psychologist or psychiatrist, followed by an Australian Federal Police vetting. And while our intake officers do a property audit prior to service, there's always the chance things might go wrong. Inefficient as the pager is, as wavering as my phone reception can be in Canberra, these little things offer security. And I *need* to feel secure if I'm going to do my job well. Vulnerable people act irrationally— human nature 101—and nothing churns already troubled waters like having the dead stride into the homes they once resided.

My house groans in the wind. The radio is off. Just the rain. It's warm in here, soothing, a womb I don't want to be dragged out of. Yet I go, holding my coat in place as I run, the Braintrees' file in an over-the-shoulder bag. Doc Martens splash puddles and I slide into the car. The air is barbed enough to slit a throat.

With its wide yard observable through a secured fence, the regal three-storey house doesn't so much sit on the land-scape as wound it. The Braintrees don't want for space.

Hedges chatter as though they, too, are cold. Not wearing gloves had been a deliberate move. My nails are still tacky to the touch.

"Come on in," comes a man's voice through the intercom.

The gate clicks free, revealing a hundred-yard stretch to the front door. I steel myself, kick the gate shut behind me, and knuckle into a trot. My shitty nine buck umbrella inverts and any chances of scoring a leading role in the Canberran leg of Mary Poppins are gone with the wind. In some other life, a life where I'm snug in bed with Pranav, I laugh at this. That life, however, isn't this one. Here, I push through sleet.

Mr Braintree meets me halfway with his own umbrella. It fwhoomps above me like hawk wings, bringing with it a rush of his heat. We beeline for the building, and within, I apologise for treading mud on the floorboards.

"Oh, that's fine."

He closes the door, blocking out one sound to grant entry to another, the thrum of water against wood, a nice country noise. Mr Braintree folds up his umbrella and deposits it in a holster by a side table, a far cry from what I'll be doing when I get home. Straight into the bathtub, it'll go.

He slips free of his loafers and steps into the light barefoot, hand first. Our palms dance, and it begins. His smile is an armour. Here is someone who has had to protect himself from individuals like me, people who read others like prose, whose job it is to look behind the smile to seek out the abscessed teeth beneath.

I don't begrudge Richard Braintree his aloofness.

Filling this silence would be the easiest thing to do. I hold off. I need him to make the first move. The tall man's blue eyes flitter from charmed to confused to scared, settling on some distant cousin of humbled. He remembers to smile. "Right through here."

Mr Braintree gestures towards a better-lit kitchen—better lit, yet cooler. I've taken off my Doc Martens, which he's noticed—a glance that might as well be the freezing of lungs. His daughter wore those same shoes. Back then. When she was alive.

We move on, purple socks wisping over floorboards as I enter the adjoining room.

Mrs Braintree perches on a stool by the kitchen bench, feline, gorgeous. She's in her late fifties, hair coifed with braids, dressed in earthy greens and browns. She tenses as I approach, window light making the peach fuzz on her cheek glow.

I offer my hand. At first, Mrs Braintree doesn't take it.

"Hi, Mum," I say.

She tilts her head, crow's feet wrinkles threading her face, furrowing her brow. I ache for her but can't show it.

In my mind, a wall pieces together brick by brick. Without it, I'm weak. When I'm weak, it's the Mr and Mrs Braintrees who suffer. I don't want that. That's not what I'm in this game for.

I feel Mr Braintree beside me, the soles of his feet pat-pat-patting about. I remain zoned in on his wife. She nods, and I breathe a sigh of relief. We shake fingers, not palms.

There we go, darlin'. We got there.

"Cup of tea?" asks Mrs Braintree.

In my current role, I accept what I'm offered even if I don't want it, even if it constitutes as a gift. It curbs their anxieties, allowing the owners of these homes to exert dominance within the room. Trust follows suit. So, yes, take the tea or coffee even though many of their houses are in a terrible state, mugs chipped and gummy with old sugar, even though the entire time I'm wondering if I'm going to glimpse not-quite-dissolved Rat Sack at the bottom of the drink.

I often think I should be paid more.

"Please. Black, no sugar."

Mrs Braintree gestures to her husband who goes for the kettle. The appliances are as antiquated as the house. I smell fresh bread. Emma Braintree would find it easy to be loved in a place such as this.

So, why did she suicide?

My muscles clench when Mrs Braintree stands to stride into the living room by the unlit fireplace, scissor legs snipping, gesturing to the leather couch. I slip off my jacket and drape it over the stool she left unoccupied, revealing my purple top.

Cushions exhale sad air as I ease my weight against them.

"There," she says. "That's better."

The old woman sits beside me, tilted so her knee flirts with mine. I don't back away. Her glare is intelligent, though my presence strips her of the qualifications and experience notarised in certificates adorning the walls. Photographs of Emma hang here, too.

We study them together, smiling.

Emma as a child with sparklers in hand, ice cream coating her chin and cheeks. Emma and an awkward boy standing by the stairs in the Braintrees' corridor, her wrist blooming a cheap corsage. Emma throwing a graduation hat in the air.

"Gosh, I miss this place." My words are calm, deliberate.

She whips her head at me.

Yes, I want to tell her, but don't. *We're doing this. And it's okay, darlin'. It's okay.*

Mrs Braintree's face is narrow and peaked, as though from her earthy nature a plant has grown to seek out the sun. But never finding it. Her yearning is everything.

Richard offers me tea in a china cup, served on a saucer. He sits on my left so I'm piggie-in-the-middle. We're mostly still. I sip. English Breakfast, maybe. Hints of vanilla. After trudging through the weather outside, it's warming.

"Thank you so much."

They watch me drink. I know they've seen the nail polish. I take one more gulp and place the cup and saucer on the table in front of us beside copies of House & Garden.

Tock-tock-tock goes a grandfather clock in the corner of the room.

I turn to Mrs Braintree and a silent, electric thing compasses between us. It shifts something in her. Her sigh waivers. She offers a nod.

"Mum—" I say.

"Sh-hhh."

I do as I'm told. Mrs Braintree lifts a shivering hand to my face and touches my wig. "Do you mind?" she asks. A thud of vulnerability detonates inside me as she lifts the damp wig. Cool air tickles my scalp, toes curling within my socks. The wig sits lifeless in the old woman's hand. "Oh, Richard. It's—"

"I know, Bern. Sweet Jesus."

They embrace me from either side. Mr Braintree's guffaws are brutish, a man who has been trying to keep it all in for far too long, given here, in the hush of his own home, the privilege of revealing those hurts. Mrs Braintree, Bern', Bernadette, wife of Richard Braintree and mother of dead Emma Braintree, weeps in a refined way. I hug these two people back, acknowledging the agony that defines orphaned parents even though they don't want it to, and rarely admit.

The wig slops to the floor.

"I'm sorry for what I did," I tell them. "You both didn't deserve it."

They cry harder. I can't let myself feel guilty.

"I struggled. I should have left a note, at least."

"It's okay, baby," Richard tells his daughter. "Do you forgive us, too?"

"Of course, I have, Dad. You, too, Mum."

My voice snaps. It's a crack in the wall I've erected. The fissure stems from the love these people have in their hearts for the woman who slit her wrists upstairs. There must have been so much blood. The psychologist's referral said Bern found the body.

Something writhes on the other side of the wall, bricks crumbling.

Grubby fingers emerge.

Not now. Please, not now.

"We're sorry for everything we did," Bern says, grip fierce. "We wish it had been different."

The room rolls white. Lightning strobes the sky.

We three turn our heads to the windows, breaths held, waiting for thunder. Water beads the glass, snaking shadows across the room.

One Mississippi. Bricks shift again. Two Mississippis. A face pushes through, breathing dust. Three Mississippis. It's my mother on the other side of that wall.

Thunder makes us flinch as one.

It crosses my mind that I should wait until the storm passes, but now that the job is done and brief fulfilled, I want out of the Braintrees' house as soon as possible. They stand at my back as I slip into my Doc's, trying not to fall in the process, holding the wig with one hand and jimmying on a shoe with the other.

My exhaustion is fever thick. I'm flushed, too, a flurry of embarrassment—partially for me, mostly for them. I've been on their street, in their house, in their heads. There is no naked that compares to that, more naked than the day they were born. We don't come into this world grieving. That, we accrue with age.

Leaving is best, even though it's cold and wet and I might be struck down by lightning. The married couple have sucked me dry. Again, I don't blame them. Pain makes vampires of us all.

"Sure you don't want to stay for a while?" Bern Braintree asks me.

Laces tied, I stand. "You're both very kind but I should go."

"Quite right," Richard says. "Take my umbrella."

"Oh, I couldn't."

"Please, I've got many. Keep it."

"That's lovely of you, but—"

"Let her go, Richard."

"She'll get the pneumonia."

Bern knits her hands. She's slender, half her face illuminated by the kitchen light, the other devoured by shadow. "It's fine." Her voice is clipped. I'm worried about her. Leaving the number for the counselling hotline isn't just a formality but an essential part of my consult.

"Thank you," I say as Richard opens the door. Winter reaches with clammy hands and I let it take me. No looking back now.

I switch off my emergency pager and message Sakura in the car. **All done. Homeward bound. Feeling sick.**

Wind shakes the car as I drive. Canberra, the city I volley between loving and hating, rolls by. I turn onto my street and skirt into the driveway. Tears come before I have a chance to get inside. A call to Lynn, my clinical psychologist, sounds like a good idea.

Not yet, though. Shower first.

4

The state might own the townhouse, but Mum has marked it as her territory. I can tell this from where I stand by my car, handbag under one arm. Leaves fly along the Ainslie backstreet, twirling over a bike by her front door, onto ceramic gnomes.

A watery day. The sun, elusive.

I go to the mailbox and wrestle free bills and envelopes marked with Housing A.C.T.'s insignia. The rain can have the rest.

Richard Braintree's umbrella is in the backseat of my car.

The bell doesn't work. I knock hard, hoping she won't answer. Moments stagger by. My heart leaps when my mother's door opens, sour air escaping.

We sit at the table.

Everything reeks of cigarettes. The ceiling is dead fingernail-yellow with grease and nicotine, a gravy that come eviction time (because eviction is never far when it comes to Mum), will be an absolute bitch to scrape off. The table is clear, though. She knew I was coming and wiped it down. Our stalemate continues, an island of two surrounded by crates of computer parts, towers of paperbacks she'll never read. And shoes. Innumerable shoes, some hers and some—no doubt—stolen from verandas throughout the neighbourhood.

Behind her, a bench separates the dining quarter from the kitchen where dishes squirm with bugs. The bench homes cat figurines and ceramic pigs, McDonald's Happy Meal toys from God only knows how long ago. They all, too, are yellow.

She's hunched in her chair, wearing a tattered beanie. The coat is enormous on her frame. Two terriers curl on her lap, ratty and dewy-eyed. They're less dogs than bundles of fur on chopstick legs that Mum puts in the basket of her bike to whisk around town as she hunts for her next score. Everyone in the community sector knows Valerie and her munchkins, Sid and Nancy. Times like these, I'm glad I'm not a social worker per-se. Women like Valerie Desmond end up my clients. And those twains just can't meet.

"Talk to me Mum."

Sid — or maybe it's Nancy — issues a bark.

"Enough," she tells the dog. Her expression shovels my resolve aside to prod at the sympathy beneath. Pretending to hate her is difficult.

Once upon a time, my mother was Queen Mary riding rough seas but keeping afloat. Now she's driftwood. Bonfire materials for kids to set alight on a beach and dance around. Good for them.

"Is it money you need? What are you going to use it on this time? Who do you need to pay back? You've got to stop with all this, Mum."

She stares, and the dogs stare. Even their blinks are syncopated.

"Thought about rehab?"

"People likes me cants afford no rehab."

"It'll come out of your disability pension."

"What'll I eats?"

"They feed you there, Mum."

"And whats about Sid and Nancy? Who'll look after them. Yous?"

Whatever retort I'd had handy is lamed. The dogs shiver, and I despise myself for feeling more affection towards them because they're cute than for the woman who birthed me. I can't believe this is our lives. Sid and Nancy lick their lips. Hopeful.

"I'd look after them while you were in," I say. "It doesn't matter how long it takes."

"I'm not goings to no rehabs."

"Then why am I here? I asked you not to reach out. Do you know how hard it was for me to put my foot down? I can't do this. It's not good for either of us. I can't depend on you, and you shouldn't be dependent on me. It's — oh, never mind."

"You cuts your hair."

"What?"

"And you've lost weights. Don't get too skinny. I don't want you to look likes me."

There are memories I have of us and Dad being happy, memories like Polaroids in a tip going to rot, rotting like my father, the husband that left her after her fifth overdose, buried in the Phillip cemetery. I haven't been to his grave in two years, and the shame I feel about that, here in this squalored room, makes a tiny thing of me. Small enough to fit into one of the shoes piled around the place.

"I'm in troubles Kaylee."

I can see us in our old home in Downer. Dad with a beer and his leg draped over the arm of the chair he sat in after work. The man was a wizard with anything computer-based, skills that skipped his daughter and hadn't rubbed off on his wife. All these years later, Mum has gathered bric-a-brac to piece together a monolith of wires and keyboards and broken mice to honour him. Him. *Dad*. The guy who accepted Valerie Desmond in ways I can't.

A golem of trash.

For the briefest second, Bern and Richard Braintree are in front of me. They loved their child and ache in her absence. They even paid to hold the echo of her for an hour on a stormy day. My mother loves heroin and ice more than me. That's a tough pill to swallow or inject. God only knows how many syringes are tucked away in the crannies of this townhouse.

The Braintrees fade. I wish I was loved as their dead daughter was loved. When I look at Mum, I don't see someone who wants to hug me. I see someone who would knock the fillings out of my teeth to hock for a gram of scrag if given the chance.

We've been down this road before. We parted ways after she was caught selling her methadone on Northbourne Avenue. Mum had been taking her allotted dose in paper cups, which she'd then tip onto her tongue and sell to buyers outside the pharmacy by spitting into their mouths. I almost convinced her into going into rehab after that, but my wrangling didn't stick. Whatever promises were made that day had been broken by now.

I told myself I'd never give her another cent. Yet here I am, opening my handbag, Sid and Nancy perking up, and drawing out an envelope containing twenty one-hundred dollar notes. As I get up to leave, I notice a photograph of me from my graduation on the wall. Nicotine sludge obscures my smile.

I stamp out a quick text to Pranav at the traffic lights leading to the city.

You busy tonight?

Tonight. I need him to know what I mean.

The lights change from red to green and I snag a parking spot—the Sunday crowd thinner than any other day of the week. Hunger has me with its hooks.

I cross Garema Place, head tilted against the wind, bee lining for the Vietnamese restaurant on the corner. A passer-by clips my shoulder by the sculptures that look like they've burst up through the ground and bronzed in place. The shock of the collision yanks a yelp from my mouth, and I spin to offer a quick apology.

The girl keeps going. She doesn't recognise me, but I recognise her.

Monique.

Mon'.

She runs in the direction of her apartment above the shops, an apartment I know intimately, and then I'm the only person in the square. The cold has driven everyone else away. A plastic bag catches on one of the statues, flapping like skin on a wound that will never heal.

There's nobody around to confirm I exist at all.

Pranav comes over later, having taken the bait. We don't drink as much wine as I want to. When he asks me to wear one of the wigs, I whisper 'no' and ask him to make love to *me* for the first time in months. I don't need a man to have rough hands to turn me on, but that night, I want to be fucked as if he has rough hands. I invite this in too-hard kisses that leave his face shiny, in the way my body presses against his, like I'm trying to penetrate him, get under his skin, all in the hopes of piecing me back together.

5

Our work demountable backs onto a park where children never play.

George is there when I slip outside to go to my café for an afternoon fix. He sits on the swing, coffee mug in hand, surrounded by trees and empty beer bottles. No drunks yet. George looks like shit. His eyes are red, face white and small under two jackets.

The path leads straight to him.

"You okay, buddy?" I ask, teeth chattering. "You'll catch your death."

George glances away, lips trying to climb into his mouth. His knuckles are purple against the coffee mug. He nods to say yes but that nod says no.

I ease onto the swing next to him, rusty chains giving a cry the wind carries off. The leather harness is freezing. I'm not going to use counselling nudges on him. He'd see straight through them. Instead, I wait until he's ready, and when he is, everything spills out fast.

"Michelle's up and left me."

"Oh, George."

He toys with the mug that used to annoy me so he can read the inscription again. I LOVE MY DADDY. "The kids are a wreck. Hell, I'm a wreck."

"When did this happen?"

"About a week ago," he says.

"Shit."

"It's fucked up. I fucked up. Jesus."

"Have you spoken to anyone about it?"

"Not yet. I—I was thinkin' of calling my best mate in Brisbane tonight."

"When's the last time you two spoke?"

"Six months ago," he says, stopping to cough and clear his throat. I offer him a tissue from my handbag. "Canberra's like that, though. You get here, pull up stumps, and try to keep in touch with everyone you've left behind. It's tough. We're in the middle of nowhere."

"I'm sure your mate—what's his name?"

"Bill."

"I'm sure Bill would love to hear from you. I'm sure he's sorry about not calling you, too. That's life for you, right? A two-way street."

George blows his nose. "Yeah." He sounds dog-tired. "I'm embarrassed. I didn't want Sakura to see."

"That's cool."

"Where're you off to? Getting a coffee?"

"Was the plan. Why don't you come with me? We don't need to talk about Michelle and the kids unless you want to. We don't need to talk at all. But let's go together. You can hold my arm as I walk. It'll keep us warm."

George fights the offer at first but relents. We stand, brushing off our coats, the swings giving another one of their metal-on-metal groans. The light brightens and dims again as clouds rush over the sun. We shuffle off together.

"Oh, your mug," I say, stopping. He's left it on the woodchips by the see-saw.

"Forget about it, Kaylee. I don't want it anymore. I just don't care."

He takes the lead, trees closing into a hollow. My heart twinges for him, for Michelle and the kids. Good people. The offer of dinner a month ago—a 'keeping up appearances' default perhaps. Twenty-year marriages rarely unravel over a four-week period, or so I guess. What do I know about marriage? Zilch.

A twist of guilt over my fickle annoyance of his coffee mug, and how I wished someone would give me one so those around me would know I was appreciated. Is that what I need from people? Maybe I should try looking in a mirror instead. Sometimes, I think I'm such hot shit when it comes to reading others. But you never know anyone. Humans are upright jigsaw puzzles showing off all the pretty things that don't matter. The pieces we omit make us who we are. The lies and the deceits and ugly jealousies and our need for validation.

We buy coffees on my coin and take our time wandering back to the demountable. George doesn't end up talking, and that's fine. I feel him tense on my arm as we approach the park, which now that it's almost dark has been reclaimed by the drunks. One of them uses George's abandoned mug for an ashtray. They offer 'G'days' as we pass them by.

Inside, George packs up and leaves early. I lock the door behind him and switch off most of the lights. It's been three weeks since I did the service for the Braintrees. Three weeks since Pranav answered my texts. I know I have every right to call, but I'm worried about what he'll say. It aches that I've let him think he's better than he is, that in our best moments I sort of loved the bastard. I'm worthy of a goodbye.

The demountable door leading to the rest of the building opens and Sakura walks in with another manila folder. "Oh, good," she says. "Caught you. Is George gone?"

"Yeah. Just then."

"He's been quiet. Everything okay?"

I don't know how to answer this, so I upturn my palms and shrug.

"Anyway," Sakura begins, "I've got something for you."

"Another curly one?"

"You tell me." My boss places the folder on my desk. The moment my fingers touch the cardboard, I know. An icky feeling nudges the back of my neck.

"Is this what I think it is, Sakura?"

"I've already told their psychiatrist this'll be the last referral we'll accept from them. He agreed. No dependencies, please."

"The Braintrees want me back?"

Sakura draws her finger into a trigger, shoots me. "You're going to have to stop doing your job so well, Kaylee. You're helping them. You must be."

The icky nudge turns into a hold, shaking me until my heart thrums. It's not the Braintrees that worry me. God, no. They are kind, broken people. It's the dreaded pre-and-post briefing with Lynn who knows what Sakura doesn't. That I'm close to buckling. That I'm close to being unfit to do my job.

Speak up, I tell myself. *Closed mouths don't get fed.*

"Is everything okay, Kaylee?"

My fingers curl around the manila folder and draw it to my chest. The file is nothing but paper and staples and a photograph or two, yet feels heavy as stone.

6

Friday afternoon is clear. Cars shine on the street. Breath plumes escape my mouth like ghosts, all the people I've been in my years with the team. Purple clothing beneath my coat. Doc Martens. I didn't paint my nails this time. That might have been a bit too much, a tad desperate. No wig. I know I'm more like Emma Braintree without one.

Now that my ankle pager is switched on and alert sent to Sakura, I march to the gate and announce myself. "Come on through, sweetheart," Bern says through the intercom, her voice crisp and more confident than last time.

Hinges squeak as I close the gate behind me.

The house, the whole Braintree estate, is different in fine weather. It has its own pulse, the rhythmic swish of windchimes and the trees. With its peaks and windows, it holds a witchy otherness that's quite charming. The air is without scent. I find that odd, a kind of hospital nothingness that winter leaves behind, a world stripped of pollen and nectar.

I'm walking toward the house, only my mind remains in the morning I've left in the cemetery at Phillip. The flowers on my father's grave were dried natives. They would last longer in the frost, I figured. Standing in the graveyard, sunlight carving the fog, I wondered where they buried Emma Braintree. Was she here with him? Did they share worms? There was a weird comfort in the thought. I don't cry at Dad's plot anymore. Those tears stopped coming when I ceased remembering what he sounded like. Memory is corrosive. There's survival in that, maybe. It helps us to let go.

Richard greets me at the door. "No need for an umbrella today, right?"

"True, that."

"Weather for the ducks last time."

"Wasn't it just?"

He steps aside to let me in. I take off my Doc's and sit them by the wall. "Come on through," he tells me. "Bern's in there."

I lead the way and round the corner, finding Mrs Braintree where she'd been last time, on the stool next to the kitchen bench. Things are smoother this time. The woman stands and shakes my hand with both fists, her skin like rice paper.

"It's so great you came back this one last time," she says. "Tea?"

"Sure."

"I'll fix it," Richard says, moving around the counter.

We exchange pleasantries but the whole time I'm wondering. A child without parents is an orphan. What is a parent who has lost their child? I search for the word and fail to unearth anything appropriate. The closest thing is, 'bereaved'. That fits—just. It seems unfair that there isn't an appointed expression for those in such a situation. I guess it speaks more to how we, as a culture, struggle to address those we've lost. We don't know what to say, and the bereaved don't appreciate that. They've suffered, and as a result, part of who they were vanishes, identities shattering. Worse, we can't quantify their *standing* with a title. This plucks a chord in me and sadness sings, a sadness I put behind the brick wall for fear of slipping out of character. I imagine the word I want to honour them with exists in other languages. They say Eskimos have fifty ways of saying snow. Surely, they could help me out. Assuming we westerners can stop clutching our pearls for five minutes to listen.

Death happens. Nobody gets out alive. We all share worms in the end.

"Cheers, Dad," I say to Richard as he hands over the tea. It's served in what appears to be the same cup and saucer. I sip a few times and tell him how lovely it is.

Bern takes my hand and her own tea, leads me to our place on the couch. I know she appreciates that I didn't wear the wig. Socks wisp over the rug. We sit.

"You're beautiful, Emma."

"Thanks, Mum."

I smile, riding crests and dips of emotion I don't have to dig far to find. She drinks her tea again, gestures I replicate. Doing this helps build rapport. Richard takes a seat by my side.

"Did you see your trophies over there?" he asks.

Caught off guard, I swallow a hot gulp. "Whereabouts? Oh, yeah."

"We brought them out from your room," Bern says. "I think they add something, don't you think?"

"Sure do." I put my cup and saucer on the coffee table and walk to the mantelpiece above the fireplace. No freshly baked bread today. I miss that homeliness. My eyes scan five trophies, all polished.

"Third Place Runner up in the Telstra Ballet Awards," I read, admiring a gold-painted figurine caught mid-pirouette on the heavy, wooden base. "Second Place at the Canberran Ballet Awards. Oh, I remember that. I was so nervous in the lead up to it. I wanted you to be happy with my performance."

"We were, sweetheart," Richard tells me. "You were gorgeous."

"What was the song again?" I ask, eyebrow raised, rolling the dice hard. "The one I danced to?"

The mother and father I'm being paid to be the dead daughter of look at me. They are scarecrows in a field, haggard things despite the tautness of their stitches, picked at and ignored. Black button eyes. My father speaks. "Tchaikovsky's The Sleeping Beauty."

"Richard," I hear my mother say. "Catch her quick."

My head strikes the coffee table and I register pain, but it's dull and cloudy. Oxygen escapes me, wheezes coming thick. Something wet on my face. Something warm. It drips into my mouth. At first, I think I'm crying. The taste is too metallic for tears.

7

It bleeds out of the dark. Slow. A rising sun. And like the sun, it brings the birds. They are cheeping. Warmth. This exhaustion is unlike anything I've experienced since I was a child with glandular fever—or at least I *think* it was glandular fever. Someone tended to me back then, palms against my forehead, bringing damp towels. I watched a lot of television. Its static is here with me now.

A swallowed-sand-itchiness fills my throat. Pain in every joint, its blade trying to pry my skeleton apart.

More than anything, the weight of fatigue is terrifying. I feel thick under its pressure. Dense. Maybe there's too much blood in me. Maybe I should be bled out.

The blur takes shape through a squint, wet and wavering. The room is foreign, too. I'm on a bed with no give to it, the pillow stinking of mothballs. When I tilt my head from the shape over me, I notice wallpaper. Criss-crossing vines over a purple weave.

"Tell me more about you," a man's voice says. He has a lisp. "Tell me efferythung."

God only knows if there's sense to my slurs, but words spill out just the same. His voice is officious, it's an anchor. I'm grateful he's with me. That gratitude might be why I let it all out, purging answers to every one of his questions.

Vines uncoil from the wallpaper and wrap around my limbs and throat. I'm bound to the bed. Jesus. It doesn't occur to me to scream. A moan is all I can manage. The vines tighten in response. "No—"

"Thank you," the man says, having obtained what he needs. The blur of him comes into focus, the sun risen, birds alive with song. Bluebirds. Two of them. They are nailed to his face where his eyes should be. Wings beat his cheeks—not that he's concerned at all.

One of the birds pries free and flutters onto the bed. It hops across a knitted quilt, the kind a grandmother would craft to fill her time. The little head with its little eyes twitch. I think it's studying me, weighing me up. My body tenses when the bird lashes out to bite the crook of my right arm. The beak pinches skin, breaking it.

"Th-ere, now," whispers the man, this stranger. "Thh-ere, thhh-ere."

Vines tighten as I thrash, but the heaviness increases. I'm drowning in cotton and grandmotherly wool. His face blurs again, the sun going down. Throughout, the bird bites and bites.

Its prick isn't what I thought it was. It's a needle. I've never been more alone.

8

"Thir-sty."

This, I say. Or, at least, I think I say.

Regardless, the word is solid, a rung on the ladder I'm using to drag myself out of sleep. This is why I repeat it. "Thirsty. Thirsty. Thirsty." My mantra wakes me up, arm over arm, higher and higher, rung after rung and each more solid than the last. "Thirsty. *Thirsty*."

The dreams lose their hold, images of dancers and lispy men with blue bird eyes and a coffee mug in an empty park and pages that make no sense and wigs in a closet and shoes—God, so many shoes, a whole mountain of shoes, and in each crawls spiders and maggots. But it's fading, the fragments that are pleasant and the nightmares both, an iris opening to reveal this strange room.

I can tell I'm up high from the slant of the roof, on the second or third floor of a big house. Wallpaper on either side—vines over purple. The memory of being held down lashes at me, yet by whom, I can't recall. None of this makes sense. Floorboards stretch from the end of the bed, across the space—more a loft than a room, or maybe a converted attic—to where a dresser sits, its upright mirror annotated in theatre bulbs. The one in the bottom left-hand corner flickers. Its strobe is an itch I can't scratch.

Combs and brushes and photographs. Makeup cases. Magazines, books, cheap figurines—the kind a nervy high-school boy gifts a girlfriend when he doesn't get girls yet.

An old woman is slumped in a wheelchair next to the dresser. The glare of the bulbs—that damn flicker—masked her presence in the room until now. And it *has* been a while. Minutes that might have been hours with me on this bed saying how thirsty I am.

"Hello?" I croak, straining to lift my head.

The woman is a hundred if she's a day. Her near-bald scalp doesn't so much reflect the light coming through the window so much as absorb it. Hollowed eye sockets. Bulging cheeks. Tufts of hair pepper her head, knots like upholstery through a slashed seat. Her mouth unnerves me most, a toothless cave, an O of gums.

"H-h-elp," I say. "Help me."

She jolts. Crabby arms drawing across her nightgown. The woman bellows wordless alarms. One of her feet thuds the floorboards, rattling trinkets on the dresser.

"AAAUUGGHHHHHHHHHHHHHHHHHHHHH—"

"What—*cough*—the fuck?"

Thump-thump goes her one mobile foot.

"A G H H H H H I I I I I I I I I I I I I I I I I I I C C C C C H H H H H . THIIIRRRSSSTTYYYYY—"

The old woman in the wheelchair runs out of oxygen and slumps again.

"Breathe," I tell her. "B-breathe."

As though she's even *capable* of listening, those lungs kick into gear. I watch her toes curl, the nails yellow and overgrown. *Wolves teeth*, I think. *The better to eat you with.*

Footsteps. Yes, there's a door. The handle is crystal, or something like it. My breathing quickens, and I flinch as the handle turns. A man *I think* I've met before strides in.

"Bern," he shouts over his shoulder. "She's awake!"

The man takes a few steps towards the bed. He's so tall.

"Where am I?"

"Sh-hhh."

The crone lets another groan sail about the loft and the man rushes to her side as another woman I'm *almost* sure I've seen before joins us. "Oh, Richard," she says, hands at her mouth. They're shaking. I wonder if I can lift my own. No. It's like someone I can't see is on my chest, keeping me in place.

"She's bloody wet herself," the man named Richard says. He's crouched over the wheelchair, fists on his hips. Fury radiates off him. The contempt he has for the old woman is evident in his face. He slaps her across the jaw with the back of his hand.

"Stop it!" I cry.

"Don't strain too much, Emma," Bern tells me, closing in. "The doctor said you have to rest."

Doctor.

That blur with the bluebell eyes. The beak and its bite. The lisp.

Emma. The name sits uneasy on my tongue, like a boiled knuckle, slimy, soft and hard at the same time.

Richard wheels the woman out of the room, ammonia-stink sweeping me in the process. "Where are you taking her? Why'd you do that? She didn't—she, she—"

"No more talking, darlin'." Bern perches on the side of the mattress by my side. "God, you're beautiful."

"W-what happened? To me?"

Bern tries to hold her emotions in check—not that she's doing that great a job. They are slippery things. Slippery as my name. Emma. Emma Something on a bed in a room I'm not convinced I've been in before. My panic must show because Bern is rubbing my chest, right under my throat. I don't realise how cold I am until I feel the heat of her touch. Soothing. Despite myself, I lean into her forearm. "C-confused."

"A'course you are, darlin'. It'll take time to get better."

"Where?"

"Your room. Don't speak, okay? Wait until you father gets back."

Confusion yanks at my head, left and then right and then left and then right again, a tug-of-war where I'm the knot in the middle. I want no part of this. No. Surely, I said no.

"Water."

Bern nods and leaps to my right. A pitcher and glass sit on a bedside table.

A shard of memory: shattering teacups.

The woman in the earthy clothes, the one with a face of haggard worry, tips liquid down my throat. Water it may be, yet it ignites me. Jet fuel. I lay back on the pillow a couple of splutters later. A web of cracks spindles across the ceiling. Mould.

My room?

Hurried footsteps draw my attention to the man, Richard, who joins Bern's side. She's on the bed again. His hand curls about her shoulder, and she reaches to touch him without glancing from me. Tears drip down their faces.

"Your father has something he needs to ask you. It won't be easy."

Tugging to the left again. Tugging to the right. Something inside me rips.

"D-dad?"

Dad?

Tearing.

Dad.

Coming unsewn.

"Why'd you do it, Emma?" Richard asks.

Whatever has been straining in me snaps, and in the darkness on the other side, an origami face unfolds sad eyes and the kind of smile that maybe never knew happiness, a face that could never have dreamed of being as loved as I am right now. Emma Braintree.

"W-what are you t-talking about?"

Bern scrutinises every inch of me. She grips the quilt keeping the cold away. Fingers twist fabric until her fist shakes.

"Maybe not yet, Bern," Richard says. "She's been through hell."

"Oh, she's the one who's been through hell, huh?"

"Bern, stop."

But Bern doesn't stop. She yanks the blanket back and heaves up my lifeless arms to reveal wounds snaking my fish-belly white skin from wrist to inner elbow. The stitches are neat. The stitches are clean.

My mother leans in so I can smell the musky wine on her breath. The pain in her is hot on me. "We saved you."

9

They dose out care between interludes of light and dark. The kiss of warm sponges. Refilled water jugs and broth that doesn't taste as it should. Sometimes the vines come alive. When I complain about the flickering light, Dad fixes it for me. A twist is all it takes. I've never known shame like this, shame made all the worse because I can't answer the question they keep asking me.

Why'd I do it?

No matter how I've hurt them, they still roll me to slide the bed pan under my arse. And once I'm strong enough to sit up, Richard helps me transfer onto a wheelie-commode to do my business without them around. I can't control my vomit, though. It splashes over the floor without warning, steams. Sick. So sick. This isn't living.

A razor through flesh, splitting me open. Two bloodied smiles stitched ever so tight, closing their secrets inside.

I haven't just wounded myself. I've wounded them.

Mum combs my hair. Her presence is something I hadn't known my hunger of. The magnitude of it makes me crumble. I'm a nowhere thing in a nowhere hour, and I hate that that's okay.

Tick-tock, tick-tock.

"How long have I been here?"

The comb teeth stop and dig in. Mum takes my chin to twist my face to meet her own. Her affection doesn't mean anything. Her voice is stony. "Darlin', you never left."

10

Stars announce themselves through the window, a universe without an axis to spin on.

I throw back the covers and slide onto the floor, dizzy. My legs aren't working but I'm stronger than before. Good. I hold onto that, find allegiance with it, feel an obligation to myself to get better. The gown they dressed me in wisps over floorboards as I use my still-aching arms to heave over to the door, knocking the commode along the way. The crystal door handle catches the moonlight. It's not crystal. Glass.

Locked.

Even though the exhaustion will leave me crying, I scuttle to the window and use the sill as leverage to yank myself upright. No doubt, they've heard my moans. They don't come, though. They must expect me to explore. Surely, that's a sign of the healing they've anticipated.

I jimmy onto the sill and stare. Crying comes on slow. The

moon is almost full. A wide blue lawn below. Blue hedges pin the yard in place. Beyond, a blue street where no cars are parked. I don't realise a light has been shining inside the *(my)* house until it switches off, and the yellow rectangle blinks out on the grass. The blue tapestry is complete. My forehead against the chilly glass as dogs bark. Cold creeps across my cheeks, down my neck, right into the centre of me. My hands go to that spot, between my breasts, and intertwine. I think I'm praying, but to who, I don't know.

The teacup upends at a pace that isn't natural, slipping sideways to let its contents soar. Liquid stains the dark, glowing like a jellyfish, one of those deep-sea critters from the documentaries I recall watching when I was a kid, back when my mother shot her body full of smack, a belt around her upper arm. She chased that dragon and crawled inside its gullet gladly, peering out at me through its teeth.

Mum.

She appears different in my dreams than she does in life. Less tall, less regal. More beaten and broken, hunched over and fucked up. When the mother of my dreams smiles, her tongue rolls white from the Aspirin she's chewed.

The teacup shatters and it becomes clear.

These people aren't my parents.

My Dad is dead. The flowers. The worms.

I bolt awake. A face stares in the window at me. He's floating against the blue. My hand reaches to push him away, but I slam glass. The man isn't outside. He's in the room with me. Behind me. That's his reflection. He lets his bluebird fly and its needle beak pierces my thigh through the nightgown. Wings flap and flutter, a hush that makes me want to sleep. The bird spits into my body, making the vines un-weave from the walls again.

"Mum." Weeping makes the word come out wrong. It's stillborn.

He asks me his questions again in his lisping voice. I can't avoid answering.

11

"I said, I don't want them."

Mum has me under her arm, pushing crutches to my father who props them against the wall. He's the one who opens the door with the crystal—no, glass—handle, stepping aside to let us hobble into the hall. It smells like Pine-O-Clean out here. Nice.

We're at the top of a staircase, rooms branching in every direction except straight ahead. Here, the house is scooped out, a bowl of morning sunshine so buttery you could put it to your lips and fatten. And I could do with that. This gown is loose. Am I wearing it or is it wearing me?

"Hold your horses, darlin'," Mum wheezes into my neck. There's a wiry power to her. "Have you got this?"

"Yes."

"You were always so stubborn."

I grab the balustrade on my right, breathing hard and haggard. "I—need—shower."

"Not yet. You're too weak. The steam will make you lightheaded. We just need you to get your sea-legs again."

"No. Shower."

"Would you listen to me for once?"

"Jesus."

"What?"

"Down."

"What's that?"

"I need to sit down!"

The immediate withdraws, fearful of my voice, and the distant takes its place. My father pushes the wheelchair underneath me. I fall into it. "Oh, fuck me," I say. "Damn. D-damn."

I lean to the right, leather harness twisting, and rest against the balustrade. Wood polish. Please don't spew, please don't spew. It doesn't come. When one of my parents touch my shoulder, I shrug them off with a shout and soak up the brightness. I need it. I need anything from the outside world. Even though it's winter—that much is easy to tell—I crave sunshine.

"You did well, Emma," Dad tells me. "We'll have you dancing in no time."

Only trophies in my mind, girls caught in forever poses—no, not only caught. Threatened. Hold that pose, sweetheart. Hold it until it hurts. And if you buckle, if you let your stance go, the crowd will lose its faith. That's what the audience wants. To trust you. Hold your arms up, even though your shoulders scream. Pinch your toes, bones be damned. Don't let them see you fail.

In the distance of this distance, someone knocks at a door.

I watch my father bound down the stairs, trailing silhouettes. Everything turns into an echo. I hate feeling so anaemic and dependent. There's no other choice: I've got to force this haze to pass because, again, this is no way to live. Sure, who I was before this is still lost, but I know in the marrow of me, that I'm stronger than my parents are letting me be. I can't wait to be devoted to myself again.

Dad's talking to someone. I hear wind chimes.

"Who—"

"Quiet now," Mum says. A rollercoaster jolt kicking into gear as she whisks me into my room where the walls are my favourite colour, purple, and the door closes. The haze thickens. All I can see is the glass handle shimmering, bright as the brightest ornament on the Christmas tree, under which I must have sat with these people to open presents year after year. I can see myself tearing away wrapping, all that paper and cellophane. Mum and Dad watching with pride—and twisting the blade of guilt repeatedly, the sharpness of having betrayed them by trying to kill myself— as I yank the lid off a box.

Revealing emptiness.

12

"There's something I want you to see," Mum tells me after dinner.

I place the fork against the china plate and set it on the bedside table beside the jug of water. Bright and chirpy, I swing around, socks skidding wooden boards laid top to toe, all wedged together to ground the world as I know it, a space of six by six yards with a canted ceiling and theatre bulbs and makeup I sometimes put on for sport.

This enthusiasm is alien. I'm not sure why things aren't relative—and relative, I can sense, like a blind person seeking familiarity of the dark, was important to me once. In this new place where I'm appreciated and fawned over, there's only happy or sad, nothing or something, excited or I just don't-give-a-shit. Binary is liberating.

"Sounds awesome."

Mum and Dad smile. He opens the door and I trundle out on newborn deer legs faster than I should. These people don't judge me. That's what good parents do. And they are goodly. They've forgiven me in ways others wouldn't. They stitched me up when I did the terrible thing and loved me just as strong afterwards.

I take Mum's hand as she leads me down the hall, by the staircase twisting into black. Rain hammers the house tonight. The sound is a hug telling me everything will work out. My left leg works better than the right, but I push on. This is important to them. Dizziness makes the wallpaper beyond my bedroom writhe, yet the vines stay put. I think it's my will keeping them in place. Pride dims memories of blades cutting, birds biting.

Dad opens another door further up on the left, passing, first, what must be a bathroom separating my quarters from the next. I hear flushing in the night, the groan of pipes. He stands before that last entrance, light pitching half his face into darkness, making him appear a part of the shadows of the house, a creature of flesh and wood, tin and teeth. He points for me to go in and look. I do.

The woman on the bed doesn't move. She's ashen, a face of frost.

She's being watched over by the ancient lady in her wheelchair in the corner of the room, which unlike my own, is painted white. Her eyes watch us as we shuffle in one by one. She issues a groan of acknowledgement.

"Quiet now, Nanna," says my mother, behind me now.

Nanna quietens, drops her swollen foot to the ground. Thump. The bandages are ochre in places. Squish. She would've been with us at the Christmas tree, too. Must've been.

I yank my sight from the old woman, down to the somewhat younger lady on the bed. Her woollen beanie looks comfy. "Is she sleeping?" I ask my parents.

Yes, Mum tells me. "She's very tired."

"Do you recognise her?" Dad's voice is a notch above a whisper.

I study her sleeping form, the way those skinny hands are linked. The semi-dark cradles her as a parent cradles a child. She isn't just comfortable, isn't just at one with the shadows. She's of the shadows. In some ways, I envy her that.

"No." My word is a mild exhale. Mum grips my arm. Squeeze-squeeze.

"Good," she says. "We can get you back to bed now. Wrap you up snug-as-a-bug-in-a-rug. Just how you used to like it when you were a tot—"

"Are the lady's doggies sleeping, too?" I ask anyone willing to listen.

"Yes," Dad tells me. "Now kiss Nanna goodnight, too, while we're here."

The ancient lady in her chair reeks of shit.

13

It isn't a real orchestra on the CD, though it acts like an orchestra. Synthesizers work into overdrive without breaking a sweat, without strings having to snap. It's nothing, the spirit of something that never was.

Mum and Dad are in their chairs against the wall of my room, watching. Their backs taut and tall, hands gripped together. The moon through the window shines on their faces. Only the theatre bulbs are on.

Music rushes and ebbs. Flutes quicken. I spin to match their beats, even though I'm giddy. The theme flattens into dread, then a rush of delight—the excitement of dragons snapping, and you, the dancer, pirouetting from danger. A second of silence follows, but it's not enough. I have to get up again. And again, I spin, hair flailing, sweat flying.

The floor rushes up to meet me. It isn't that my legs gave out. It's because this is part of the dance Mum and Dad requested I perform. The Sleeping Beauty by Tchaikovsky, they said it's called. Even though I don't remember what to do, the moves come. I've done this so many times before. In dreams.

Slowly, I bloom from this position, arms rising to show off my scars. They are a part of me now, something I invited, as I did this fake music. I'm up again, turning—not for me. For them. Because their smiles, the tears in their eyes, the hope they have for me as I do what my trophies said I can do, is worth it.

When it's over, breathless, I bow. The song ends.

They cheer. They cheer for me. I'm forgiven. There's no way I can express my gratitude, except to dance when they ask for it, every day of my life if that's what it takes. They rise and embrace me.

"Emma," Mum says. I smell alcohol on her again, and the sickness it's masking. "It really is you."

"It is Bern," Dad tells her. "My God. My good God in heaven."

They draw away, the music drifting into quiet again. The old CD player in the corner discovers a scratch on the disc. It skips. Skips. Skips. Over and over again. The pulse of this house. My house. Our house.

I've never been so strong.

"We love you, Emma," my father says. "Now more than ever. I can't—I—I can't believe it."

"Of course, you can believe it, Richard."

It's not just me that has been dancing. The vines on the walls joined in, too. They shimmy, writhe, and peel off their planks to wave.

"Now, Richard," Mum says, not breaking eye contact. "She's real now. I can feel her *in* me." Her veiny hands trace the curve of her belly to her navel and beyond, cupping the space between her legs. The air she sucks from the room draws a gasp from me, like she's taking something back that I'm not ready to give over.

"I can't," Dad says. "It won't work."

Mum turns away, leaving a black stain on the room I can't rip my eyes from. The silhouette shimmers, strobing as the bulb in the theatre display strobed when this began. There was no time before that. Just the dark they drew me from, when they saved me.

My mother puts a long-bladed razor in my hand.

"W-what?" I say.

"Undo your stitches," she says through clenched teeth. Her eyes tell me nothing—an absence that sends a bolt of concern from my head down to my toes. "Cut."

The blade is icy, icy as the wind outside must be icy—not that I've been outside. Not once. An image I can't place breezes over my body, welcoming goose bumps.

(*A young man, his skin dark and beautiful, his collar turned up against the breeze. Shooting stars of rain as he switches on his headlights. Tree shadows reaching out to grab me when he reverses out of a driveway I've been down more than once.*)

"Cut." Mum's word freezes, all edges and burns.

I dip the blade low, its side catching the lamplight. Consuming it. The squared-off edge plays the primary stitch. I don't want to do this, but I can feel myself doing it anyway—*because why wouldn't I?* They are my parents. They are goodly. They know what's best. I can't betray them twice.

Skip-skip-skip-skip-skip, goes the CD.

Only there is no pulse to this place. The house is dead.

Mum, sensing my uncertainty, grabs my wrist and pushes the razor down for me. Metal slits through string and sinew to strike the bone beneath. The pain brings broken teacups back together. My scream doesn't sound like my voice. I cling to that otherness, even as I push my parents aside, blade slitting downwards and across, blood zooming into the air. I cling to that otherness as I'm clinging to the pitcher of water from the bedside table, the one I'm bringing down on Mum's face as she reaches to finish what she needed me to start.

Glass shoots in every direction. Some slivers make their way into Mum's face. Her cheek is a butterfly of flesh spreading its wings—cartoonish, something you'd see on a dresser in a little girl's room. I don't relate to that. I can't. *I'm not that.* I don't think I ever had the chance to be a girl. The skinny woman with the needle in her arm and the belt strap in her mouth saw to that. The woman on the bed up the hall, watched over by Nanna.

(*Are her doggies sleeping, too?*)

Bern shrieks and stumbles back, flipping onto the bed she'd spent so much time—how much, I'm not sure—tending to me on. The knocks I'd heard downstairs the other day must have been someone—someone whose name I can't pin down—searching for me. That name will come later, if I let it.

My fingers pinch the razor imbedded in my arm to yank it out.

Tic-tac-toe. I draw red lines through the old man's face as he lunges, making a smile for him where there hadn't been one before. He still comes, heaving, forcing me back. We strike the wall together and a crack rockets up the plaster. Vines scramble. I feel drugged.

I am drugged.

He pushes against me. I bring my knee into the bastard's middle, leaning to bite his ear at the same time. Wetness gushes into my mouth. The taste isn't pennies. It isn't dirty water drunk straight from the tap. It isn't poisoned broth, either. It's hot blood.

The vines reach out from the wallpaper to snatch the blade from my grip—but I refuse to let it go. For every millisecond I hold onto it, the void I think I've been living in fills.

(*His name is Pranav, the Tinder fuck-buddy I didn't want to leave, yet who always hurts me in the end. The lake glimmers under the moon in his absence. Through the trees. The house I can't afford to buy. An umbrella in a bath stall, splayed like a raven with a broken wing. Finding the bluebird on the ground. Crushing muslin bags of lavender between my fingers.*)

I spit out Richard's meat as he dives at me once more.

"Who are you?" I cry when the blade parts the air, when it parts the right-hand side of his neck. Blood so black it looks like he's bleeding night shoots again, raining down on me—

He gave me that umbrella. Him.

The memory of lightning and having to take off the Doc Martens I chose for them. Because I'm not their daughter, yet I'm paid to love them like a daughter.

I knock the CD player to the floor. It doesn't break. Instead, the disc skips back into alignment and triggers the beginning of the track.

Vines wiggle in retreat. Only wallpaper now.

There is no joy in me at the sight of Richard dancing, throwing red around the room, blood that sizzles against the bulbs and hisses. He clips his shoulder on the doorway, gagging. He's confused, as I've been confused. By them.

Who the fuck am I?

He stumbles into the hall. Hunched over, hair draping my face, half the room now bright red from the bloodstained lights, I hear him strike the landing.

Pain beams through my scalp and neck. Everything upends. I'm ripped backwards from behind. Bern has me by the hair and pins me to the ground. My head strikes the floorboards, making my jaws snap on my tongue. An explosion of bone-white pain.

"Fuckin' bitch!" Bern screams. Blood from the holes I've opened in her spills over me. I don't realise I've got the blade in my hand until that hand rises again and sinks its edge into her eye, which deflates and sludges into my mouth. It tastes of cloth dampened in kerosene and tingles on my tongue like a popping candy slug, a familiar tingling sensation from another time—but damn it, at least that other time belongs to me again. I don't know how not to swallow her mess. The slug taps, pops at the end of my tongue, wanting in. I cough. The eye slug gloops down my throat. Into me. Not even fear can dim the shame. After all, there's so much for me to hate about myself.

Bern arcs onto her back, legs striking my jaw. Something crunches, and I pray it's her and not me. Luck isn't on my side. The pain will come, I just know it. Pain always does.

This gives the woman time enough to pounce. She forces me onto my haunches. But I'm strong. Of course, I'm strong. They fed me to be strong. The vines turn into wallpaper again. I draw on every remaining energy reserve in my body to push back against that weight, driving Bernadette Braintree (yes, that's her name) across the room, past the bed on the left and the dresser on the right.

And through the window.

It peels outwards in a silvery mouth. Her hand grabs my forearm, yanking me at the sill, teeth of glass. A twist of my neck saves my life, for what it'll be worth once this is all said and done. She holds on to me, slicing my arm open in the process, skin peeling back, skim off cream. I grip the sill with my free hand, the gown I'm wearing splitting up the back. The woman's hold on me vanishes. I fall one way, and she, the other. I hit the floor. She hits the ground three storeys below.

For the first time in I don't know how long, I hear the clock somewhere down the hall. Time has found me. Time is the only family I need. Winter air scrambles at my feet, my legs, my torso, at my old scars and scars-to-be. Groaning, I peer over the window edge and at the blue yard where the woman who said she was my mother (but wasn't) is sprawled. Clouds pass over the moon, their enormous shadows peekaboo her busted face. There, and then not there. There, and then not there again.

Richard Braintree is on the landing in the hall. I stand over him and watch the life drain through the holes I opened. I wheeze a scream that doesn't carry. Not here. Not in this awful house.

He glares at me. What is he thinking, I wonder? I don't linger in that speculation for long. That speculation doesn't feel safe, and my time here has been dangerous enough.

Richard's eyes don't glaze as I expect them to, shifting instead to over my shoulder. With one bleeding arm propped against the floor, I follow his line of sight down the hall, past my room (no, Emma's room) where photographs hang in frames both handsome and tacky.

Fainting is near. I push on. I have to.

There's something I know I need to do—the last thing. After that, I can let the pain come. Pain I need to own.

I scour the photographs.

There is a young Richard and Bernadette with a child on their knee in a park, surrounded by trees and farm animals. The girl wears a purple top. Everything about the image shouts early 70s, late 80s. The next picture features a teenage girl against an acid-wash background of blues and whites, her expression is hope disciplined by braces and the kind of acne that will bring humility later in life. A purple flower in her hair.

I shuffle along, blood pat-pat-patting the floorboards. Richard fingers my ankle. I kick him away. He'll be dead soon, maybe. Like his daughter.

In the next frame there is the image of Emma Braintree as she appeared in the manila folder given to me by Sakura

(Fridays, huh?)

back when I didn't know any better. The origami face unfolding for the last time.

(got a curly one for you)

Looking from picture to picture to picture, I can tell, even though the ages are different, and the quality varies, these replications aren't of the same woman. Some brows arch, some frown. The last one features a woman with a slightly upturned nose. The second-to-last reveals a teenager with cauliflower ears. The first girl, just a child, the girl on Richard and Bern's knee, the girl in the purple tutu and the ballet shoes, well, she seems happy.

I stumble in the direction of the next door, knocking that final frame. The last photograph is from my graduation day, which until now, hung in my mother's living room overlooking shoes and magazines, with flies for guardians. It had been covered in a layer of nicotine gravy. But not anymore.

(do you recognise her?)

"No," I say. "Please, no."

A noise issues from down the hall, from the last room on the left, the one where shadows clot. Light slinks out from under the jam. The noise is a thump I feel in my guts. One Mississippi. It's followed by another. Two Mississippis. And another. Three Mississippis. Poised, with Richard dying behind me,

(I LOVE MY DADDY, reads the cup)

I lean into the sound. He spasms and goes quiet at my heels.

"M-mum?"

Thump.

"AUUGGGHHHHHHHHHHHHHHHHHHHHHHH," screams a hoarse voice. "THUUURRRSSSSTTYYYYYYY. THIIIIRSSSTTTTII-IIIIIIII—"

14

The blood on the bathroom tiles is too red. My cuts are severe but not life threatening. After I do what I need to do, I'll brave exploring the house for a phone, or my mobile and pager, anything that will let the outside world in. Red. Too red. I don't want to look at it.

That's why I switch off the light and slip out of my clothes with deliberate slowness, every twist of skin turning stings into sufferings. I moan along with the woman on the other side of the wall, the one who had been watching over my mother's corpse and her two dead dogs, Sid and Nancy. For all I know, the bodies are still in there. Rotting away. As the old woman who isn't my Nanna had done long ago, I think I've pissed myself, too.

I draw the curtain back and step into the stall, crying. Twist the taps. Freezing water gushes over me. I wash the client from my hair.

For the last time.

Afterwards, I sit in the dark, shivering, pulling on my bloodied gown once more. It sticks to my skin like sloppy kisses to which I offered no consent. I think of the girls in their some-handsome-some-tacky frames in the hall. Each smile: the replication of a crime. Like my mother with her dirty syringes and belt straps, this might be the Braintrees way of chasing their own dragon, albeit a dragon of a very different kind.

Damn them for making me their ground zero. I'm more than that.

I'm Kaylee.

Lights swish across the dark ceiling. The car's headlights switch off. Probing anticipation fiddles with my innards, making me need to shit. My skin—both intact and slit—jumps at the sound of a closing door, the creak of a gate.

Clenching jaws. Tightening fists.

Those vines, illuminated by dim moonlight, cover the bathroom walls. I squint. The pattern shifts again. Worming. Whatever drugs they put in me must still be in my system. Each strand reaches out to wrap my arms. It's hard to not welcome their touch. They yank me up, a marionette on strings, making my head swim. Blood rains over the tiles again, across my feet, my essence the only heat in the room. My groin pushes against the basin as I angle to see out the window. I rise to peer down at the yard where I know, just out of sight, Bernadette Braintree, the woman who told me to call her Mum, lays dead.

Clouds slink over the moon again, throwing the estate into bruises of dark and dim. Yet I see him down there. Him. With his black bag. He's staring up at the house. Not that he's saying anything, and not that I'd be able to hear him anyway, but I know he has a lisp.

It might be a trick of the light but I think it's starting to snow.

The vines tighten, and then I know.

He's the psychiatrist who put in the referral to my team. With a jot of his signature, our lives were joined, fated, Ts crossed, the dot of an I. There are bluebirds where his peepers should be, and they cheep-cheep Disney agonies just for me.

Cut to Care

They call it the Heart of the Nation but it's just metal and steel and ignoring. Dawn reflected in glass. Cigarette buts. Broken beer bottles. Condoms men threw on the ground last night. Vomit. The remains of dropped phones and lost keys and food picked at by birds. Unread magazines the wind ripped apart, pages fluttering through the streets, urban tumbleweeds.

This is the city, my city. It's Sunday morning and I'm in my sweats and nobody is out except me. Or so I thought.

A homeless man between two buildings rattles a soup cup of loose change, says, *hey fella help me out will you*. I slip off my headphones, jog sweat spilling down my stubbled cheeks. The sound of garbage trucks and the frog-croak of pedestrian crossing call buttons and that weird hum a nearly empty street makes. I step up to him, reaching into my pocket for coins. Hand them over. The man—bent double from a life of begging—nods thanks.

And I push on.

There's a woman on the corner looking up at the sky at the next intersection. Her hair, her face, are wild with knots. She is a story I'm not ready to read. She calls to me, arms opening, revealing that she's topless beneath the blanket. Flies swarm. I wonder how long she's felt invisible. It must be hard, how people don't look at you when you're like her, how it's better to keep moving and consider yourself lucky. The woman shivers. I didn't want to read her, but I do. I see the system stacked against her. This could have been my mother if she hadn't been so fortunate. I sigh and take off my shirt, apologising for its woofy dampness, and hand it over. Flies lift and soar, some landing on my muscled skin, sucking salt off my nipples. The woman takes the shirt and scurries away. I'm cold in the city but that's okay.

And I push on.

There's a one-handed kid on the next corner sitting cross-legged on a piece of cardboard. A baseball cap in front of him, a five dollar-note at the bottom. He's tapping an empty ice cream container with a chopstick. He's a human greyhound with coals for eyes. I think of the sons I never had, tell him to hold on, and run across the road where a newsagent is flipping the sign of his store to OPEN. Inside, behind the counter, are cigarette lighters in the shape of naked ladies and Powerball scratchies and novelty bottle openers. There's a Swiss Army Knife. I point. Offer a thumbs up.

Buy it.

Run across the road, still no traffic. I kneel in front of the kid and it's like he's frightened at first, but then he sees what I'm doing and is relieved. The longest of the blades is what I require. Doing good dulls pain better than any drug, and I hardly feel a thing as I begin to cut off my left hand above the wrist. Blood lathers our faces as I saw, tendons yanked tight and snipped in two, a smile of meat, bones splintering and cracking and breaking, generosity spilling across the cement in a ruby rain. I hand my hand to him. The kid takes it. He's moved to tears, *says, thank you mister*.

I'm happy.

And I push on, leaving behind swishes of blood on the concrete.

The wind is frosty and blows from behind, bringing with it shavings off the snowy mountains. Dust swirls. A brown paper bag slaps against the shin of a one-legged woman perched on a milk crate with a sign on a string around her neck reading, **NEED MONEY FOR DIZABILITYS N FOOD**. I stand over her, stare. She's like a living breathing black and white commercial asking for donations that come on around dinner time. She moves in slow motion, gumming a toothless mouth. I can't imagine how difficult her life must've been. Yet here she is. Living. I wouldn't give the best of me away to just anyone, but it's easy to see what a fighter she is. What a survivor. She's earned this. The flies find me again and swim in the blood I'm shedding as I bring the knife to my mouth and slide it between each tooth, twisting the blade, plucking nerves that make everything screech. Flies rub their arms, flatten their wings. The woman's face is slick with my gore as she takes each tooth I gift her and forces them into her gums. She drops one, slippery thing, says WOOPS and it's okay, it's nothing a light brush-off won't fix and 'ten second rule' anyway. The woman is crying, she's *that* grateful. Good. This isn't a waste then. Choking on blood, but determined to keep going, I stab my thigh and slit myself open. It takes a long time and it's so much harder than I thought it could ever be. I ask the woman for help to break through the bone, which she does by pushing her knee against it and throwing her weight down. The snapping sound is thunder off the tall buildings around us. Pigeons coo from a ledge, looking at us as the woman climbs onto her milk crate and accepts the leg I hand over. I put the knife between my teeth as I tie off the end of my sweatpants. It bulges with blood as I hop away, struggling for balance but getting the hang of it. Always been a fast learner—well, that's what Dad says.

And I push on.

I round the corner, stopping for breath, and see the old man with his fort of cask wine boxes. He's pissing into one of the silver bladders through a gnarly stub of thick cock. I shake my head. It's too much. All of it, too much. Somewhere in this man's past, fire reshaped him and this was how he set. Webbed where he shouldn't be. Wet where he should be dry. Hairless where there should be hair. And because of the tautness of his cheeks, he smiles even though tears trickle from his eyes. I can't handle it—that I have so much when he has so little—and I love the man for saying yes when I ask if he wants my skin.

There are screams as I slit and pull and uncoil myself from my muscle, screams echoing everywhere, but they feel like someone else's screams, someone else's pain. I'm anesthetised with the dopamine rush that comes with giving and that giving being acknowledged so warmly. The wounded man says he loves me he loves me he loves me as he slips inside my skin, as he wears my face so well and snug. He's handsome, I think. Well put together. He's got a chance.

Unable to walk, I crawl across the ground, homeward bound. My hands slap the concrete, dirt and glass shards and discarded needles coating and spearing my exposed meat and veins as I push on and push on. Tired. It's a kind of relief, tiredness, like giving up. I scuttle into one of the alleys opposite the park where the morning's first kites are raised, leaving behind my red snail trail. The ding of cyclists on their bikes. The clip-clop of workers stepping off buses. My city is waking. I lean against a brick wall, cushioned by bags of yesterday's food, cats sniffing at my wounds. Clothed in flies, I watch the day stretch its legs.

Tallow-Maker, Tallow Made

1

"Tallow-maker, tallow made
His wick burns in the grave
Wax won't rot, a plot unnamed
Tallow-maker, tallow-maker."

This song haunts me to noose-day and beyond. People hiss it, boys on their way to the schoolhouse, their nasty chanticleer read to them by their parents. It was published in *The Bulletin*, four lines in neat font like something from a hymnal, right between chatter of Federation and war with the Boers. Most of those snake-tonged kids can't read themselves. They know meanness, though.

If we do go to war, I pray it takes them with it. Little fingers to set Pommie traps.

It has been five days since Daddy's death.

Our town isn't big enough, not overflowing with sin enough, to have warranted the construction of gallows. The law hung him from a lightning-scarred tree off main square instead. I, along with the other townsfolk, watched the executioner toss his rope over the white branch and slip the noose about my father's neck. Daddy didn't elect to defend his honour when granted the opportunity, nor did he cry out from beneath his hood. Not even at the end. The crowd, however, yelped on his behalf when the ladder he teetered upon was kicked out from under him, followed by the crack. I watched Daddy tap-dance to music only he could hear, until the stilling came. Quietness swelled within us, we observers of governed capital punishment, all infection-hot and in desperate need of bleeding. Only that bleeding—and the relief it brings—wasn't awarded me that day. The others turned away one by one, and I stood before the lifeless tree from which a lifeless noose was strung with a lifeless man at its end. Daddy had been living not a minute beforehand. Now, this. Wind thrashed away tears, the winter dress billowing on my frame. *This can't be real. It all must be a dream.* But then the sound of waxy knots groaning against wood made its way into my ears, inched through every vein like roots in search of water, taking seed at my core. This was no fiction.

Screech-screeechhh. Screech-screeeeccccchhh.

The policeman refused him a plot at Saint Mathew's. My father's marker spears the dirt beyond the graveyard, out amongst the bushrangers and Protestants. Executions aren't free, either. Daddy had to pay for his noose and the cost of labour in advance, and had he not sterling in pocket, the law would have settled his debts by staking claim of our livestock. 'Hangman's wages', I'd heard this called. The colonies were rich with it.

Excluding the funeral, so much as it was, I haven't braved mass since before it happened, before the tracker led Policeman Edmund to the door of our homestead. We're not wont for snow in this part of New South Wales, but there was a dusting of it that night. I saw their lanterns through the window bobbing in the dark. Lucy, our mare, alerted me to their presence with a bray. At first, I assumed it was Lowry's fence-making boys come 'round for grog again. And I would have given them Daddy's moonshine, it being frosty. But I thought wrong. It wasn't the fence-makers, stinking of old sweat and even older eucalyptus. No. I peered through the glass and saw Edmund, the burly bastard, stepping onto our veranda, flanked by his men and the barefoot half-caste who'd steered them to this part of Queen's Country, here where we're not wont for snow. Mostly.

"Daddy?"

Only Daddy didn't come.

I lifted my hem, spiriting from room to room, wondering

where we'd left our pistol. He wasn't in the parlour where he'd been stuffing his pipe earlier, stopping every so often to brush the dandruff from his lapels. Just the empty rocking chair.

Each crackle and pop of the fire notched my pulse like slaps to a horses' hide.

They caught Dudley Harris, my father, out back where he'd been making a run for it. He didn't fight, all told. The write-up said he'd confessed. Daddy didn't speak to me again, not even when I pleaded with him through the bars, and he took his goodbyes to the dirt beyond Saint Mathew's. And there they lie still. For now.

He's gone left me an orphan at nineteen.

Ole Ma passed four years ago. I don't hold a grudge for her as I do him. She died screaming, split open on the barn floor birthing a stillborn brother Daddy told me we weren't allowed to name.

"Easier that way," he'd said.

Daddy was by Ole Ma's side when she passed, threatening me with wallops if I didn't march back to the house as told. But I've never been the obeying type, even then. I watched through a crack in the wall, and what I saw put the fear of God in me over ever getting in the Family Way. Returning to the house and waiting for my father to come inside to tell me what I already knew, proved the worst moment of my existence. Until that first night after they hanged Daddy, and I found myself alone for the first time. Two deaths with the bulk of my childhood wedged between. I have no idea what to do. I've wept enough to fill two brooks.

"Tallow-maker! Tallow-maker!"

Their echoes like rope over branch, neither yielding. Neither feeling.

Screech-screeechhh. Screech-screeeecccchhh.

I sold Lucy to tide me over, though it's hard to say how far the bob will stretch. It took me three days to fool myself into thinking I was stoic enough to brave town, to check on Daddy's tiny store and muster groceries. Setting off after noon had been a good idea. Chillier then. Less folks about.

Plus, the bitter boys were tied up in tutorage, saving me their hisses.

The death tree, however, remained in its spot, unmoving and leafless. Only its shadow moved, creeping with the sun. It was a scar on the day.

It'll be a while until I open the store, if I ever do. I hope, someday, people will see me as Genevieve again, and not the daughter of a candle-maker who slaughtered three swagmen. Assuming they'd accept a lady proprietor in the first place. Mr Livery, a former headmaster from Victoria, spat at my feet when I scurried onto the street. I wonder if he'd been waiting for me. Regardless, I wasn't shocked by his conduct, being from the Mother Country. "You can't trust an Englishman," Daddy used to say. "The bastards live for the cold and shit in the streets!" I left Mr Livery to his scowls and spit and went about my business without paying him much mind—on the outside, anyway. Groceries weren't going to shop themselves. Afterwards, I went home to milk Nessie and Tessie, our cows. Though all along, I kept hearing the coo of Daddy's death tree, rope over bark.

Screech-screeechhh. Screech-screeeecccchhh.

He killed the three men in his craftery.

Yes, that's what my father called it.

The craftery is at the rear of our lot across from the barn, opposite the outhouse and dam. I never liked it in there. Heavens know how many spiders Daddy sealed in the wax he cast and had me cart to the store Wednesday and Saturday mornings. 'Country' I may be, but country don't always mean grit. I treated anything with less than two legs and more than four with an appropriate amount of trepidation. And why should I not? We lost two goats to snakes the summer last, and Granddaddy Harris was killed by a spider he carried into the house within the tip of his boot. Not that he knew it.

Until the moment it bit him.

Daddy's craftery was mostly empty now, save a wick or two, supplies beneath a film of winter dust. Most of it was overturned, destroyed, lorried away by Policeman Edmund and his men, evidence to strengthen the conviction they said. I would've thought the confession, combined with the witness, would have been enough. Only what do I know? I'm but the lowly daughter of a candlestick maker turned murderer, and I've no schooling but the farm.

The witness, Craybrooke, caught Daddy mid-act, hammer in hand and wheelbarrow by his side. I'm told Daddy brought the dead back by night. There are those who don't believe me when I say I had no knowledge of what Dudley Harris was doing back there. Guess that's their cross to carry. Such betrayals will never cease stinging, I imagine.

He beat them with that hammer, carried them in his wheelbarrow, and then waxed their skins in the craftery, corpses entombed inside a husk that would have split come spring. Candles branched from their shoulders and arms like toadstools after rain. Human chandeliers, the three of them.

I know this, and still see it in detail these weeks later, because Policeman Edmund had me dragged to the craftery to see the remains. Guess he hoped the sight would beat a confession out of me, too. It didn't do the trick, there being nothing to reveal — so Edmund tried his knuckles instead. It was the half-caste tracker who dragged them off me, there where I'd been thrown at the feet of the dead. I flinched when the strange man put a hand on my shoulder, tears on his cheeks as he whispered how he believed me. I'd never been touched by a man I didn't know before, least of all a black-skinned copper's hop.

The men's toenails had grown through the nubs of their waxy casings.

I've heard tell that our hair and nails continue growing after we die. For a while, at least. I do not understand death.

M'guts tell me it's the half-caste tracker who leaves me the bucket of goods on the veranda every morning, every second at least. Herbs, roots, mushrooms, a rabbit. Who else could it be? The last had been delivered day before last. He'd skinned the meat and picked it free of buckshot, covered it in a glaze that tasted like tobacco, the workings of someone with something to say. And I guess I heard it true. *'I care'*. But being believed is pale comfort when eating alone. My stomach may be full, but I'm left drunk on his pity. After dark, I return the bucket to where I found it and wait at the window to see if he'll come. Haven't caught him yet, though. Not that I'd know what to say if I did. 'Thank you' is too hard a thing to muster, and oh so small.

Wind off the ranges makes the house planks groan about their nails. I wake nightly, often weeping, sounds not for the sharing. Only in these moments do I appreciate the solitude Daddy gifted me, warranted or not. And perhaps I do deserve this.

I should've known what he was up to.

Someone threw a rock through the parlour window yesterday, the crunch-crunch of feet over frost as the coward made for the trees. I patched the hole with ply from the barn, not utilising the hammer Daddy had been fond of. Edmund took that away. I used the butt of our woodchopping axe. Afterwards, I kept the tool by my side for the rest of the night on account of sounds I didn't much like out there in the dark, scuttling that made my chest seize. Touching the axe handle soothed me a wee bit. Though nowhere near enough.

At some point, I crawled into Daddy's chair and howled, hating myself for thinking those three dead men were transients only, whiskey-hounds who'd hitched the wrong trains into the wrong town at the wrong time, men who must have burned their bridges elsewhere and were not worthy of anyone's time or pity. Thinking that my father had done them a favour. That they would not be missed by anyone of virtue. The only thing to do was take a knee in the bedroom, kick aside the chamber pot, pray for forgiveness I'm yet to see acknowledged.

Father, please. A sign. Tell me what to do.

There on my knees, the room spun. Then it was as though a hand I couldn't see reached down my throat to drag the vomit out of my stomach. Every breath tasted like game and tobacco and earth. There should have been relief. Only there was none. I scrubbed away the mess, leaving behind a humiliating patch on the mattress.

Tonight is dark and cold and lonely as yesterday. And the yesterday before that. I'm quite sure I want only to die.

Where there is no forgiveness, madness wells. I know that now. It fills you with appetites you want to deny yet cannot. The drip-drip-drip of an unbreakable fever. And drinking is easy, the easiest thing in the world, its madness sweet enough to rot you to the bone. Perhaps I should use the axe on myself—fall on it face-first and kiss the dark.

Daddy?

Daddy, are you there?

I'm afraid.

He doesn't answer, though I do hear the *screech-screeechhh* of waxy rope over tree branch between dreams. Dawn snaps night in two like kindling over a knee, and I went outside for air. The bucket was filled again.

I looked down at the rabbit, skinned except for its head, ears draped over the tin rim. Its paws, too, were untouched. Fur gloves peppered with beads of glaze. Morning frost had clouded the animal's eyes, reminding me of marbles the boys in town played with in the dirt when they weren't busy hissing rhymes at passing women. As I knelt to retrieve the bucket, I wondered if the rabbit's claws had continued to grow after it was shot. If fur spindled from its neck and snout even though its heart no longer thrummed.

And if it had, for how long?

"Is there still time?" I asked the rabbit, not expecting an answer. My voice was foreign in my ears. Slurred. I felt as though I'd spent the night on Daddy's moonshine, that its effects hadn't worn off. A sudden hunger for the tracker's glaze and the mushrooms he'd picked, the desire to run butter over those yellowed gills, the springy resistance in the cap before teeth pierced flesh. I needed it. And that need sprung the sweat from my skin, odd considering the chill. I flushed just the same. All over. Both inside and out.

"There's time," the rabbit said without moving its mouth. *Screech-screeechhh. Screech-screeeecccchhh.*

"But not much."

2

Saint Mathew's is a mile from the house, through fields with untended fences.

No torch is needed, there being moon enough to light the fog. Once or twice I stopped in my tracks, startled by a shape unfolding from the mist. It was just a tree, its girth wrung with faces crying sap. It couldn't be any more different from the one Daddy died on. Sickness took me over. The death tree in town is bone white, except for its lightning grafts, and smooth as a sheep's belly after shearing. And this I know because I'd walked into the square and touched it the night before, kneeling before it as though asking for a conspirator in crime.

Pleading forgiveness in advance.

I don't want to hang from you, dear tree. But this has to be done.

There's still time, remember?

I slit Ole Ma's wedding dress before setting out. Daddy kept it in his tallboy under a film of paper. Scissors butterflied the gown. Its silk now glides across the grass with ease, though it's only weighted with a shovel. I would have brought the wheelbarrow, only the law took that, too. Or maybe I wouldn't have.

Foxes watch me come and go. I approach the cemetery from the east.

My father's marker has been uprooted, snapped in two, pieces punched by bullet holes. I lay on the soil and hope the fog will thin enough to let in the stars and a little common sense. The fog is stubborn, as Daddy said I always was.

There's comfort in its glow.

The dig commences. Shivers. Panting breaths.

Screech-screeechhh. Screech-screeeecccchhh.

The new day bleaches the sky as I drag the corpse on the wedding dress into our lot. No flies yet, though the trip took longer than anticipated.

I bury Daddy under the house where the snakes sleep, under wood-beams that will be garlanded by webs once the weather turns. The ground is soft, and by the time the deed is done, I'm a mess of mud and Daddy's flaked skin. Something in me is both dead and alive, a candle burned at each end. And whatever's left, I have no choice but to own.

Days pass.

Mornings begin with another bucket from the tracker. The concept of coming outside to find it empty as I'd left it is enough to make me scratch at my skin. It has come to the point where I'm going to bed thinking of the mushrooms and glaze I've consumed, waking in anticipation of the mushrooms and glaze to come. I'm not sure this is any way to live. But I am living, and I'm not as afraid. Even the axe is back by the woodpile where it belongs.

No more thrown stones. That, at least, is something.

Boys sing the tallow-maker rhyme until I threaten them with a backhandin' when I head into town. They aren't in school, hardly dressed for church. This is how I piece together that it must be Saturday. I should be more patient with people than I am. Their stares are difficult to tolerate.

The store is fine, cavernous without its rightful proprietor behind the register a cousin brought with her from Tasmania after Ole Ma died. I made a mental note to scrounge through Daddy's papers to find her address and draft a letter. There could be, I hoped, a fresh start in the far south. Might change my name, though I feared the way shame had a tendency to stick.

Still, this sliver of hope helped me through the week, indeterminable as the passing days prove to be. And knowing that Daddy's close to me again, warmed by dirt, conversing with the mice beneath the floorboards, that I'd gotten to him in time, also helps.

"Tallow-maker, tallow made," I sing into my mattress on the eve of that letter being sent. My hand dangles off the side of the bed. I splay my palm against the wood until it warms, a token for Daddy down there under the house.

I think he's a'stirrin'.

Screech-screeechhh. Screech-screeeecccchhh.

The shrieking birds of morning.

I empty my chamber pot, piss steaming on the lawn. Chickens fed. Coffee brewed. Eggs boiled. Nessie and Tessie can wait for their milking a little longer.

A gasp snags in my throat as I head to my bedroom to dress.

I raise a hand to the wall and touch what has grown through the plaster—and not in one spot, either. It's all along the length of the corridor. I study the stalks, cradling air within my lungs as I would a pup. Roots push through the plaster with a thin screech, moving at a snail's pace. Wrist-bones *click* as I lay my palms against those pointed tips, delighted by their sharpness. A smile sits foreign on my face. I can't help but welcome it.

You should be afraid of this, whispers a tiny voice in my head.

Only fear is the last thing I feel.

It's not roots I touch, though they grow like roots—and from a single source, too. *They're coming from under the house.* The stalks are hundreds, even thousands of Daddy's fingernails, some thick as tongues, others fine as twine. And they have branched even further by the time day ebbs into dark again, curling towards me and giving off a brackish whiff, a wound you're not repulsed by because it's your own.

I sleep better that night than I have in a quite some time.

And there's a bucket waiting for me on the veranda.

The rabbit holds its tongue.

Indulgence has always been rare as hen's teeth for me. But I need a treat. I've earned it.

The bath is drawn.

Plus, I have ambitions of opening the shop come Monday next, hopeful that a trade might be mustered from the curious, scented wicks of controversy for people to take home and tame like brumbies. Standing behind that register would require courage I believed to be beaten and broken, though hardly dead. Baths, on those occasions when I did something good for myself and had them, nurtured my body into decent health and preparation for change. Elements meeting elements, bubbles frothing with the fleecing that is letting something go.

I suspect further indulgences ahead.

I've hurts aplenty.

It takes fourteen bales to cover my nakedness, and the home-made soap is fashioned from goat fat scented with last season's lavender. Steam curls the air. Wind doesn't moan. It complains. And I let it. This is *my* time. There are cracks in the ceiling where there hadn't been cracks before, that's how the wind gets in. Well, let it. Let it come. I ease into the tub, which cants to one side as though the floorboards are off-balance. Come to think of it, the whole room is off-balance.

I'm not worried by this at all.

There is strange luxury in these changings, the way the house has warped around me, shifted like a sheet under which its owner rolls in his sleep.

You should be afraid of this.

A half-hour passes, long enough to prune. Candles flicker. Rested, I reach for the plug chain to drain the tub. Find it. Pull it. The gurgle is loud and throaty. Grey water swirls through pipes behind the walls, deposited on the garden outside. Daddy used to say soap kept the slugs at bay. He was right.

Weight settles on me as the water-level drops. I don't hop out immediately—the cold beyond the steam is an intimidating thing. The water is milky with suds and filth, dropping below the moons of my kneecaps. A tapestry of black hair is revealed— only none of that hair belongs to me. I jolt, wondering if I'd been bathing with snakes all along.

I grip the tub on either side.

Water gurgles away and the wet pelt lathers my legs and torso, a second skin, strands of it clinging to my breasts. I lift my arms, braids draping, releasing the faint aroma of tobacco and spit after a pipe is emptied, old newspapers and tonics. My father's scents.

You should be afraid of this, comes the thin whisper again. A whisper through cracks and canted floorboards. And yes, I *am* rattled. But I'm also awed.

"Daddy," I say, bursting into tears. "You're really here, ain't-chya? Stay. Please, stay."

Knees against chest, the cold an afterthought. There is heat in the knots of hair. I wear it like a gown as I step out of the bathroom and shuffle down the hall, dripping water, bending under the criss-crossing fingernail stalks. His smell is everywhere. Everywhere! I sit before the fire in the parlour, steaming and full of lightness, welcoming the deepest sleep I've experienced since before noose-date.

I break from sleepless black a few times during the night to screams on the wind.

They are trying to tell me something.

Screech-screeechhh, goes rope over death tree. *Screech-screeee-cccchhh.*

It's louder now than before.

A nudge of light. My eyes creak open.

The floorboards on which I've slept have bulged in the night. A crack slivers through the opposite wall, and a faint cry dies in my throat as I struggle upright, bones snaking into realignment. Wind jangles our slowly tilting homestead, filling rooms with a tuneless whistle.

Daddy's hair has dried to my skin in a pelt, fronds wisping over uprooted wood as I scuttle for my bedroom. My palm flush against the door, pushing.

Inside, everything leans to the left, overturned trinkets on the mostly threadbare armoire that Ole Ma once sat at to braid her hair, singing. It's impossible to number the days I've longed to hear the sound of her voice. But her imprint long faded away. I'm a tally of forgotten things. This makes me appreciate the pelt I'm wearing, the fatherly stink of it. Being alone is someone else's problem now. Because Daddy is back in some form, even if his long-dead wife is not. It's as if she never had a voice to sing with in the first place.

Screech-screeechhh. Screech-screeeecccchhh.

Snow flurries in my bedroom.

I glance at the ceiling, hands lifting to hold the tiny flakes. Only no, it's not snow. Nor is it peeling paint. It's dried skin. Tiny pieces of him by the thousands, his whittlings. Daddy's dandruff.

Long, drawn-out cries issue from outside.
I'm too content in his storm to care.

3

I don't open the store that Monday as planned. The homestead has swung even further off its hinge, furniture bundled against the left-hand side in piles. There's glass everywhere from where the windows have burst free of their frames. I lurch from room to room in my shawl of hair, strands I've ornamented with ribbons and twine. Rats scurry between my feet to nibble at spoiled rabbit and mushrooms my body ejected at some point.

Hours writhe by. Pissing hurts, burning at my core that filters out with a wince. Blood in the back of my throat, too. I stumble from the outhouse and onto grass that feels like a million frozen splinters, the door clattering shut behind me. I glance back to my—our—home.

Screech-screeechhh. Screech-screeeecccchhh.

From this angle, it's easy to see how the whole building has been pushed off its piers from the fingernails, as though long ago the foundations were erected on an acorn, triggered now and blooming at breakneck speed, stalks desperate for the sun and willing to cast the building aside in order to attain it. Some of those nails reach high. Some buckle under their ambition and curl into pinwheels. But they all clatter in the breeze. My love for this place has never been more severe because Daddy is a part of it now, a tree of protein branch and hair willow and skin spores, more living than the one he'd been hanged from, the death tree, eyes bulging beneath his hood and rope knots grinding like teeth over white bark. I twinge, happily, at the sight.

Something moves through the trees on my right.

Screech-screeechhh. Screech-screeeecccchhh.

A swish of movement, and then it's gone. I climb up into the house through a window near the vegetable garden. The slugs got it after all.

Twilight in pursuit. I leave behind the corpses of dead chickens that foxes ripped apart, paying them no mind. Nor the screaming, either. There is only this. My need to be home with him.

The *chomp* of a raw potato between my teeth, forcing it down. Attaching bells to the hair-bows so I'm pretty for him. Pissing brown waste into the chamber pot after dark. The bed doesn't feel right, so I push aside the furniture and curl up where the wall of my room meets the floor.

Rats come and go, fog seeping in through cracks and around architraves.

Blackness inverts, dreams of chandelier men creeping towards the homestead. The death tree, pale as the white around an eye, enormous behind them. Daddy's noose dangles from its extended bow. The chandelier men lumber on, drawn to me, their wicks blowing out. I still hear muffled voices beneath the wax, screaming and singing.

I wake to find that the night isn't through with me, nor my grief.

A slow-moving sludge inches across the floorboards in my direction, ebbing to my knees from on high. It is warm, and pools about me like honey about a spoon. The sensation of its tide doesn't alleviate hurts, of which there are many. Rather, it strikes me as made of hurt, and that, perhaps, is why I feel at home in it. This is an embracing I don't know how to say no to. So, I don't.

You should be afraid of this.

I nestle against my hair-coated arms, skin flakes twirling in the air, fingernails sprouting from between the floorboards to knit me a shell in which to hide. The sludge rises bit by bit, sweating from the wall on the other side. From the dark.

Falling asleep has never been so easy. No dreams on the other side.

A thud in the house. Light filters into the room. I'm still on the floor.

"Hullo, miss?" comes a voice from down the hall.

The clatter of a dropped bucket.

I flinch, trying to get up, the realisation that I'm mostly naked lashing at me. Only I can't move, not even a little. Every part of my person, excluding the upper half of my face and left shoulder, is sealed beneath the sludge.

Wax.

It has hardened.

Panic swells, and again, I try to move. Tendrils of my father's hair, the freckling of his skin flakes, are mixed with the wax pinning me in place. My breaths come short—have to. There's hardly wriggle-room for my lungs to expand, and my lower jaw is set in place.

A moan escapes me as those footsteps draw nearer. Curses as the man approaches, the wicker-snap of fingernails brushing as he forces his way through the almost sideways hall. To here. To my room. To me.

Please, I long to say, even though I can't. *Turn back! Don't see me this way.*

Rats dodge into hiding as the half-caste tracker stumbles into view. He wriggles through the canted architrave to glare in at me, railroad spike eyes within the shield of his face. The house trembles. Daddy's hair constricts beneath the wax and I gasp.

(She's mine. Not yours, stranger.)

"Missus?"

He crab-walks closer, and I am ashamed. He extends a hand.

"Uhroo," I whine at him. *No.*

The half-cast tracker stinks of bushfire and the lamp and the grog we white folk have bred into him and his people under threat of their lives. He snatches back that hand, affronted. As he should be.

I'm not ready.

He tries to free me again. I scream for him to leave—throat raw. The tracker backs away, confused. He tosses me a look before slipping back into the hall, that of a man who has seen you at your most naked and can't differentiate disappointment from pity. I didn't ask for his honour. No, not once.

You should be afraid of this. Afraid of what you've let yourself become.

I sense that he'll be back, and maybe not on his own. Perhaps he'll bring his boss, Edmund, a man who'd relish the opportunity to see me done for good. Have me convicted of something and hanged from the death tree, too. *Please, not that.*

Hours pass, or at least they might be hours. Nobody comes, after all.

The decay of the day.

I weep for my father and for the men he murdered out in his craftery. My prayers are mumbles, tongue-clicks. Though I'm sure the good God in Heaven understands the language, even if His lack of reply is a drowning.

I love my father. But I am not my father.

There is no help coming. If I'm going to get out of here, it will have to be of my own will. Figure the Lord must be tied up. And why should he bother with me? I'm just an unschooled orphan of the land.

I stare at the rats staring at me, expecting one of them to stand up on its hind legs and talk to me as the skinned rabbit had done. To tell me that there's still time.

Only the rats say nothing.

Push! Yes. Push harder.

Wax begins to yield. I burn within, desperate to escape it all, to escape *him*. Let me go, I want to scream. Only, no.

It is I who must let go of him.

I'm sorry, Daddy.

My legs move, a hair-coated knee breaking the seal. I clamp my jaw and spit out a chunk of waxy skin. It takes everything I have in me, every ounce of energy, to heave from the mess, through the burrow of fingernails, and untangle myself from the knots of a dead man's hair.

Because, yes. He is dead. And dead means there is no coming back. Just ask my mother. Ask my nameless brother whose bones are buried in the lot, assuming the foxes haven't dug them up. I hope Daddy dug him deep.

Though I don't trust he did.

I get there. I push and push and make it through.

Shivers wrack me on the uneven floor where I sprawl without clothes. Another crack climbs the wall, raining dust. My companions, the rats, scatter as I limp to the broken window and spill out onto the ground. Winter has teeth and chews from every direction. A partial moon has faded into view above the tree line, a cosmic wink of knowing—and I'm angered by its contempt. In the barn there's enough hay for me to rest on, burlap sacks to wrap myself up in for the night. The smell of loam in my nostrils.

The fever breaks at some point.

I wait for the *screech-screeechhh, screech-screeeeeccchhh* of waxy rope over the death tree to come again. And I wait.

And wait.

There are goodbyes that I moan into the hay. Stars above, their light in the barn. It is then that the screaming outside starts again, a sound that has been with me for so long I've almost failed to hear it. A bellow from across the field. It comes into me. Into me deep, through the veins where the roots had taken hold but are dead now. I bolt upright, the burlap slipping off my shoulder, heart trip-hammering. Fear makes everything brighter.

"Oh, no," I say, realising what I've failed to do. "Heavens, no."

My feet crunch grass as I step outside, guilt for a guide.

Nessie and Tessie continue to mewl as I draw closer, their dumb eyes unable to comprehend what has happened to them or what they did to deserve such torture. Their udders bulge from a lack of milking, huge sacks of neglect. Weeping, I drop to my knees and take them by the teat. The two cows scream and scream until I'm done doing my job, and I'm screaming along with them, our noises a dance that reverberates through this part of New South Wales, out here where we're not wont for snow. Mostly. I'd brought no bucket with me from the barn, so I kneel in their steaming milky slop until everything is quiet again.

I'm afraid. How can I be this afraid, yet live?

Close to dawn, I climb inside the house for clothes. Buttons through buttonholes. Laces through shoe. Not even water washes the taste of meat from my throat. The dress I chose hangs from my frame like the remains of a broken kite, but never mind. There's only one thing to do now, the only thing. I'm blind to all else. I head for town and the lightning-scarred tree at its heart, taking the axe with me. A nasty chanticleer slips from my mouth, soon carried away on the breeze.

"Tallow-maker, tallow made. His wick burns in the grave…"

And whilst it might be my imagination, I think I'm watched from the dark. Though perhaps, by caring eyes.

The bush is dead around us, and spring so far away.

Nona Doesn't Dance

Skyroad after skyroad revealed billboards in the toxic haze, only the advertisements had changed since last time. Even at eight years old, Sienna knew how quick the world was to update itself, to find something new to sell and distract itself with. They hadn't visited Nona in twelve months. Almost three whole school trimesters.

Class was back-to-back hours of information processing— demands to learn it, remember it, recycle it. Monday to Friday. One big countdown to the weekend. Those gaps between trips to her grandmother, however, stretched without comparison. They were the empty spaces, and sometimes, in them, Sienna forgot about Nona altogether. Guilt cures weren't advertised on the billboards they flew past.

But it was Christmas, as Da reminded them before loading up the cruiser, like she could forget. Christmas meant you do what you must even if you don't want to.

And I don't want to, Sienna conceded. Then, before then, now.

Nona always smelled funny when they went to her pod after the show, like dried spit on a pillow. Then there was The Home itself, with its long corridors and security drones levitating from room to room to ensure nobody had fallen from their beds. That happened. People even died. Sienna processed this fact—and others—in articles at school. Getting old made no sense, and she often wondered what Nona did to deserve it.

Another billboard. Another. They shone red and green, colours Sienna enjoyed when viewed independently but made her queasy when together, as though she'd scoffed too many sweet emulators in one sitting, regardless of her mother's cautions. Ma was always at her. *Do this. Don't do that. You'll regret it. You'll thank me someday.* She sat in the front seat now, poised and tightly-wound, watching reindeer holograms loop in the smog above the sport stadium. Some advertisements featured a skinny smiling Santa, his gaunt cheeks too red, teeth far too white. Neat teeth, Sienna thought. Baby teeth. Sienna tapped her own with a fingernail. She turned from the window. "Ma? Are teeth just skeletons sticking out?"

"What a question."

"Yes, love," replied her father as he steered the cruiser into a tunnel, toll beepers flaring, overhead fluorescents turning into a string of ruby and white. Coca Cola branding. Sienna smiled. She'd processed information about the drink at school.

The little girl nodded, content. For now. Her fingers inched around her face, sussing out the sculpture of her bones.

Her snoozing brother beside her, head lolling. Boys were icky, except Da who got a free pass. Damien was two years her senior, not that many people could tell. Damien still wet the bed, forgot how to speak every now and then. Damien sometimes did a lot of things that other kids didn't. Sienna didn't think her brother would have to worry about getting too old, not like Nona, a fact she tried to ignore as best she could. And failed every time.

She sighed, shuffling in her seat, squinting as they flew from the tunnel and into the valley where trees no longer grew. Sienna hated this part. All those rocks and pebbles and cracks below like an almost dead beach breaking itself apart in search of water. Santa would have to wear his safety mask and goggles on his sleigh. The haze could kill anyone.

Toxic had been one of Sienna's first words.

Irritable, she triggered the concave depressors in her wrist and the ring on her forefinger beamed a cat hologram across the back of her mother's seat. The cat licked its paw, glanced around as though a digital fly had flown by. Tweeny, she dubbed the cat on her birthday six trimesters ago. The name was a hug and didn't need to make sense.

The cat waivered, static threatening.

(Stupid thing!)

Bad word, she thought, scrambling. *Even in your head. Someone's always listening.*

(Silly thing. Better.)

Sienna hoped Santa brought her a new depressor. She hadn't asked for it, nor had she sent him correspondence as kids were supposed to—but he knew these things, right? Sienna had been a good girl this year. You had to be good, always. That's what they said.

Tweeny followed its unseen distraction and leapt over her brother's sleeping face, seeming to scratch at his freckles before slicking across the interior of the windshield.

"Damn it," her father yelled, swerving with shock. "Turn that off."

"Sienna! What have we told you about using that thing in here?"

"Sorry." The eight-year-old deactivated the simulator and shrunk in her seat, a fast-blooming flower in reverse. "Jesus," she almost said aloud, pocketing the word in the back of her brain instead, cushioning it between images of virtual reality horses and memories of Da saying he loved her drawings. The word was outlawed, big time trouble there.

Ma gave Sienna one of her glass-cutting stares.

"Enough of that," said Da, gripping the wheel. "Damien, wake up. We're here."

Always the same stories as they approached The Home. Da's voice loud in her ear through the microphone in Sienna's mask.

"When she was young, my mother used to make the best Christmas cake. We'd all look forward to it," he said, guiding them from where he docked the cruiser and through the haze. "I miss it, you know. She'd always be singing, and when she didn't know the words, she made them up. Your uncles and I used to laugh over that. But there was nothing—and I mean nothing—that compared to how Nona danced. That was her job, back in the day."

Sienna held her brother's hand as they walked, drones projecting bird holograms over the haze, only the projector kept looping the footage in a clumsy time trip. She bit her lip, imagining what it must be like to be as old as those inside the nine-storey building in front of them. Damien groaned at her side.

That Nona ever danced seemed an impossible thing. There had never been a time in Sienna's life when her grandmother appeared younger than she was now. She recalled learning about insects trapped in amber in programming class, captured as they had died, young forever. And shuddered.

A memory from their last visit:

There in her pod recliner, industrial droids spinning their cogs to shovel slush into Nona's mouth. A grunt from the ancient woman. Expelled a bowel movement. The mess vacuumed through tubes in the seat. There hadn't been a smell, and that unnerved Sienna most. Where did the poop go? *Into the empty spaces, maybe. That was where everything she couldn't see or remember or understood ended up.*

If you couldn't process it, it didn't exist.

Doors to The Home opened to let out the hospital air. Dust speckled Sienna's goggles. She rubbed them clear and caught her brother staring at her, sensed his disquiet. Once the doors slammed in a gasp of compressed gas, projections of fields and grazing cows resumed on the chrome walls. They slipped free of their masks after decontamination. Drawn-out moos echoed from speakers they couldn't see and birdsong played too loud. It hurt Sienna's ears. Damien squeezed her hand.

Drones zoomed down the corridor to greet them.

"Here we go, kids," Ma told them. "Behave yourselves."

Sienna did as she was told and hoped Santa took note.

With their identities approved and retinas scanned, the hologram of a woman in hospital scrubs blinked to life before them. She was too tall to pass as real. Like Santa on the billboards, her teeth were neat and crowded, white as the joints of the boiled chicken bones in the broth her mother made when Sienna was unwell. Sienna was often unwell.

"Merry Christmas to the—**Dunlop-Spruce**—family," said the nurse, shifting her clipboard from under one arm to the other.

"Welcome to The Home. We all hope your travels were safe and that you're not too tired. We've got a lovely event planned for you. Oh, yes. Well, now that we're all together, let's go find— **Eleonore Dunlop**—for you."

The voice stating the names didn't match the rest of the hologram's sentences, similar to an auditory cut-and-paste from one of Sienna's school sessions. A chill scuttled up her spine, playing bones that would grow out of her mouth like an instrument.

"Let's go," said the hologram nurse. Cheery. Her feet didn't touch the ground when she walked. Still, the Dunlop-Spruce family followed their guide down one of The Home's gun barrel corridors, passing sealed rooms where the elderly were tended to, passing windows overlooking hologram fields where hologram workers looked up from their picks to wave. Sienna felt the fake warmth from the screens on her face as she walked by.

Maybe forgetting Nona is better? Or melt the amber and set her free for good.

They didn't speak as they went, studying the hard walls that didn't reflect the light instead. Footfalls didn't echo, either. Like the building was designed to not absorb sound. Sienna hungered for Tweeny again chasing her tail, toying with simulated balls of twine. Triggering the cat required no effort, and the temptation was right there. One meow to make Sienna happy, a flitter, a peekaboo to carry her through. Her brother would enjoy it as well, she thought. Damien's phlegmy breaths itched at her ears. His eyes were too dry, red.

"Here we are—**Eleonore Dunlop**—is through here," said the nurse with a giggle. She waved her hand over the door display. The portal widened in an expanding iris.

Darkness on the other side.

"Have a lovely day—**Dunlop-Spruce**—family. Happy new year. I'll see you once the show is over."

One by one they filed into the theatre, choosing front row seats before the stage. Blue velvet curtains ebbed on a breeze that shouldn't be there, The Home being airtight as it was.

"This is like a cinema," Sienna heard her mother say. "Remember them, Lochie?"

"I think I do," Da said. "But. No. Maybe. Maybe I don't."

Sienna turned in her seat to watch a holographic audience fade from the shadows of the dimly lit auditorium, cerulean shapes filing in and settling around them, wavering like cruiser headlights through steam in the city. She couldn't wait to get back to their apartment, to her room. Better to fold all this into the empty spaces again until next year with all the days of programming and weekends full of fun between.

The auditorium filled, overlapping voices issuing from unseen speakers. A hush fell as those curtains drew back, wheels turning and the whisper of heavy material. An acute beat of excitement punched through Sienna, but then she remembered where she was and how she'd felt last time they had been in this exact spot. About to see this exact same show. Memory turned her throat to sand as those who had never lived applauded all about her.

"Da, I want to go," Sienna said. He didn't listen. He rarely did.

Damien reached across the arm of his chair to snatch her leg. She felt him quivering. Sienna took his hand, boy-ickiness evaporating, and saw a scared boy she sometimes loved as she was expected to.

Voices receded. A chorus that didn't exist began to sing. Sienna recognised the tune. *Come, All Ye Faithful.*

The hologram audience swayed in tune to the music, weeds in a tide tugged this way and that. Meanwhile, the Dunlop-Spruce family remained motionless. Sienna stared, braced.

Dry ice bloomed in the upper left hand of the stage as Nona descended from above, swinging onto the floorboards. "Jesus," Sienna whispered, not caring about the consequences. She knew all the naughty words. Memories were fluid in the empty spaces between visits but turned to spears when drawn into the present. That sharpness pierced her now. *Here we go. Again.* A machine Sienna thought of as 'the spider-claw'—not that she'd ever call it that aloud—conducted Nona's movements like a puppet master.

Metal stilts clipped and clopped as the machine twirled the old woman in ways she could no longer manage on her own.

Nona used to dance. That was how her father's story went. Year after year. Every time they trundled to The Home for Christmas.

Danced like you wouldn't believe.

Pistons fired. Prongs eased Nona's head to the left, forcing her to arch, legs extending as the music swelled. She wore a gown of delicate lace. The spotlight illuminated the calligraphy of varicose veins beneath the hem. Sienna wondered where the red ballet shoes came from. Those were new. Bundles of wire constricted the old woman's arms, dragged her limbs into a pirouette. The spider-claw spun on the end of its long arm and scuttled across the stage. Flawless programming. Smooth. Not at all like Tweeny with his twine and static.

Sienna watched, mouth open. And her family watched, too.

Damien's hand tightened on her own. She squeezed back. *I'm here.*

The spider-claw arched forward so they could see Nona's face through a criss-cross of tubes and shadows, the music rising to a crescendo. Button-sized spades on the ends of needles inched from the metal halo around Nona's face to hook the insides of her mouth, drawing backwards to open the old woman's mouth like yet another theatre curtain. A curtain of skin. Brackish gums. Sienna wondered if this was meant to be a smile.

Nona's eyes locked with her granddaughter's. Tears on that wrinkled face. A moan which might have been more than that, escaped her.

Help me, said the old woman's look. *Help me.*

Sienna tried to get out of her seat, but her mother pushed her down. "You can't leave," she said. "It's tradition. We have to stay. There's nothing wrong and Nona's fine. Look, see. She's dancing. Nona loves this. This is what Nona wants—"

"Look at her, Ma. She doesn't want this. She hates it! This is for you, not her and—" Sienna's protestations died in her mouth. Her brother pressed close and asked her not to leave. Sienna stared at the wet patch spreading across his crotch and almost said something, but the audience laughed and clapped so loud nobody would hear. *I want to disappear*. Only, no, they forced her to sit and watch the spider-claw force Nona into arabesques, extending her arthritic fingers, pinching her toes beneath red shoes. A swan of a neck exposed to the light, and the hologram audience roared. Some stood, arms raised. They cast no shadows.

"I want to go—"

To the right.

"Ma!"

To the left.

"Da!"

Only Da wasn't paying attention. His head was directed at the stage, eyes shut. It was difficult to tell from that angle, but Sienna thought he might be weeping. *If I have to watch then so do you*, she wanted to scream at him. *Who is this for, anyway? It's a trick, all of it a trick. A trick on her!* She hated him then. Wanted to reach across her brother and mother and slap him until he opened his eyes and admitted that everything about this was wrong.

Nona doesn't dance anymore, Da. And you can't make her—

Sienna didn't get a chance to say what she wanted to say, or even finish her thought. Electricity crackled at the top of the stage behind the curtain and sparks zipped like the shooting stars she'd heard about in processing class but had never seen in real life because of the smog. The spider claw jolted, and jolted Nona with it. Pinchers gripped her lips again for a show-stopping smile ahead of a curtsey but withdrew too fast. Skin ripped free of its gums. Bright blood hit the stage under the spotlight. The metal halo tipped, pistons firing at the wrong angle this time. Instead of tilting Nona's head it speared through her cheek and ripped the jaw clear off her face.

It wasn't just the old woman's screams in the auditorium now. Sienna and her family joined in too, carollers of a different kind. Throughout, the hologram crowd continued to sway and cheer and sing and laugh. Da's eyes were open now. He leapt from his seat to clamber at the stage, shouting his mother's name, only to trip and strike his head.

Nona's blood decorated the air as the spider-claw twirled and bound, trying to complete the performance as automated, only each of its movements mistimed. Wires pulled too tight. Hinges swung too far. The lacework of Nona's dress never stood a chance. It ripped as her old flesh ripped, all of it an apron of red upon red.

Wetness splashed Sienna's face. On her tongue.

Ma tried to pull Da back, the two of them silhouetted against the sparks and clouds of smoke. She had never heard sounds like that from her mother. Feral.

Sienna watched Nona's skeleton pierce up through her flesh, the machine making mouths of her joints, and every one of those kisses had new teeth coming through. White spears that gnashed, that clicked.

Damien let his sister go and ran.

Take me with you, Sienna ached to say to him. Only she couldn't form the words. Couldn't move at all—not to escape, or get help, not even to wipe the blood dribbling down her face. It was as though, like Nona, Sienna were held in place by a machine, crafted by flickering light and dark and tradition that wouldn't budge. They had come here to see Nona dance.

I have to be here.

Blood tasted salty.

Come All Ye, Faithful ended, curtain falling. Nona rose into the rafters, up where the light couldn't reach. The pitter-patter of gore dripping over a hardwood stage. Electricity.

The holograms, ghosts of those who never were, stood, gathered hats to shield them from suns that would never burn them and picked up coats that would keep chills from non-existent bones. They marched out, some fading and others blinking into nothing.

All the lights died. Screams. Damien thumped in the dark somewhere, she heard his cries. Sienna almost depressed the simulator on her wrist that she wanted replaced, for illumination if nothing else. She didn't, though. It just wouldn't be right. Tweeny, stupid Tweeny who didn't really work anymore wasn't worth the risk. Da might turn on her, his face busted open from where he'd struck the stage, lashing out as he sometimes did, his scolding whittling her down to size, down to nothing. So, she sat there as everything played out, trying to be a good girl because Santa was watching.

Little Balloons

We were in the backyard watching the kids. Skeletal mothers and fathers posed in lawn chairs with their phones, Diane Arbus photographs waiting to happen. The lawn was so lime it hurt to look at without Ray Bans. I sighed, dressed in a shirt that fit me a week ago and a pair of short shorts. A gust of air snatched the umbrella from my cocktail flute, but I didn't chase it, was distracted by a Frisbee thrown too wide. And then Dave lost control of his tongs and a sausage escaped the grill. It didn't get far. Barkley saw to that.

A good dog, always had been.

The sausage—speckled with confetti, blackened by Dave's need for us to know what a dude he was—never stood a chance.

Gulp, gone.

"Attaboy," I said, ruffling the Labrador's mane. Our eyes locked. We were almost indistinguishable from one other. Over-domesticated and sad.

Barkley was Dave and Linda's dog, funny when you thought about it. Linda, my sister, hated dogs ever since we were tots when Brett McAllister's poodle took a nip at her arm one afternoon. We'd been at their property eating berries straight off the vine. I should've been the big brother my parents wanted me to be, especially when Linda screamed, when Brett laughed. But I hadn't been that good big brother and my sister still bore the scars to prove it. My scars, however, are where nobody can see. Remorse chimes loudest at night.

The Frisbee returned, clipping my mimosa this time and

throwing pink slush across my shorts. I should've known better than to wear white to a six-year-old's birthday party. Linda's friend, Belinda, dived at me as Barkley had that poor sausage, napkins flying, dabbing, trying to undo what couldn't be undone.

Fussing. Always so much fussing. Sometimes, I can't take it. The Valium I popped earlier helps, but nowhere near enough.

"It's fine, it's fine," I said, handing the glass to her husband, Kiran. He gave me a refill and thumped me on the back as though I'd swallowed one of the kids' toys instead of being de-mimosaed by one. He issued a cringe-worthy comment that they all giggled over, a joke that was heavy on the in-your-end-do but light on wit.

His voice challenged me. Eyebrow raised with expectation. "Well, you know what they say, don't you, Larry?"

Dot, dot, dot.

Subtle as bullet holes in a speeding sign.

I realised, then, that he'd thrown me a comedic bone to chew on. It was me who was supposed to finish his joke. My zinger didn't measure up. I just scraped by.

Just.

A terrible fucking word.

Ask what I ate for breakfast, and I'd struggle to tell you. Ask me about every self-conscious slight or gaff over the past forty-five years of my life and I'd be able to recite them syllable for stuttering syllable. This particular 'just', spurned by Kiran's obvious disappointment (or maybe it had been a trap) was another deposit in the bank. I'd spite myself later on, back in my apartment as I tore my eyes from *Law & Order* reruns to watch the air-conditioner tickle an artificial fern in the corner of the room into the imitation of life.

Everyone glared at me from their chairs, from behind their grills and oversized sunglasses. Like dragging out the grand piano at one of my parent's infamous dinner parties, expecting Liberace but getting Latoya Jackson instead. I hadn't performed. If I wasn't Linda's brother, I'd be worried they'd soon trade me in for a newer, more functional gay. Like Barkley, fags make good pets. So long as they sit when asked, shake paws when commanded, and don't shit on the carpet.

I sat back in my chair, Kiran trotting off. Everything smelled of barbecue. Clouds over the sun stained the eight kids in the yard. It was Duncan's party, my nephew. He made my heart swell. The boy was less a boy than an advertisement for boys—that's how perfect he was. Duncan and his friends shrieked things I didn't understand, cried over currencies I'm just too old to trade in. (That word again, 'just'). I felt like the lone survivor in a plane crash, washing up on the *Lord of the Flies* island. Should one of the kids in the yard cry, "piggie!", I'd Uber to higher ground at breakneck speed—Code Blue. And I knew all about Code Blues. Dave was a doctor, something I never heard the end of from Linda. Being a real estate agent, I was an unfortunate reminder of her blue-collar roots, which like the splatter on my shorts, proved to be a stain that couldn't be daubed away. I wondered if she disremembered my pulling, my snipping, and my bowtieing of strings to help her score this condo by the beach.

Mutton dressed as lamb, my sister. The girl I used to know would laugh at the woman sitting across from me today.

"Did you hear?" said one of her disciples. "They're putting in a public housing tenement building over on Cayman Close."

"No," said another friend, exasperation unmatched. "But that's a gated community."

"I wouldn't lie about such a thing."

"It'll bring crime into the area. Don't they ever stop to think?"

"I wouldn't worry. There's a petition."

"Well, sign me up then."

"I'll text you a link to the app to register your vote on the website."

Nasal voices faded as I turned my attention to the children again. They were safe and unpretentious and hadn't mastered the art of lying. *Yet*. A block of ice migrated from one side of my mouth to the other, shrinking in size. I'd left my flat in the city, my old friends who didn't judge me for my limitations, my whole life, to come to the coast and care for our mother in her final years. Every defining thing melted away. I missed Mum endlessly, even though she turned mean in the end. Cruelties were hugs in disguise. Neurons firing in a dying brain. Darts poisoned with family secrets shot from her lips. She told Duncan to piss off. Linda couldn't take it when Mum called her a bitch.

My eyes settled on Duncan, life of the party, there with his friends. They danced over cloud shadows.

And the woman, the clown, kept an eye on us all.

"Hidey-ho-ho-ho, kiderinos," she said from behind grease-paint. "Who wants a balloon?"

She smiled her double smile, one real, one fake, relishing in the kids prancing to her popcorn cart in the corner of the yard. Behind the plexiglass, catching the midday sun, she'd propped three industrial cannisters. Helium. I saw their taps from where I reclined, surrounded by people I didn't really know who talked in a language I didn't really understand as they tried to tell me who I really was without saying a thing at all.

The clown gripped those taps with chubby fingers. Twist. Twist. Twist. She grinned again—though you can never quite tell. It doesn't matter if you don't get the joke, clowns stare like they know you skeleton deep.

"Want a balloon?"

"Yes-sssssss!" screamed the kids. Their cheers evoked a strange chill, despite the barbecuing weather. I turned away, something flittering in my guts.

"Where'd you find this clown?" I asked my sister who was busy showing Brenda or Sandra or whoever something on one of their phones.

"Huh?"

"The lady?"

"Oh, isn't she fab!"

"Who is she, Linda?" I said, stroppier than intended.

"Don't get your knickers in a knot, Larry."

"All I'm doing is asking who she is."

My sister glared, affronted, and straightened her back. She would have paid good money for this glorified babysitter with her cart and cannisters. Linda returned her focus to the phone and picked up her conversation.

Kids mulled about the clown's stand, pushing and shoving.

One by one, they turned our way, ogling for validation. *Isn't this the coolest? Tell me it is, Mum, Dad. Confirm it. Tell me what I already know, and then you'll be cool. A dude. Just like Dave.*

Maybe it *was* cool. And maybe I *was* overthinking things, and the chill that wouldn't go away was just—as my mother used to say when she had her faculties—me being 'a little bit Larry'. And if that were the case, it might explain Linda's sly, feline stare.

"Hey, Uncle Larry!" Duncan called.

I toasted him with the remainder of my drink that I hadn't already nervously downed. I was so thirsty, kindling inside. Too hot. Everything was too loud. The clown's outfit and her smile were too bright. She was round of body and face, locks of hair mushrooming from under a pointy hat. It was impossible to tell her age.

"You okay there, big fella?" Kiran asked me.

I cleared my throat. "Right as rain, buddy-o." Latoya Jackson, I thought again. Piano strings and prayer.

The clown handed over her empty balloons. They weren't inflated so why the helium cannisters then? Limp multi-hued nothings snatched by kids who would never stop to question what might be happening.

(And what is happening here, Larry?)

It was my mother's sick voice in the back of my head. In those tones you heard the scratching of steel wool on gums. Heard it, yes. But felt it, too. Tasted it.

(You've done what Linda always says you do. You're looking too hard because you've got nothing else to look at, seeking drama because you've got none of your own. You're desperate to be noticed, because at the end of the day, you're easy to gloss over.

You're you, Larry.

Just.

You.)

The children ran about, Barkley yapping. Automatic sprinklers turned on and made rainbows for everyone to dive through. Parents put down their drinks to snap pictures, a kindergarten of Instagram filters and hashtags and TikToks.

I sat, still. Mimosa melting.

One by one, those around me returned to their chairs and gossip, mermaids on their rocks again, too afraid to do anything with their lives in case they grew legs and had to slum it like the rest of us. Was I bitter? Sure. But my bitterness wasn't without reason.

I hadn't always come to these barbeques alone.

Sound faded, their chatter, the sizzling grill, birdsong and the R'n'B music pounding from inside the condo. Soon, all that remained was the pft-pft-pft of the sprinklers, feet over grass. It was like seeing in black and white—except for the balloons the children were inflating. And the red smile of the clown as she huddled behind her cart.

Kiran's son blew into his balloon until it was almost at bursting point, and I watched, shocked, as his eyes rolled back in his head and he hit the ground. The rubber balloon, bright orange, an almost bile hue, pinwheeled through the air before puttering to the grass.

Nobody noticed but me.

Two more kids went down. Thud. Thud. Balloons sailed like daytime shooting stars only the Uncle Larrys of this world get the privilege of seeing.

The drink slipped from my fingers as I leapt from the chair, which flipped backwards and whip-cracked terracotta tiles. "Jesus," I said. *"The children!"*

Someone yelped behind me. "What the hell, Larry?"

Another child fell.

I ran through the sprinklers, water beading off my thighs. I saw what I saw and knew it was real. A chill took hold of me, burning from the inside out.

Right before the kids lost feeling in their legs, they puffed their cheeks and blew, funnelling themselves into the rubber skins the clown had given them. As I ran across the lawn, I noticed that the balloons in the mouths of the remaining children were full of more than (just) lung-dumps of oxygen.

They were full of the people the children would become.

Futures swirled in smoke beneath the rubber, only in the smoke, lost in that smoke, faces scrambled to be. *Help,* I almost heard them shrieking. *We're not ready.* Some of those phantom faces were handsome, others ugly. There were funny women and awkward men. I could see all their successes, all the opportunities they pissed away.

Thud. Another child down.

I was among them now, Linda and Dave and all the other parents shouting as reality punched through the eggshell façade they lived within—part fear, part disciplinary. Only they didn't know what I knew. That this was no game. The kids on the ground were dead.

One girl (I wished I remembered her name—to honour her, if nothing else) sprawled at my feet. To think this child had ever lived (let alone only seconds before) now seemed a fiction. Her cheeks were sullen, jaw unhinged to show off teeth she must've been proud to grow into. Her eyes glared with knowingness, as though they had seen things at six that they were not meant to see—let alone comprehend—until older. This dead child, all the dead children, knew themselves fully now. This terrified me and filled me with envy.

"NO!" I shouted as another balloon whizzed by my ear.

I spun to see another girl go weak and drop. I reached to catch her. Dead weight, an embodiment of wrongness that made my head spin. Keeping her upright was hard. She was too heavy. Down she went, another pigeon in the shooting gallery, or a tot in a preschool once the gunman ensures his hurts are heard. The girl faceplanted my shin before landing on a sprinkler, the spray filling her mouth and shooting out her nose.

Parents swarmed around me, screamed.

I heard none of it.

Nothing but the little boy exhale filling the green balloon in front of me. It swelled. I knew it was Duncan not because of the oversized sports jersey he wore, or the knees with the X-marks the spot Band Aids. I knew him by the spirit he filled the balloon with, all his potential. Because I had seen that potential in him, too. Uncles saw not what was aspired to or hoped for but what will be. These smoky images swirled under the taut rubber as I rushed at Duncan, almost tripping. Swishing faces inside the balloon, all the people he would love and be partly destroyed by, those who would force him to grow. In the balloon, there was every exam, every fumbling in the backseats of cars, there were the funerals and the weddings, and a world of pandemics and fires and collapsing buildings. It was there, all of it, the life of the boy I cared for more than I cared for myself, the echo of me, the best part of me, Duncan. As those hands went weak and his balloon set free, I watched, helpless, as the boy's eyes rolled white, just like all the others. I caught him, but he died in my hands.

People everywhere, knocking me over. They grabbed their children. Linda snatched Duncan away from me, glaring as though I'd done this, as though I were involved somehow. My fingers clutched at nothing.

I turned, tears mixed with spray, and pounced at the popcorn cart in anger. I overturned it, the burning ice flowing through me, splintering up through my pores. Empty helium cannisters rolled across the grass. Where I expected to find the clown hunched, hands rubbing together like a fly, her double smile stretched from ear to ear, there was nothing. Just the shadows of clouds as they chased the sun, but never catching it.

Barkley, such a good dog, howled. I howled with him.

The air-conditioner hummed in my apartment, its breeze stirring the artificial fern. It swayed back and forth. A plastic leaf tapped the white wall, a metronomic sound, the marking of time, the hours and minutes and seconds I'd stared at the television without seeing a thing.

My sister and brother-in-law were done with me for the day. The police had had their fill, too. I was one with my couch and felt crunchy with burning ice that wouldn't melt no matter how I willed it to, its shards criss-crossing my chest like Pick-Up-Sticks through Play Dough. Breathing was difficult and I was in a perpetual state of thinking I was dead until I blinked, and then it all cycled again.

Blue light from the television. Tin-can studio laughter. Photographs on the mantle of my mother and the friends I no longer saw and the men I've been damaged by. The glass that trapped them within their frames also glowed, reflections of sitcom happiness, characters in shows written to know who they are and why.

Imagine that, I thought. *Imagine knowing your place, and the pleasures of understanding who you want to be when you grow up.*

Blink. Cycle. Blink.

(*Go to bed, Larry*, said my dead mother from the place she resides in my mind).

I listened to her and pieced together the will to schlep myself off the couch. My feet in a V before me, grubby shoes still matted with grass. I reached to slip off my sneakers, tossing them on the carpet. My left shoe rolled onto its side, revealing something stuck to its tread.

I froze, seeing children's eyes rolling in the sitcom glow again, their bodies hitting the ground one by one. Sprinkler rainbows. Cloud shadows. The barking and howling of dogs. Police sketches and eraser dust swished off a tabletop by a hand. Fingerprints. All those body bags with their zipper clown smiles. Duncan and the man he would have become trapped within smoke, the look of knowing who he was before he died. I peeled the worm of purple rubber off my shoe and squeezed it.

Just a balloon.

Eels

1

Miranda thought she understood shame.

There was Ananya, the girl in high school she'd crushed on, who sought out Miranda's insecurities and announced them to the world. Commenting about her pockmarked skin. Her stretch marks. Wounds without a hope of healing. Ananya embarked on this mission once she learned who slipped the letter into her netball bag, that offending page ripped from a notebook, a letter Miranda signed with a heart above the 'I' where the dot in her name should be. Xs and Os that might as well have been a target.

"Do you love me, too? Tick yes or no."

Two months of smears followed. "Lezzos go to Hell, you know. She's into girls 'cause she's too ugly for a deep dicking. Maybe she's boy!" Two months waiting for that letter to be acknowledged, for the tick.

Just give me a fucking answer. Please. I'll wait.

Even though you're killing me.

Ananya died on Christmas Day, struck down by a drunk driver who assumed he had the right of way. Though the scars of her betrayal still stung, Miranda wept at the funeral. There had been more to their relationship than anyone could know. The life they had shared in Miranda's imagination.

Those invisible kisses. Handholding nobody else saw.

(I'll wait.)

Stinking heat in the church. Some of Ananya's relatives flew in from India, explosions of colour among the dandruff-lined suits.

Someone fainted, In Memorium booklets flying like startled birds. Girls snickered at Miranda from behind their hands.

"That's her," said Charmaine Newberry. "That's the dyke who liked her."

Miranda glanced up from the mahogany casket, her tears nothing to them. And saw her. She. The whisperer who wanted to be heard. Always.

Everyone knew Charmaine Newberry. The kind of girl who couldn't flick through something as innocuous as a chemistry textbook without announcing her personality to the world in some spectacular way. Went everywhere with a little Pomeranian called Squeak. The reflections of stained-glass martyrs painted Charmaine's face in a kaleidoscope as she sat on her pews at Ananya's funeral, dog in her lap. Squeak never made a sound. Ever. Miranda couldn't help but wonder why.

They locked eyes. The two young women across the aisle.

"Her."

Charmaine Newberry would carry the torch for the dead friend Miranda loved. "Watch your back," she'd say at any given opportunity to anyone who would listen. "Whoever she crushes on dies. Have you seen her skin? The stretch marks on her arms? She rides a skateboard, you know. Besides, lezzo cunts go to hell, everyone knows that. Ananya probably drove herself into that car because she couldn't take being obsessed over."

I'm not going to punch you.

I'm NOT going to punch you.

Even though I want to punch you, Charmaine Newberry.

And then there was Tyler at university, Tyler with the Holden Torana he'd resurrected from a junkyard. The craftiness of his hands was something Miranda knew better than most. She'd experienced his callouses up close. Springs beneath the backseat singing along with that old 'Til Tuesday song on the radio, the song that insisted she shut up now. He tasted of Guinness, tobacco. The way his penis looked. Long and thin—useless. He called Miranda a dumb shit, said it was her fault he couldn't get it up.

"'Cause you's ugly, that's why. Ugly as fuuuucccckkk."

I'm not going to punch you.
I'm not going to punch you.
I am NOT going to punch you, Tyler.

Miranda didn't finish her degree. Her thoughts were cracking ice cubes in lukewarm water, the chewed ends of pencils, tin between teeth. Her thoughts groaned, snapped, ground together. They were asphyxiations. And they rarely let in any light. She saw a tired doctor with certified qualifications in indifference framed in expensive plywood on his walls. He scribbled prescriptions for the ' —ines'. Fluoxetine. Sertraline. Paroxetine. They mostly worked. Mostly. Ice cubes held their shape. Pencils hardened. Tin, swallowed. Miranda could breathe, sometimes. One thing remained constant throughout.

Shame.

Bear-trap vicious shame.

Miranda could've sworn she knew its ins and outs, the way it tended to lie dormant, rusting, and then coming out to play when you least expected it. The way it stalked you, an old hurt.

Only she was wrong.

Miranda didn't understand shame because she didn't have any of it left, a fact that revealed itself at Lula-Bell Lake in the winter of 2020.

It was the kind of cold day that ripped the moisture right out of your skin. The Australian sun shone on anyway. Miranda was thankful. When it was overcast, this part of Ku-ring-gai Chase National Park was obsidian waves carved by wind, faces in trees, spiders and their traps. It made for some decent photography. Only *decent* wouldn't cut it. Her project required beauty. Honesty. Nothing short of perfection would suffice. She didn't need that degree to be happy, so long as she did this and did this better than anyone else.

Don't give up, Miranda. Do not give up.
You. Must. Win.

The competition deadline was three weeks away and she still had to have the as-yet-captured images printed on canvas and sent to the judges. Miranda would be cutting it fine, as she always seemed to be. If she cut it at all.

She'd been at the cabin for five days, longer than anticipated, waiting for the right combination of weather, light, and motivation. Like shame, she was patient. Not that the owner of the property, who lived in the neighbouring town of Long Swamp Bay appeared to care.

"Stay as long as you have a mind to," he'd said through dentures too big for his mouth, giving her a once over, trying not to focus on her tattoos and piercings. "Business isn't exactly boomin', in case you hadn't noticed."

Miranda's patience paid off and the camera in her hand was heavier as a result. It was, she thought, as though the amalgamation of metal and plastic and itty-bitty springs were imbued now with meaning that hadn't been there before.

Because the day was the postcard to a place everyone had to visit.

Miranda said it again. Her mantra. Her promise.

Nothing less than perfection will do.

The person judging the competition was someone from her school years, proving, again, that the universe was tiny and unfair. She'd been Charmaine Newberry back then. Now that she was married and had kids of her own, she went by Charmaine Richardson.

Such a neat, domesticated amendment, Miranda thought. *How flawlessly expected of you, Charmaine.*

Twitter, Instagram, and Pinterest revealed that Charmaine Whatever was still the Class-A knockout she'd been as a teenager. A knockout with three hundred likes per post who curated one of Sydney's most well-regarded galleries.

Prove. Her. Wrong.

The glare off the lake was strong. Miranda stared through the viewfinder of her SONY digital NEX-3 as opposed to using the display screen. The camera was compact, its ruby casing making the skin of her fingers pale by comparison. She used the 18-55 e-mount long lens, which gave wonderful depth of field on details when flicked to micro settings.

That wasn't appropriate here. Some landscapes were designed to dominate. She should've brought a wide-angle lens, something that would assist in personifying how she felt: tiny and submissive in comparison to nature, a flick of charcoal on an otherwise untouched canvas.

An ancient shed to her left, some corrugated relic. To her right, a swamp bird. It was starved, a mustering of ribs and feathers and tics.

Miranda took a couple of snaps. The shutter sent her heart skipping. It might as well have been a thunderclap. Quiet followed, awkward as silence after a bad joke. And that was what the playback screen proved: images so bland they weren't worthy of laughter, let alone the validations the Charmaine Richardsons of the world gifted.

The bird strode away.

A breeze whipped the collar of her jacket. Miranda sighed. Lula Bell's waters around her ankles, jeans rolled up to the knees. No drama here. Not yet.

Patient. Remember? You can do this.

(You've got no fucking choice.)

Exhausted, she stepped out of the water, pebbles massaging the soles of her feet, sat on a log by the shore. This lump of wood had its own majesty. It resembled a giant hand, perhaps the one that had carved this landscape into being, only to be thrown away afterwards, made useless by the arthritis that had contorted it into its current, gnarled state. Everything rotted in the end. Ananya would be bones by now.

Miranda grabbed a picture. Checked the playback.

Nope. Not right.

Even with the sexy depth-of-field, she struggled to link the camera with the images her mind saw so clearly.

"I'm a goddamned joke," Miranda said. "Fuckin' Christ."

She defaulted to an old familiar line, one that traced the shape of her scars: *Charmaine was right. Charmaine was always right.*

And then Miranda heard it.

A light aircraft zoomed over the tree-topped peninsula that lent Lula-Bell her privacy. From this distance, the plane resembled someone's toy thing.

Flying low there, buddy. Better pull up.

But the pilot did not pull up.

Miranda watched, gasping, as gravity snatched the plane from where it waivered, dragged it down. Threads of smoke billowed from its undercarriage, a dirty streak against the blue. Miranda ran into the water, waving her arms—though to what purpose she had no idea. It just struck her as the thing to do. The only thing, maybe.

"Watch out!"

Her shouts were of no use. The aircraft with the words **BETHIE'S NEW HEIGHTS** inscribed above the wing swirled into a nose-dive. The wasp-whine of useless propellers, an almost cartoony sound.

"No. *No! NO!*"

The plane struck Lula-Bell twenty yards from shore. It didn't slide beneath the surface as Miranda expected it to. It tumbled across the horizon like a discarded crucifix on a church floor, up and over, breaking apart. Flames. The lake swallowed debris in plodding gulps.

"—oh shit, oh shit, oh shit, oh—"

That breeze picked up again, an awful cold driving her to blink, and when she did, tears slipped from her lashes and froze on her cheeks.

Miranda backed out of the water. Glanced up and down the shoreline. To the nearby cabin. To her car in the crushed oyster shell driveway. Nobody around to help, not that help could be offered.

I'm alone out here.

Even the swamp bird had taken flight, dropping scat as it went.

Waves lapped at her heels, *whhiisshhed* over the bank like someone hissing for silence, someone who feared a secret was close to being revealed.

The pilot broke the water's surface where the wreckage sunk. The woman may or may not have gone by 'Bethie'. Regardless, and no matter the heights she'd aimed for, one thing was certain: this person was busy dying. Miranda watched her roll, screaming, exposing the remnants of her left arm. Mangled above the elbow, forearm and hand dangling on an elastic tendon. Blood fountained, pooled. Whitecaps rolled red.

Miranda exhaled a quiver, menthol cool, and it left a pit at the middle of her. It caught her off guard, that emptiness. Miranda didn't dismiss it, denied the denial. She sensed the moment presenting itself and reached out to touch it, and found herself shocked by its texture, the shape of it, its contours and opportunities.

Now.

Now or you'll miss it.

She brought the camera to her eye. The lens clattered, snapped, snatcher of sights. She zoomed in, framed by all that beautiful landscape, and saw the burnt, dismembered woman.

—Click—

A quiver in reverse. Miranda recoiled. The woman thrashed, rolled

—Click—

and glared straight at her. Eyes white amid the blackened skin.

(Well, are you? Going to help her?)

How? What could I possibly do?

Screams from the lake. "Help! Help! Help me! God! God, no—"

—Click—

(Swim out to her! Bring her in. You can swim, damn it!)

But she's beyond help!

—Click—

(Nobody's beyond help, Miranda. Nobody.)

The pilot's fingers clutched air with no saviour to be found. Not here. Not on that perfect day, with these photos to be taken. Bubbles amid the gore and oil, and then the woman went under for good.

Miranda stole a breath, clean air. The camera dangled from her grip. Beneath this thing of itty-bitty cogs and microchips, beneath the plastic and metal casing, the pilot's last moments were captured in detail. Like ice so cold its burn couldn't be differentiated from heat, Miranda couldn't tell if it was beauty or horror she'd captured. But it didn't matter in the end. It had been real. It had been genuine. And now it belonged to her.

2

Miranda watched them drag the woman from the water, all her clothes torn off, an eel slipping from her mouth. Tow-truck drivers fought over wings and hull fragments before leaving with equal shares of the loot.

They draped the body in a white sheet.

She documented everything with the NEX-3, stopping to answer questions, to sip from coffee someone handed her in a Styrofoam cup. A marbled cloud of oil over the liquid. She gulped it down. Bitter. Coppery, tasting of the tap. Miranda wondered whose job it was to bring hot drinks and those space blankets at emergency sites. What professional qualification did such a role require? She envied this person's importance, their purpose in the machine. The empty feeling at her core lingered on.

Now that her statement was done and the interview with a Sydney anchorman had wrapped, Miranda was alone again, naturally—as went the song she remembered from her childhood. Her parents loved Gilbert O'Sullivan. A needle over the vinyl groove, melodies she'd never shake. Miranda's parents were long gone. The song never died. It wasn't fair.

News helicopters flew away, taking the last of the light with them. An ambulance carted away the carcass one of the scuba-diving rescue teams had fished from the lake. *No.* Not rescue. Retrieval teams.

She went back to the cabin, sick to her stomach.

A northwesterly made the walls groan. Wood against wood. The sound almost obscured the chittering of Miranda's conscience. Almost.

You disgust me.

(I had to do it).

You could've helped that woman.

(She didn't stand a chance).

You'd exploit your own children, if you had any, to prove your worth.

(I didn't mean to. It all happened so fast).

Miranda stared at the camera. It sat on the coffee table in the living area, anchoring a pile of lifestyle magazines, which explained, over and over again, what it was to be a woman. See, this is how you smile. This is how you lie. This is how you don't get tattoos when you're drunk or sometimes drink beer in the shower when you're sad or ride skateboards to forget about love and hate or let everything get to you or succeed. *Jesus*, Miranda thought. *Shame is a trap made by people who have no shame.* She huddled in a wicker chair, upset, a blanket across her knees. Nausea thrummed again.

Sighing, Miranda drew herself upright. She reached for the camera to see, for the first time, what images were within—but stayed her hand.

The pilot's expression, the realisation that she was about to die, was fresh in her mind. Miranda saw it in the shadows of the room. Carved into the walls. Everywhere.

Not yet.

Miranda turned off the lights and crawled into bed. Curled up, muscles constricting. The cramps were the worst.

Moonlight carved the bedroom into light and dark with the precision of a blade. A ticking clock somewhere, crickets. Miranda tossed and turned.

CRACKING ICE CUBES. CHEWED PENCILS. TIN BETWEEN TEETH.

The night was long. It was like she could feel time pushing back on her. Trying to crush her. And there had been no dreams to wake from because there had been no sleep to begin with. Only aches and hurts, sweats despite the chill.

I give up.

Miranda thumped the pillow. Was it full of rocks herded from the shore and not the duck feathers mentioned in the promotional material? Sure seemed that way.

Why should I be surprised? Nothing listed in the pamphlets reflects the experience I had today. 'Enjoy nature and serenity,' it said. 'A respite from the modern world,' it said.

What a crock of shit.

Miranda buried her face in her hands. The camera called.

She swung out of bed, feet brushing uneven floorboards that creaked when she crossed the room. The dark in the adjoining kitchenette/living room had no depth, as she imagined Lula Bell Lake to be. Her eyes adjusted to make out the cabin's architecture by the time Miranda reached the coffee table. Shadows danced in the periphery of her vision, something scuttling just out of sight.

Miranda picked up the NEX-3. Before switching it on, she chanced a look out the bay windows. Lula-Bell was dead calm, fog blurring the line between horizon and sky. No stars. The lake didn't so much fill the landscape as create an absence in it.

The camera's ON/OFF dial under Miranda's thumb. Flicked it. It whizzed, screen flashing. Brightness made her squint, pain behind her temples. It was worth the discomfort, that terrible glare. There would be no sleep until she reviewed what had been captured. Because this was why she was here. This was why she'd come. To catch beauty by the wings and pin the moment for display like a butterfly on a board. Only this butterfly wasn't dead. Miranda swore she could still hear it screaming.

(Help! Help! Help me! God! God, no—)

She lifted the camera. Ready.

The first photo was the last one she'd taken: a police car heading in the direction of Long Swamp Bay. It wasn't a spectacular shot, kind of sloppy. The shutter speed dragged those taillights into ruby squiggles that made Miranda think of doctor's signatures as they signed off prescriptions for the 'ines'. Her heartbeat raced. CRACKING ICE CUBES. CHEWED PENCILS. TIN BETWEEN TEETH. CRACKING ICE CUBES. CHEWED PENCILS. TIN BETWEEN TEETH. She trembled, inched closer to the display. Looked closer.

Closer.

The naked, bloodied pilot stood in the corner of the frame against a chorus-line of trees. Alive. And she was staring straight into the lens.

Wind rustled inside Miranda. It was laced with ice shards that speared her lungs and frosted her breath. Pain twisted in her guts again, harder this time.

"Oh, fuck."

Water slid across the cabin floor and gushed between her toes. Lula-Bell had opened one of its veins and bled just for her. Miranda smelled its stink and was repulsed. Deadfall. Old tea bags. Mould. Larvae. Ammonia. Earth. Armpits. Sewer rot and honey. Bandages. Cum. Spit. Dead mice in a cage. Wet hair.

Moonlight flushed the room.

The dead woman stood across from Miranda. Her lifeless left arm dangled from the elbow on a tendon pulled so tight you could *ping* it and strike an off-key chord. Leaves plastered her burned and blistered skin, the remains of her clothes melted into flesh. What remained of her hair was slick against her scalp, swished across her collarbone, falling between breasts. No expression, head tilted ever so slightly.

Miranda tried to speak and failed. Tried to run. Couldn't.

She watched the woman raise that one remaining arm to her jaw, fingers curling around her lower set of teeth. Yanked it down. Bones dislodged with a pop. An eel greased out through her lips and slapped against the cabin floor, splashing electric figure eights in the water.

3

It had been two weeks since Miranda last saw the pilot. The days were intolerable. Every moment curdled with the expectancy of the dead woman's return.

She always came without warning, or provocation.

Limbo left Miranda anxious and sharp-tongued, traits that made her co-workers at the industrial building supply factory where she'd worked for the last two years uneasy. Their glances reminded her of those at Ananya's funeral. The whispers. Cupped hands.

What's going on with her?

Gosh, she's lost weight.

Is she sick?

Food didn't taste as it should. Miranda wondered if she had a cancer. That was how her mother died. Memories of the slow rot, the shrieks that came at night. *"Is it time? Is it now?"* her mother would yell, terrified that the aches were going to end her right there and then. They didn't, though. The ending came later in hospital when she shat herself to death. That was the writing on the wall for her father, too. He never recovered. No wonder the memories she had of her family were so fucked. Miranda learned pretty quick that death and forgiveness are the same thing, that both are the hardest thing you will ever do. Nobody goes quietly. The end is loud. Maybe that was why she knew to take the photos of the pilot in the first place. The drama of it all. Miranda knew she could live with herself without having to forgive herself.

You don't have Cancer.

(You're not that lucky.)

The last visitation came when Miranda was showering. She'd been washing her hair (which she did almost compulsively now), thinking about her plan for the exhibition, and glanced down to see the eye of the drain clogging up.

Dirt. Twigs. Leaves.

An eel threaded over her toes, twisted, beating itself in electric desperation. Scales against her skin like lapping tongues. The woman from the lake appeared beside her, staring as she always stared. Unblinking eyes dappled with dewdrops. Her expression was the same: *Why are you afraid of me? Why do you run?*

You wanted *me.*

Didn't you?

The days in the lead up to the show were noted by Paroxetine capsules. *CRACKING ICE CUBES.* By rotting food in the refrigerator. *CHEWED PENCILS.* Mould spores on the ceiling of her Sydney apartment. *TIN BETWEEN TEETH.*

Having a plan helped. That, more than anything. And maybe that alone.

It was so weird that the days had been so slow, yet the night of the exhibition had come so fast.

Miranda forced herself to get dressed and apply her makeup the way the magazines said she had to. Cake it on, a mask of lipstick and foundation. Her fingers wouldn't stop shaking. She played the words in her head.

Hi, Charmaine. Remember me?

She snatched up the keys and locked the door behind her. Vertigo. Excluding work and grocery detours, this was her first outing since getting back from the cabin. Miranda hated being out in the open now. Sydney roared after dark. The loud cars and their impatient drivers. The construction sites. The parties in apartments. The drunk people running across the streets, laughing and howling. Buildings huddled in to block out the sky, but clouds could still be seen, slowly passing over the moon. Flowers on the branches of trees like dusty earrings and pearls ornamenting skeletons. She rode her skateboard, soon finding her groove. Or maybe that was just the beta blockers kicking in.

Ice cubes melting. Teeth marks uncurling from the end of a pencil in reverse. Pulling out the tin from between her teeth.

A soft pattering of rain swished over the city and Miranda lifted her face to meet it. The city's edges blunted for a short while, and she managed to smirk. Well, half a smirk.

You're almost there, Miranda.

No going back now.

Do it.

Miranda stepped off her skateboard, tucked it into her backpack, and entered the gallery, Doc Martin's clopping up the steps. She paid her admission to the man at the door, handing over her backpack. "Welcome," he said, apathetic, waspy, looking at the skateboard sticking out of the bag's unzipped mouth. "Feel free to wander. There were some great submissions this year. The winner won't be announced for another hour, though. You get one free drink at the bar."

"Thank you," Miranda said, accepting her change and an old-school carnival stub. "Is... Charmaine here?"

"You'll find her hobnobbing around the room. Catch her quick, though. She's fast. Like a ferret. Have a nice night."

Miranda grinned.

Have a nice night.

She planned to do that very thing. Sure, Miranda hadn't been bold enough to submit the photographs she'd taken out on Lula-

Bell Lake, but that didn't mean Miranda couldn't go up to the girl who had handcrafted her Hell one insult at a time, and prove, beyond all doubt, that she was worthy of admiration.

See, Charmaine. My acne is gone. What a shame. I've lost all that weight, too. Can't call me 'thunder-thighs' anymore, can you? Woops. I've severed all the ties that bound me to the person you said I was. I'm proud of that. I'm beautiful enough now. And I came here tonight to tell you that I hate you *for convincing me and everyone else that I was ugly.*

You've earned this fucking punch.

Maybe a punch was one step too far. A haunting was problem enough without the added complication of an assault charge. The one free drink that came with her admission would be the one free drink Miranda threw in Charmaine's face.

"I'll have a Pinot Noir," she told the bartender. Her breath was slippery and hard to catch. Dark red wine sloshed within the glass—stains guaranteed. "Thanks."

She moved through the crowd, eavesdropping. An oil-on-water mix of professionals, friends of friends, bloggers. Perfume and pot smoke, a heady mixture that nudge-nudged the headache at the back of her skull, sending it around to the spot behind her eyes.

Miranda stopped, swallowed. Her throat was straw.

There she was.

Charmaine Newberry, the knockout she'd gone to school with, the woman who had grown into Charmaine Richardson, a matured—though just as stunning—version of her younger self. She was dressed in curve-hugging blacks, chopsticks holding her hair in a bun. Her laughter was perfection. Men and women swanned around her, salting the ground over which she walked with adorations and accolades. As they always had. As they always would. That was the existence of Charmaine Richardson.

The more things change, the more some stay the same.

Charmaine held a Pomeranian in her arms. It couldn't be the same one from when they were in high school. *Couldn't be.* That dog would be long dead, surely. Squeak. Yes, Squeak had been its name. This made Miranda feel ill, on top of everything else.

Behind Charmaine were a revolving door of dead dogs that she had maybe loved and certainly replaced like shoes, accessories to garner a crowd. Dogs that were never allowed to bark, bred to be seen and never heard.

Miranda strode across the room, glancing at black-and-white and colour landscapes and portraits on the walls. Trees. Hills. Brick walls. Homeless men and women. Abandoned buildings. Newborn babies. Lips. Eyes. Breasts. Cocks. Flowers. The elderly. Hallways and corridors and vanishing points. Some of the photographs weren't too bad. Others were like the shots Miranda had taken before the plane went down—try-hard and weightless nothings. Her head was full of a dying woman's screams. Miranda's focus shifted to her reflection in the glass. The rain had flattened her hair and made her makeup run.

The glitterati parted before her.

Stop, Miranda. This isn't you.

(It is).

What you're about to do is grotesque. *If you go through with this, you'll become what those bitches always said you were.*

(I can't turn back now. Don't you see that? Anger is all I've got.)

That's not true, you're—

"Hi, Charmaine," Miranda said. "Remember me?"

Eyes turned in her direction. Including those of the woman she'd spent the worst years of her life with. Miranda wished her father were alive to see this, all the medication he overdosed on pouring back into their bottles, his ashes reforming to make the shape of a man. Someone who must have smiled, once upon a time.

"Yes?"

"Looks like you've come far since the last time I saw you." Miranda tried not to weep. She could almost smell the flowers and incense from Ananya's funeral when they were young and assumed things would get better. "I have, too. Don't you think?"

Charmaine's entourage gawked at her, expressions unmoving. Squeak panted, showing off his pink tongue and neat teeth. Downlights highlighted the crowns of everyone's heads, throwing faces into shadow. Eyes into pits. Wine danced within the glass.

Do it now.

(Don't.)

Throw it!

(Have you no shame—)

"I'm sorry," Charmaine said. "Do I know you?"

A beat.

"It's me. Miranda." Heat waves inched up her neck. "Your sister."

Nobody said a word.

Miranda gripped her glass tighter, knuckles turning white.

Charmaine issued a polite giggle, an eyebrow raised, and turned away, taking her 'friends' with her. Squeak looked back, barked, and Miranda thought she saw Charmaine pinch the dog's underbelly. They were parasites, all of them, feeding off a woman without talent who had succeeded, as evidenced in the art around them, by accumulating the skills of others. That was perhaps the only thing Miranda and Charmaine, siblings to the end, had in common. Both of them were thieves. Profiteers. Survival was an ugly thing.

Ugly as fuuuuccckkk.

Miranda downed her wine. It tasted cheap.

The room swam. Overlapping voices, music filtering through speakers—it all receded from her ears. Everything except her pulse.

Who are you, Miranda?

(I wish I knew)

Water splashed her shoes, bringing with it the putrid stink of the lake.

The burned pilot was on the other side of the gallery walking towards her. Each step pitched sagging breasts this way and that. The arm swung on its string, spinning. Leaves stuck to her thighs, black stars against a whitewashed sky. The woman whose name might have been Bethie drew near, unseen by everyone else in the room. Everyone except Miranda. Feet slapped the cement, sending bloodstained water up in a spray. As before, her head was titled in confusion, eyes screeching, *I'm here like you wanted. Why are you afraid of me? You wanted me, didn't you?*

That's why you took me.

Miranda thought she might faint.

The dead woman curled her fingers around her lower set of teeth and dislodged the jaw with a *thock!* An eel birthed in crackles of Saint Elmo's fire.

Miranda ran to the cloakroom, retrieved her backpack, and escaped.

Outside, evening air scoured her face. She had her skateboard stuffed under one arm, gasping, tears peeling off her cheeks. Her wine glass still gripped in one hand, a sad trophy. She stopped and hurled it into an alleyway, roaring out her hurt, people on the other side of the street yelling out, "You fucking loony, bitch!"

Sydney carouselled about her, flashing lights and faces that couldn't see what Miranda could see: Lula-Bell's tide as it swept after her. And the dead woman in pursuit, close as a shadow.

Miranda didn't bother putting on the lights. She knew she wasn't alone.

CRACKING ICE CUBES.

The dead woman was with her, in the corner beside the television set. The carpet was saturated. Water dripped the walls, prominent as the veins in the dead pilot's thighs. And again, the stink of filthy water in which things lived and fucked and died and turned cannibal.

CHEWED PENCILS.

Miranda huddled on the couch with the camera, her back to the visitor.

TIN BETWEEN TEETH.

Weeping helped. Only the relief was fleeting, at best.

She almost flicked through the photographs taken at Lula Bell Lake, which she hadn't viewed since. But held off. She wasn't brave enough for that. Miranda thought she might vomit if she did.

Blood fell from the bone of the dead woman's arm.

Plop. Plop. Plop.

She stood there. Watching, watching. Joyless eyes glimmering in the dark. Her fingers reached towards her mouth.

Miranda sighed and studied the camera glaring up at her, its lens an unflinching iris. Within it was ugliness so strong it could un-write laws and logic. Miranda placed the camera down. Had to. She didn't need to see the photographs to recognise them for what they were. Though the tortured face drowning in Lula-Bell's waters belonged to someone else, her art—beautiful in its honesty—was every bit a self-portrait.

Wet slitherings in the dark. Another eel.

Is it time? Miranda Newberry wondered. Maybe even said aloud. *Is it now?*

The Acknowledged

1

Mountains weren't without their demands.

Keep our secret, they whispered in the sway of trees, in cicada song. *Maintain the lie that everything is perfect out here.* I'd been on the trail for ten minutes and had already been made a conspirator.

Shhhhhhhhh.

Well, fine, I thought. *I can live with that*, a commitment signed in sweat and shin splints.

Mid-morning heat pounced as though in waiting. I'd committed to the two-hour Green Loop. If the temperature continued to climb, I'd have to turn back. That would make Mum happy, at least.

"I'm just letting you know where I'm going," I'd said to her on the phone back at the motel. When cornered, my mother's love made your skeleton want to flee its body. Going home for Christmas had never been on the cards. I'd taken enough of a beating over the past thirteen months to put myself through that. Maybe I deserved her punishment, those reminders that I was an eight-hour drive from where I should be, in the townhouse she shared with my stepfather, a nub of a man long eroded away by her worries.

"People die out there, Thom," she'd said, her attempt to make me feel a child ageing her. "Don't you watch the news?"

"It's Bungonia National Park, not the outback. I'm in Goulburn. I've eaten too much over the holidays and want to break up the trip to Canberra. Jesus. You'd think I was confessing to murder.

Can you let me exercise without the guilt trip, please?"

"Bungonia, he tells me. Bungonia! You know who prowled those parts? Ivan Millat, that's who. A serial killer. He picked off people right there. *That's* murder. Let yourself get fat instead."

Switched off the light. Drew the door shut behind me. Spoke through a security keycard pinched between my teeth. "Stop being a worry-wort, Mum. I've got water, hiking boots, and my phone's charged. This is me being smart. 'Don't go for a hike—even a tiny one like this—without giving someone the heads up'. That's what they say, right?"

"You're as stubborn as your father." Defeat crept into her voice. "Call me once you're home. I don't want your face on the side of milk carton."

"I'm lactose intolerant. Not the legacy I'm aching for, Mum. Deal."

I checked out at reception and climbed into the Toyota Hilux awarded me in the separation. The breakup. The atomic bomb dividing who I was and who I became. Just thinking about what happened prodded the pink baby rats of anxiety at my core. They were with me, always. Their eyes pinched shut, and constantly teething.

There was Fag Rat. There was Why Me Rat. The rat that forgave nobody. The rat that didn't know when enough was enough. Fat Rat. Too Skinny Rat. The rat that feared being hated above all else. Spite Rat.

They had their nest in my gristle and spirit, every inch of me crowded with their scratchings. Mum had prodded at them that morning, too. Christmas by the beach with my family would have been back-to-back diversions and pretending my ex never existed. No thanks. Everything hurt enough as it was. I knew I'd made the right decision to hide from them all. And now, to run.

Running kept the rats still.

Shhhhh, went those trees again. *Shhhhh*.

The mountain resembled a volcanic skull with a jawline made for exploring, teeth crumbling under my boots. Lizards cut across a path that didn't resemble a path let alone the designated route. Coded markers bleached by the elements. Insects. I wrapped a bandana around my neck, baseball cap low, the sleeves of my shirt high enough to display tattoos. Water didn't hydrate as it should, and the sweat steamed right off my arms.

Rest, I heard my mother say. *Rest or you'll go belly-up.*

Only thousands of ants made sitting risky. And I knew I was watched by spiders and snakes. Even though I couldn't see them.

Coming to the National Park had nothing to do with over-eating (though to be honest, I had put on weight). I'd dreamed of Stuart and woken in tears—that's all. The rats had been gnawing since. Through a stale breakfast. As I sat in the car out the front of the Sutton Forrest Motor Motel where I'd shacked up for the silly season, treating myself to solitude and air-conditioning, luxuries not afforded me at home with my roommate, Arthur. While staring at the parking lot, keys dangling from the ignition on a chain my ex gifted me after one of his trips. I unhitched and cupped it. *Where had Stuart picked it up again? Manila? Or was it Abu Dhabi?* Multi-hued beads on cheap twine. The memories attached to it defined me once.

I tossed it out the window. Drove off.

Step, step, repeat. Muscles strained as the wind scorched. My rats kept to their nest. This exertion was better than the doctor-prescribed anti-depressants or the self-prescribed wine I'd downed over the week, sloppy toasts to the television.

Merry—fuckin'—Christmas.

I stopped to catch my breath, soaking up the enormity of the landscape. The mountains made a tiny and insignificant thing of me, just another ant. And if I were that small then my problems were smaller still. *Good.* I normally listened to music when walking. It might have been the heat that made me rip the earbuds out. Or perhaps a playlist of crunching stones and zooming flies suited my mood better. This was the first time I'd felt healthy in weeks, a million miles from the paperwork in my cubicle at the Taxation Office, and even further from my parents' home.

Keep going—
(the rats squirmed)
—*or you'll start to think*—

(they bit)
—*of him.*
"HELP!"

The voice shook me from the outside in. I spun, glancing at the bluff I'd passed. It opened onto a shimmering valley. The bush roared with wildlife trying to mask another "HELLLLLLPPP", Bungonia's secret spilling, after all.

We trusted you with our lie, Thom. You didn't obey.

"Hello?" I shouted back.

"DOWN HERE!"

I didn't think, only moved.

The man was sprawled on his back ten yards below the cliff's edge, a leg snapped to the side, bottles and electronics scattered about. He was my age or younger, in his early thirties at least. Thin, wiry, and ginger-haired, someone who broke easily. His pale face was a blot of desperation on the outcropping suspending him over a fifty-yard drop like a peppermint on the tip of a stony tongue. The Australian bush had tried to eat him alive, as it tried to eat people all the time. Just ask my mother.

"I'm coming," I yelled, manoeuvring the bluff. "Don't move."

"IT FUGHIN' HURTS! AHHHHHHHH—"

"I know, mate. Stay put. It'll be alright."

Rocks shifted as I wedged feet into every crevice, crab-walking. Fingers strained into gaps between rocks—hiding spots for snakes. I snatched my hand back. The snake in my imagination sprung from the shadows. The shock would send me crashing, next to the man I'd hoped to save—*if* I was lucky. Miss the outcropping and I'd keep spinning, the ground rushing up to kiss me nighty-night forever.

Rats scratched. Bit. Tore.

"I—I can't get any closer," I shouted. "I'm sorry."

"D-don't leave." His voice was wet sheets on a clothesline ripping in a storm. Guilt flooded and exhausted me.

"I won't," I told him, meaning it. I shuffled onto my side, dust in my nostrils. Heat thrashed from above and from the rocks. The sun was in everything everywhere, impossible to escape. I felt myself baking. "Shit. Shit. Shit."

"I'm hurt. Don't leave. *Jesusssssss*."

I jimmied against the bluff, confident I could wriggle to the pathway above without too much risk. One more step downwards would doom me. I twisted to grab the phone from my pocket.

Drop it and this guy's a goner. Mum's voice again.

Fingers flexed, quivered. The acidic sting of sunscreen in my eyes. There was one bar of reception, but one bar was all I needed. This was the first time in my life I'd ever had to call for an emergency response team. I thumbed oily streaks across the screen, scrambling for air when I noticed I'd been holding my breath.

We waited. I listened to him cry and moan.

"What's your name?" I asked, bending to keep eye contact, wanting him to know I cared. Phantom pain wrung me out when my gaze drifted over his leg. I didn't want to imagine how it felt, yet I couldn't avoid imagining how it felt.

Coming to the National Park had been a whim at best. I would be in Canberra by now if I'd listened to my mother.

"E-Eddie," he answered between sobs. His voice sounded real. "Eddie."

It rained spiders when the helicopter shook the trees.

I expected it all to go wrong at the last second, the rescue cumulating in a fireball that would burn Bungonia to the ground, those enormous blades impaling every bit of me. And maybe I deserved it, too.

The unit lifted Eddie onto a stretcher without incident. I saw the man I'd saved offer me the tiniest wave, so he knew I knew he hadn't forgotten to acknowledge what I'd done. I hurried onto the path, sun blisters popping on rocks, coated in dirt so thick it muddied with sweat and cracked over as I waited. The growl of the helicopter masked my whimpers as I repeated a name I didn't want to say again and again and again.

"Stuart. Stuart. Stuart. Stuart."

2

"**S**omeone's going to nominate you for Canberran of the Year," Arthur said through a mouthful of fried rice. We ate from our 'bachelor bowls', chipped second-hand pieces scored from a thrift store. Fried rice was my housemate's cooking specialty. Eating it was mine.

"Yeah, right," I said, shifting on the couch and reaching for the remote. The news was explosions. The news was screaming. The news was political decisions that pinched your guts. The news had to go. "It's been four months. My celebrity status has somewhat dimmed, I suspect."

"Maybe I'll nominate you," my housemate added, cheeky.

"You can't do that. That's, like, cheating."

"Yes, I can and maybe it's warranted. Now shut the fuck up and eat your rice. I already have one child. Don't make me parent you, too."

Arthur cooked. I cleaned. We were comfortable in these roles. It hadn't taken long to step into the avatars of who we used to be in our prior relationships. Arthur's ex-wife lived fifteen minutes away and brought his son, Brandon, over every second weekend. I was "Cousin Thom" to the seven-year-old. That warmed me. Arthur and I had bathed each other's wounds, and despite the bleakness of those early days when our lease-signing rung more of execution order ("it's real now," he'd said) than opportunity, we were getting there. We really were. The hurt wasn't any less, though. We'd just got better at being used to it.

Our house was squeezed into a cul-de-sac in Garron, a suburb south of the lake. Three bedrooms in all, landlords who let us be. We'd been nobodys to them prior to the two articles about me in *The Canberra Times*. The response time to our maintenance requests had quickened since. The adjoining photograph of Eddie and I was snatched in the backyard, set against a weave of trees and flowers.

Eddie had accepted our invitation to hang around for lunch after the reporter and photographer left. We ate pre-packaged salads and steaks Arthur grilled outside to avoid wrangling Eddie's wheelchair up the stairs. Brandon and his mother, Tiff, were there. We raised beers. Eddie either held eye contact a beat too long or avoided it all together, a man without a middle ground.

Brandon broke a stretch of silence to ask our guest about his pain.

"What a thing to ask," Tiff said, flustering. "I'm so sorry, Eddie—"

"It's fine. Really. To answer your question, it still hurts." Eddie drew his hands off the table, rested them on his lap. "I'm getting there. It might be the itching under the leg plaster that's worst, believe it or not."

Brandon laughed. "Liar, liar, pants on fire."

Eddie smiled and glanced my way. "Maybe a smidge."

Tiff took her child home afterwards. Arthur cleared the table and set to washing the dishes by hand. Eddie and I waited for the community service van to pick him up at the curb. The quiet we shared wasn't as uncomfortable as before. Like legs beneath plaster, the quiet itched.

"There's no way for me to repay what you did, Thom," he said.

"You don't own me anything."

Emotions slid over Eddie's face. "I'd be dead if it wasn't for you. I wouldn't exist anymore."

Eddie turned, hand flirting with his chest—not the first whiff of effeminacy I'd caught that day or back when we'd been interviewed at the hospital. The man in the wheelchair carried himself as though always wrestling an urge to confess, yanking his shoulders into a hunch, chin sucked into the back of his throat. I wished he'd tell me he was gay so we could laugh it off. A relationship wasn't on the cards—though I admit I indulged in the fairy tale every now and then.

"How did you guys meet?" people would ask at dinner parties. *"Didn't you know? Thom saved my life. Still got the scars to prove it!"* Oh, *those wedding speeches.* The Canberra Times *would have a field day.*

Attraction didn't factor into the situation at all. Eddie would always be the one I'd saved, and because of that, he'd love me more than I could ever love him. I'd experienced enough lopsided relationships to last me a lifetime.

I was glad when the van arrived to take him home. Guilt lingered in his absence like the scent of smoke you couldn't wash from your clothes fast enough.

The newspaper our article was featured in lay on the coffee table in front of the television. I kept putting it on the bookshelf, but Arthur returned it day after day. I guess I was too uncomfortable with myself to reconcile his pride in me.

"Want more rice, Mr Future Canberran of the Year?" he said.

"Fuck you, amigo. And yes. Top this bachelor bowl up, pronto."

I came home from work three weeks later to find a casserole dish on our doorstep.

It was May and the weather had started to turn, creeping chills an insidious thing. Wind blew the season's first dead leaves over the WELCOME mat the meal had been left on. A card wedged under the base—not that it required reading.

There might as well have been a voice on that wind, a whispered name.

Arthur slouched into the house at seven-thirty, his shift at the university having run long. He poked his head into the living room where I sat with a book. "What smells good in here? Did you get take-out?" He slipped off his tweed jacket and tossed it over the back of a chair. "I could eat the arse out of a low flying duck right now."

"Well, you're in luck then. Eddie cooked for us," I said, trying not to laugh. "Well, I assume your name was implied on the card."

"He left a card? Isn't that domesticated of him! I guess he's walking now."

"Quite the recovery, hey?" Words floated over the book's pages like rainbow smears on grease, formless and pretty and impossible to digest.

Arthur picked up the card where I'd left it on the table. "'Thank you again,'" he read aloud, pontificating, stroking his hipstery moustache. "Bit late for a Valentine. Look, it's up to you, Thom, but I'd pop a cap in this quick-smart. Nothing worse than a cock-tease. Put the boy out of his misery if this isn't going to be a thing."

"Yeah. I just feel bad for him."

"There's leftovers, right?" Arthur asked, changing the subject.

Hairless baby rats ruffled their paws, sharpened their teeth within me.

Eddie lived in Belconnen on the other side of the city, his one-bedroom apartment bare except for a bile-hued plant by the futon. No photographs on the walls, no portals into who he was beyond what we'd already shared. I knew he was a pharmacist—but that was pretty much it. The empty casserole dish sat on the table between us. I toyed with his card, flipping it to where the address had been scribbled.

Steam curled from our cups.

"I know it wasn't much," Eddie said. "Just a gesture. I guess I don't want you to forget how grateful I am for what you did."

"It's cool, mate," I said, that word—mate—making Eddie cringe a little. "Like I mentioned before, you don't need to repay me. Great as the meal was."

Eddie limped into the kitchen to bring the kettle back to boil. My cup was still more than half full, so I assumed he mustered out of nervousness or to show how he'd healed. A cane propped against the wall by the front door, not that I'd seen him use it.

"Such a weird feeling," he said.

"What's that, mate?"

"All this."

"I know, Eddie. Something for us to tell our grandkids, right?"

"Grandkids," he said. "I hope you tell yours how important all this was to me."

"What was?"

"Falling," he said. "Being trapped on that ledge. You coming along when you did. It was the most significant thing that's ever happened to me. I'm not sure people get how *filling* that is. The papers don't do it justice."

His words jarred, puzzle pieces I didn't know how to align. I wondered if I'd flirted with him without realising it. My ability to process company with other men—let alone gay men—had warped after Stuart left me. I could hardly stand to be hugged by guys because it made me think of sex.

It was a small apartment and Eddie struck me as even smaller inside it. His black sweater stark against white cupboards, ying searching for its yang.

Winter grabbed Canberra by the balls. I dreaded leaving the warm bed.

Jordan—assuming that was his real name—snored into my armpit. Stubble tickled my skin in a way that turned me on and I contemplated putting my hungover horniness to good use. Nah, better to leave him with the memory.

9:46am.

I drove to McDonald's and chowed down breakfast, replaying our fuck in my head, rather chuffed. Fighting families and couples who stunk of alcohol in the surrounding booths must have thought me mad. I smiled as I ate, and we all knew that shit didn't taste very good.

My phone vibrated across the countertop. Jordan had messaged my Grindr account as I'd hoped he would. As I kind of knew he would. The memories I'd left him with mustn't have been half bad, after all.

Fun times. Here's my number. Don't lose it, OK.

Canberra peeled past the windows as I drove. The thin Saturday crowd jittered from building to building to escape the cold. I was glad Arthur hadn't put that nomination in for me and that the interviews had dried up. Anonymity suited me fine. I was no different from the people on the other side of the window, another blur on a boring day. As it should be.

I parked in the carport, only noticing the vehicle on the other side of the cul-de-sac when I stepped across the threshold and into our warm house. "Cousin Thom!" came Brandon's high-pitched voice, followed by thudding feet along the hallway. He launched, pounding the wind right out of me.

"Woah, little fella. Let me get my jacket off—"

"Eddie's here," he said, blue eyes peering from under the mop of his hair. He shrugged, begrudged in some way, such an adult slight. Brandon knew this was his time. I steeled myself as I rounded the corner, passing the kitchen where Arthur had left his bottles of homemade kombucha to ferment on the counter. I followed television noise into the living room. Eddie sat at my end of the couch, my housemate at the other.

"Look who's here, Thom," Arthur said, eyebrows arched a tad too high. Three takeaway coffees sat on the table by the newspaper with our article tucked inside it.

Eddie reached to pick up a cardboard cup. "I hope your drink is still hot. It's from Hudson's in the city."

Brandon sat on a pillow in front of the flat-screen. "Not so close, buddy," Arthur said, standing. "Your eyes will go square. How about we head out for a walk, instead? Fresh air's the ticket. We'll let the boys have their catch up."

"I hope you don't mind me coming over," Eddie said. "Unannounced."

Arthur led his son from the room after switching off the television, taking the kid's complaints with him. The hush left behind irritated me as much as the man on the couch.

"What are you doing here, Eddie? Just in the neighbourhood?"

"Not really. I thought of you guys. Who doesn't like surprise coffees?"

"I appreciate that, mate. But you can't just come over here willy-nilly. We can't have strangers in the house when Brandon's about. His mother'd be fit to be tied. I don't want to get Arthur in any hotter water than he's already in, you know?"

"Of course. I didn't think. Guess I didn't consider myself a stranger 'round here is all."

"No."

"I wanted to say thank you again—"

"Look, Eddie. You don't need to do anything else for me." My voice took on a long-overdue sternness. "In fact, I insist on it. It's making me a bit uncomfortable."

"I'm sorry, Thom. I didn't mean—"

"I know you didn't, mate. It's fine. Let's cool things off for a while, yeah?"

Eddie stared, a splinter in my skin, pointed and jarring. "I'll leave now."

"That's for the best." I extended my hand for a shake that wasn't reciprocated. Eddie mumbled apologies as he scuttled past. His melancholy was mould I couldn't scrape from the room afterwards, no matter how I tried. Eddie came here with good intentions and I'd made him feel a wrongdoer. Stuart used to say I did that to him all the time.

Brandon and Arthur came home afterwards in their matching pea coats. My roommate pulled me aside to tell me this weird shit had to stop.

I slinked into my room and studied old photos on my phone.

Someone's in the house.

The mattress groaned as I rolled onto my side, studying the not-quiet, a held breath's unease pressing on me from every side. A plate clanked. The clunk of a pan.

"Jesus."

Arthur was at his old house in Ainslie, no doubt relegated to the couch, surrounded by the ruins of Brandon's eighth birthday party.

Those acute kitchen sounds stabbed at my ears again. Fear trickled away to let in anger, and that anger made the rats scuttle to their nest behind my ribcage. I'm not sure how I knew what was going on, but I did.

You've got to be fucking kidding me.

I crept from my room and into the hallway (after doing a furtive check down the hall first). My feet wisped over the old carpet, following the blade of light from the kitchen. I approached Eddie with mobile phone in hand. He knelt in front of the cupboards by the refrigerator where receipts and bills were pinned with magnets Brandon made at school. He had brought them in for us to see, five well-crafted wooden butterflies cupped in his hands. "They're not butterflies, Cousin Thom," Brandon said, almost annoyed. "They're moths."

"You know you can't be here," I told Eddie.

He slouched, clicked his tongue. Eddie drew himself upright and turned to face me, a frying pan he could brain me with in hand.

"Put that down, please."

Eddie did as he was asked.

I thought back to that morning in our yard after the second interview, how emotions skimmed the face of the man I'd saved and never quite stuck. Since then, I'd witnessed smiles that were grimaces at best, cold eyes at their core.

The man wasn't well.

Eddie began to weep.

I held true. Had to. My relationship with Stuart came to an abrupt end because I thought it would be okay to cheat. This small rental I shared with Arthur was all I had to my name, excluding the car. And everything would crumble again if I let Eddie shift this already tenuous architecture. What was a man, even a gay man, I wondered, without a home? Fag Rat bit my insides. I hated myself more than ever.

Eddie glared, shook his head.

He has no home, I thought. *He is what happens.*

"You know I need to call the police. Don't you?" I said, breathing fast. I didn't want him to see how far he'd pushed me.

"All I wanted was to cook for you, Thom," Eddie said, putting the pan down and clasping his hands. "I remembered from our lunch. How you said you didn't like being in the kitchen." He shied from my eyes, humiliated. "I thought it would be a nice way to say thank you. I wanted to acknowledge y—"

"Eddie, stop."

"You *are* grateful," he said, moving his head in a birdish way. "Aren't you?"

A draft of icy air curled about my feet. Eddie had broken in.

"Leave," I told him. "And never, ever come back."

"Are you grateful? You owe me an answer, if nothing else."

"What planet are you on, Eddie? I don't owe you shit. Get the fuck out of this house or I'm calling the police. Look, I can see you're—that—that—you're not doing okay. So, go *get* okay. I'll have a restraining order taken against you if you come back."

Eddie twitched. I wasn't sure if what I'd said struck where it counted, yet I didn't need it to. I didn't need him cured. Just gone. Eddie limped into the hallway. I stepped back, watching him pull the latch on the side door, welcoming another gust of freezing air. I turned on the outside light and walked him to his car on the other side of the cul-de-sac, my phone in hand the whole time. Eddie stepped into his Prius, the same one that had been parked in that very spot months ago.

("Eddie's here," Brandon had said.)

"Never again," I told him through the closed window. His profile was a green etching on the dark from the dashboard glow. I couldn't hear his reply. I'm not sure he intended me to, either. The concept of Eddie being the kind of guy who talked to himself didn't evoke much shock, there on the street in my winter pyjamas.

I called our landlords the following day to have the living room fly-screen Eddie broke in through repaired. "A bunch of kids were throwing stones in the night," I told them. "Scared the beeswax right out of me, to be honest."

It was possible that my pseudo-celebrity status still held sway. Everything had been fixed before Arthur got home that afternoon.

I was too humiliated to tell him what happened.

3

Heat brought sleepless nights. A TV campaign urged everyone to keep an eye on the elderly to ensure they remained hydrated. We scrambled for our landlord inspection, only realising how filthy everything was once it had been cleaned. My boss grilled me about the declining accuracy of my work, fingers rapping the table as she spoke. There were the wasp nests I knocked from the awnings. Overpriced haircuts and the fibs I told when the barber asked how I was doin'. The addiction to my phone, each Grindr ding! offering diminishing dopamine returns. More receipts pinned to the refrigerator. The beard I grew. Unremembered Netflix binges and the withdrawals that followed. Unfinished books, so many of them. I loved reading. Once.

Those four months dragged by as though wounded.

My birthday came and went, too. Arthur needed consoling after a failed reconciliation with Tiff. She called and asked me to look after him because she couldn't anymore. Arthur and I drank as we always had, though I struggled to match him now. My mother said she wanted to visit. I hadn't known how much I needed her until I picked her up from the airport.

"My baby," she said, erupting into tears. "You're nothing but skin and bone."

I became accustomed to the scratching and biting of my rats. Stupidly, I texted the guy I cheated on Stuart with one Friday after Arthur passed out on the couch, a message shot from a thunderhead of booze and limp-dicked horniness. No response. Maybe that was for the best.

Mum called every few days, handing the phone to my stepfather on cue. His mumbles were a kind of comfort. The mortification of having prepared himself for a gay wedding he'd struggled to reconcile in the first place (only to have it fall apart in the home stretch) was an anchor he'd drag around with him forever.

I rang Stuart another night, too, despite Arthur telling me what a shitty idea it was. We spoke of what lay ahead, not of our best work. My ex told me I should be proud of how I'd helped Eddie, that I'd saved a life, regardless of how things turned out. "You're a good guy," Stuart said. But I didn't feel like a good guy. I felt like a skin-sack of old habits and scabs I'd picked and kept so the wounds never had to heal. You know your former lovers have truly left you when they no longer care how—or if—you're moving on. *Not* being asked was better. It didn't feel that way at the time.

I also called Justin (turns out that was his name, go figure) a few times. The sex was more violent than I wanted it to be, yet I evoked the violence. He told me to stop. I did. Too little too late, I guess.

Rats tried to chew their way out of me.

Brandon draped across his father's lap, the three of us a mess of limbs on the couch.

Arthur carried his sleeping boy to bed after the movie wrapped, limp arms catching the television glow, reminding me of late-night swims near my parents' house with friends, plankton drawn through the waves by the moon. These memories were tied to the discipline that followed, Mum telling me I should've known better than to swim at the beach so late.

Her hand on mine. Squeezing. "Don't you know sharks feed in the dark?"

It was Sunday night. Arthur and I were drunk.

Tiff had asked if Brandon could stay an extra day, although she hadn't told Arthur why. Her elusiveness didn't have to be spelled out. The knowledge that his ex started dating again was a monkey Arthur carried on his back. Brandon's school uniform hung from a hanger on the living room door, and the twinkling of reality TV stars threw its shadows across the wall, an elongated dancer waiting for a partner.

Arthur emerged from the hallway, beer in hand. "I'm turning in, Thom."

The clock by the door read 9:15pm.

"Night-night."

I stayed up until after eleven, double-checking the doors and windows, regardless of the heat I trapped inside. The flick of light switches here, there. Brushed teeth. Reminded myself to book in for another skin check, having tanned over summer. I decided not to close my bedroom door. Too stuffy. The rotary fan spun in the corner. Reading didn't work its magic, so I bummed on my phone until sleep snuggled onto the mattress beside me, comforting and spoon-worthy. I must have drooled all over my pillow because it was wet when I woke.

The man at the end of my bed stepped back, moonlight revealing a hypodermic needle. His face pinched with anticipation as he dove, those now empty fingers clamping my mouth.

Mum's voice bolted at me:

Something sharp on the ground, Thom. Pick it up or Brandon will—

I thrashed Eddie until my arms stopped working. He glared. The man I'd saved had turned my body against me, and it didn't matter that I commanded myself to fight or flee. Nothing worked. The rats did their summersaults all the same, claws scratching and scraping. They had never been hungrier. Every cry came out a moan.

This can't be happening. Every window was locked. Every door. I made sure of it. I was careful. I'm always careful—ever since that night!

This whirlpool of confusion came to an abrupt halt.

And he was careful, too, Mum said. *If you closed this place up as well as you think, it means he was already inside the house at the time.*

My brain skimmed through every possible hiding spot, as though by pinpointing the intricacies of his plan I could trick this moment into not existing. But there was only one conclusion, and it didn't change anything.

He must have been under your bed, Thom.

Another round of moans bubbled from between my lips as Eddie dragged me onto the floor and into the hall. I felt it all— every carpet fibre grinding hairs until static electricity crackled in the dim. My insides liquified. I caught a glimpse of the hallway I'd coursed innumerable times and saw the doors to Arthur and Brandon's rooms. Both were wide open, and only darkness beyond.

Sightless in the trunk of his car. Dizzying knocks of dust, engine oil, exhaust.

I prayed at some point, litanies for light and to get out of this space where I'd been folded like a picnic chair. There was relief in the tingles inching into my toes and fingertips. Only they inched too slow. Far too slow. And with the sensation came pain. I made the hurt a reclaiming of sorts. Had to.

Everything shuddered to a stop. Inertia rolled me onto my face to lick the felt underlay. A car door slammed, followed by crunching footsteps, the click of a latch and then whooshing.

Eddie was silhouetted against a billion stars, each a billion pricks of his needle. He dwarfed me in an almost cosmic way, and I'd never been more terrified. Only then did I clock the dampness between my thighs, the acrid smell of piss. Humiliation, I found out, was a luxury.

"St-op," I stuttered, worming an arm out from under my chest to reach for him. He slapped my hand away, tender as a kitten with a ball of twine. He swallowed me with his enormous shadow. Tugged to the left. To the right. I slammed the ground, dirt clouding my mouth. The stink of sweat was stronger and bitterer on my kidnapper now, leading me to suspect that Eddie was more unnerved than he wanted to let on. As before, I tried to fight him off. And as before, I failed. Even rolling was too hard, let alone getting on my feet and running into—

The bush.

A thunder of crickets welcomed us.

Eddie had driven off the road and further into the scrub. The underbrush was equal parts mulch and jagged rock. He kicked me onto a tarp he'd wrestled from the back seat, making the stars time-lapse into contrails. Vomit ejected through my teeth and pooled about my hair. Everything reeked like matter drudged out of the sink after it's been blocked for a week. Eddie peered at me, curious, watching me marinate. He beamed a torch in my face, the brightness lancing skull-deep. Coughing obliterated whatever pleads I strived for. Eddie tilted the torch to his face.

"I can't hear you, Thom," he said, voice stripped of inflection.

"N-no-oo. No."

Eddie was decorated in blood.

He turned away, leaving me to scream. All went unheard.

Eddie had brought me back to Bungonia National Park—a conclusion not drawn through recognition (it was too dark for that), but the symmetry of our story. *Of course, it would end this way*, I thought as he drew straps over his shoulder to lug the tarp, Santa Claus with a sack of bribes. Only then, as the earth grated under my dead-weight, did it occur to me that this might be the last night of my life.

The purity of that fear was cold. It surged. Harder. Harder.

I had plenty of time to think about Brandon and his father and those chipped, second-hand bowls we sometimes ate breakfast-for-dinner from. The newspaper Arthur left on the coffee table. Our toothbrushes in separate glasses on the bathroom basin. Criss-crossing receipts and statements pinned to the refrigerator by magnets (moths, not butterflies). Father and son, and how their doors had been open yet neither came running to see what all the sound was about.

Bloodied sheets and mouths carved into their faces where mouths shouldn't be. Bodies on the floor. Brandon's school uniform on the hanger going unworn, Tiff screaming into its weave and later collapsing at the joint funeral.

I tried to convince myself that Brandon, at least, got away. Through a window, maybe. Spiriting for the street. The slap of his feet on bitumen as he ran for help.

Only the fantasy carried no weight. No, not even a little.

I sensed their absence within me, a dead weight.

Tears mingled with the vomit slopping into my ears as the kidnapper groaned, heaving those straps again. This wasn't the wiry ginger I'd last seen in my house. The months in between had been full of gym visits and planning sessions and nurturing the need to make this all happen. And it was happening. I wished he'd killed me in my bed, overdosed me on whatever paralytic he injected me with, a liquid Iron Maiden to trap me from the inside out. Or slit me open as I slept (as he must have done to Brandon and Arthur), waking at the grand finale to finger the hole he'd opened.

"Don't. Do. It," I managed to get out.

"Don't speak, Thom," he told me between pants. "You're making it worse."

The torch was strapped to his belt, its beam offering glances at the backpack on his shoulders. Blood rushed to my head as we shuffled up an incline. Tingles buffered enough of the numb to let me shuffle off the tarp at last. Eddie put me back in my place, where he thought I belonged. He inspected me then, the final piece of a puzzle he'd debated for so long. Chance had no part to play in Eddie's orchestration. Knowing now that he'd schemed in my absence—that we shared the same world, the same city, the same newspaper article—was to learn you'd lived with a stranger, not a loved one, someone who with time took advantage of your leniency and blind-spots. The person who violated the most important things you'd once shared.

A name slipped across my lips.

We came to a stop. A calligraphy of moonlit dust. Air like cotton.

"Wh-what are y-you doing?"

Eddie trundled me off the crunching plastic, gravity dragging my arm to where the earth should be. Empty space greeted it instead, the sensation so similar to waking from a dream in which you were falling. "S-stop!"

But Eddie didn't stop.

His movements played out on cue, not a second wasted.

He swung the backpack from his shoulders, the cry of a zipper. The noises that followed took me back to my stepfather's shed as a teenager, not long after the divorce and before I came out, the day he tried to teach me how to spot defaults in a car engine. He tapped metal innards with a spanner. "This is where you check your water levels, okay? Are you listening? Good. This is your oil cap. Make sure it's on tight always otherwise your car will fill with smoke."

Clunk-tap went that spanner.

("Are you listening, Thom?")

Clunk-tap went whatever Eddie withdrew from the backpack.

"Puh-lease," I said. "I'm s—"

"Don't say anything. You're not meant to speak. Yet."

That final word pinged every nerve.

Yet.

Gasping, I tried to scramble through the dust, through the electric flare-ups in my joints. The valley misted in a eucalyptus haze beneath a bowl of stars—the enormity of it all snatched what breath remained in my lungs. Fingers reached for solid ground and fumbled at the bluff instead. *I'm at the edge of the cliff,* I thought, panicking. A faraway bird laughed. And why shouldn't it laugh?

I never stood a chance.

Eddie flipped me onto my back.

"It's easier if you don't move," he whispered, close enough to kiss. Those eyes were darker than they had ever been, blackness sucked from spaces between stars. Eddie greased from my sightline, though not for long. Time enough for a single inhale. He brought a sawn-off sledgehammer down on my right leg. The leaden *thwok* of snapping bones. Immediate, sun-white agony. Nothing made sense. Eddie swung the weapon a second time, breaking my other leg. *Wind-chaffed bergs on the outside of my skin, the bushfire that levelled towns within.* I was abandoned between these two extremes, confused until the exact moment I wasn't.

Eddie pushed me over the bluff. Time elasticized.

A burst of honeyed jasmine. The whistle of my fall as that bird continued its hysterics. Three distinct pulse-beats, that's all I got. Rocks have no mercy. I shattered in a dozen places. The taste of water drunk straight from the tap around the side of my parents' house filled my throat, coppery and full of grit. Oxygen didn't exist. Not anywhere.

The cliff loomed ten yards above, the Milky Way a million miles beyond it. My watery eyes warped it all into a kaleidoscope of refracted light.

You're not meant to speak.

Yet.

It had been Eddie who said that before, but the sentence chimed in my mother's voice. *You didn't tell anyone you were coming here, Thom. You knew the risks. I told you from the start that people die out there.*

They die.

"Hello?" Eddie shouted, his voice reverberating through the valley. Pain turned everything into television static, Brandon's voice flittering through those undefined stations to ask me about pain.

Yes, it hurts, I told him. Worse *than I thought anything could. A lot more than a smidge.*

"Is somebody down there?" Eddie yelled. "Hello?!"

Mum whispered again. *You weren't meant to speak before, but now it is your time to shine. Tell him what he needs to hear. Let him know you're here.*

Let him know how grateful you are.

Scythe moon cut the kaleidoscope, a conspirator caught mid-wink. I sifted for a memory. I had walked this part of the National Park and heard the cicadas, the sigh of these trees, and how they shushed me to maintain their secret. Only it hadn't been their deceit masked out here—it had been my own. *Don't let on that you know what he's up to,* the bush clattered, bark against bark, in a million insects at once. *Don't let him know that you can play this game, too.*

Because if you play right, you might get through this.

"Can you hear me?" Eddie shouted again, loud and flat.

Blood gurgled into my eyes, rouging the landscape I'd saved him from. Red. Red everywhere. The hue of Australian soil, the me beneath the skin. Agony was a catapult I loaded with the words Eddie wanted to hear. I gave him his acknowledgement. "YES! I NEED YOUR HELP. PLEASE HELP ME!"

The rats ate their own.

Too Old For Icecream

Dad called our room The Warren, and we were his little rabbits. There we'd wait for Mum to come home. You smelled her before you saw her.

Bo, the eldest of us, on the bunk above. Cruz in a cot under the busted window, tarpaulin stapled to the sill like canvas on a frame in art class. I liked art. Math and science were hard, plus I didn't like those teachers.

I'd listen to my brothers breathe in the dark, anticipating the moment someone—almost always Bo—broke and said how much they hated her. And the quiet that followed. Dad in his room down the hall, afraid.

Mum drank Taula Strong, an imported Samoan beer they stocked at The Feddy. I don't know where Samoa is, but I know beers, even though I'm only thirteen. At Dad's request, I'd fished Mum out of The Feddy many times over. He'd stay in the car with my brothers who had Coke and hot chips wrapped in newspaper from the James Bridge Takeaway. I'd look over my shoulder before going inside and see my father through the windshield biting his fingernails, spitting nibbles onto the tarmac. Heat made the parking lot shimmery. I hated The Feddy, how it stunk of clothes left to dry inside and vinegar. Mum at the bar with her friends, catfish-faced men who never straightened their backs like kids had to, the refrigerator where the beer was stocked behind them, all those labels and brands. The publican with his handlebar moustache between us. He knew my name but called me 'Blue', which made no sense. My hair was red. The old-fashioned jukebox in the renovated section was cool, though. Sometimes, Mum came without a fight. Mostly, we had to wait. Coming back to the car with my head low, asking Dad to put on the radio until she slinked over when the mood suited her. We wouldn't talk as we drove, the smell of piss on her. Afterwards, eating in front of the television with Family Feud blasting too loud, studio laughter as we chewed but didn't smile.

The quiet of The Warren in summer after Bo confessed his hatred.

Crickets outside.

Cruz slapping a mosquito.

And later, the elephant parade of Mum staggering across the veranda. Her and Dad were either doing It or fighting. It was hard to tell. You only knew afterwards. If it was sex, they fell asleep, which meant we, too, could fall asleep. If it was a fight, Mum left again—and that's what happened that night. The slamming screen door made me flinch. I peered through a gap in the tarpaulin and watched her fade into the dim beyond the Christmas lights we kept on all year round. Our house was on a wide street opposite train tracks. Everything rattled when the freights went by. Two passed before Mum came back with a sack over her shoulder.

It didn't matter that I was the middle child. My brothers turned to me to be brave. I told them to stay put as I crept into the kitchen after everything stilled, Mum's drunken snores chainsawing the walls. The bag was on the table next to the salt and pepper shakers. Moonlight made everything blue and chilly, even though it was hot. Nights like this, I often took my pillow and slept in the bathtub.

I peered into the bag. My mouth went dry.

Buzzing with panic, I ran back to The Warren, panting hard and fast. I tried not to cry when Cruz and Bo shook me, whisper-yelling for me to tell them what happened, what I'd found.

A door clunked in the house and we scuttled to our beds. The thump of feet coming our way like a storm getting closer and closer.

One Mississippi.

Two Mississippis.
Three Mississippis.
BOOM.

Mum thundered into our room with the bag in her hands and upended the kittens onto the floor. I hadn't noticed before that their heads were on backwards. We screamed. Mum glared at me and I thought I saw something moving under the skin of her face, like hands scrambling for freedom. She left. There was yelling. Something crashed. We cried harder, holding one another, when Dad howled. Mum didn't come back, so I got up to lay my Star Wars blanket over the dead kittens.

The three of us squeezed into Cruz's cot, salty-sweaty as sardines. The wind gusted, tarpaulin breathing in and out, crunching-crunching. One of the kittens wasn't dead and writhed beneath the blanket. It couldn't meow, but we watched it trying to crawl away. Paws kneaded the carpet.

I suggested putting on the radio for distraction.

"No," Bo said. "She'll hear us."

The surviving kitten crawled out and rolled onto its back, blood seeping from between needlepoint teeth. Bo told us not to look when he climbed off the cot and asked me for a pillow. I knew what he was going to do.

"Bo, please," I said. "There has to be another way."

"There isn't."

This was the most adult thing I'd ever heard. Bo was only a year older than me. He was going through puberty and had hairs on his chest and said his shins hurt all the time. But none of that mattered anymore because he was crying like all of us, all of us just the same. He put the pillow over the kitten and was gentle. I felt a part of it. Like I was above the pillow and helping hold it down, but also under it and unable to breathe.

Bo came back to bed once it was done and we waited for morning. Dad always visited us first because Mum slept late. The tarpaulin crunched in and out until sun-up. Our room smelled of damp fur. The boys were asleep. I wriggled out of bed, trying not to look at the blanket and pillow as I put my ear to the door.

Was Dad okay?

A train rumbled by. The house shook. I could hear cutlery leaping in kitchen drawers, ornamental plates Nan gave us before she died quivering on their wall hooks. I often dreamed of running across the road and jumping on one of the trains, quick as the rabbit Dad said I was. The destination didn't matter, only that I escaped. But I would miss my brothers. I turned and watched them spooning on the mattress. They were growing up, as was I. Me chasing Bo and Cruz chasing me. Time pushed us along. I wondered who we would be someday.

After dawn, Cruz got up to pee but I stopped him.

"Something's wrong," I said.

Cruz whined. There was an old plastic KFC cup in our toy chest. It was full of green soldiers. I upended them and told Cruz to go in that. He asked us to look away. When he was done, I pulled the tarpaulin from the windowsill, yanking out staples to tip the cup out. I was sad for Cruz as we listened to the splash. He'd always been the shy, easy to embarrass type.

Bo told us to hang tight. "I'm gonna check what's going on."

"No," I said. "Stay." My voice didn't sound like my own. "Didn't you see that thing moving under her face?"

Bo glanced at his hand on the doorknob. I thought he looked handsome then, like someone from a television show. "I've got to," he said. "It's my job, and I haven't been doing it right. I shouldn't have let you go last night. I'm sorry. You can have the Easter egg I've been saving in the freezer."

We watched him tiptoe from sight, the door closing behind him. I held my breath. The house seemed alive with waiting. A few minutes passed and then we heard his scream.

Cruz clutched me, told me not to leave him when I ran to the door and opened it. His fingernails in my flesh. He tucked under my arm as I crab-walked along the hallway, which stretched to a T intersection. On one side was the living room. On the other, Mum and Dad's bedroom. The door was open an inch or two, and through the crack, I saw a shadow.

An icky stranger-danger sensation of being watched filled me.

The shadow had silver eyes and stunk of Taula Strong. She jolted, a flash of shapes on the carpet, thudding over to slam the door.

"RUN!" Bo shouted.

Wood groaned under her weight. Something scratched. "Fucking, rabbit," I heard my mother growl. I was more scared than I'd ever been. Cruz shrieked as I dragged him from the house. I didn't stop to turn off the Christmas lights as I was supposed to, it being one of my chores in addition to mowing the lawn and nailing down fence posts when they came loose. I'd always thought it was chores, the do-it-only-to-have-to-do-it-again sameness that kept the sun coming up and going down, like it was the power that kept the world spinning. All chores—not just my own. Millions of people going to work, the birds hunting for their babies. But I didn't do my job, risking everything and everyone, and we ran instead. The lights remained on. All that power wasted. I expected to hear Mum screaming, or see her chasing after us, grabbing and twisting our heads backwards so she could stuff us in her sack.

She never came.

That hurt worst of all.

We didn't have anywhere to go, so I took us to the one place where people would, at least, recognise me. We dodged behind hedges when cars passed by. Nobody saw us, the barefoot kids in their pyjamas. The heat was already climbing.

I told Cruz to wait outside the big brick building because he was too young to go in—so was I, but oh well. He cried again and I hugged him in a way boys weren't allowed to. The heave and pull of his face against my chest. His breaths were warm cat ghosts pawing at my neck. I felt all the chores of other people in James Bridge keeping time going, forcing me on, ageing me. I hated it, them.

"Please come back," Cruz said. He was small in the sunlight. Fragile, a bird without feathers. I ran to the Feddy's locked doors and banged the glass until my fists hurt. It was unlikely that anyone would be there this early, and the hope was draining from me. My greasy handprints on the glass. Tears on my cheeks.

"Blue!" said the publican from the other side of the door. "What the hell are you doing here?" He fumbled with the latch and let me in.

I told him what was going on, not that it made much sense, and after a pause, the publican asked me to bring the tot inside. "Cruz is grown and can fight as good as anyone!" I shouted. This was the first time I'd raised my voice to an adult. It was awful.

The publican raised his hands. "Easy now, mate."

We brought Cruz in and the two of us sat on one of the leather couches in the renovated area out back. It still smelled, just not as bad. The publican knelt in front of us and placed coins in the palm of my hand. He said he'd be back. Sunshine through the window made the dollars glow. I knew what the money was for and asked Cruz what he'd like to hear on the Jukebox. His request was pure *him*. Music filled The Feddy.

The publican returned a few minutes later and said the police were on the way. I watched him search for something to say, his thick hands running through his hair. "Uh, do you, uh, want some ice cream while we wait?"

I hugged Cruz again, who was sucking his thumb.

"No," I said, lifting my chin. "I'm too old for ice cream."

But I wanted it so bad.

Love Amongst the Redback Spiders

By the dry and dusty winter of 1951, I'd celebrated two years of successful deceit. A joyless landmark. I swear, secrets kept me ticking.

"You ought to dress with more flair," my wife would say. "You're so drab."

Loneliness palsied fashion, jaundiced the skin, and sometimes made it hard to keep down the meals she cooked up. And then, as if compensating for my lack of hue, she'd layer her face with makeup. A china dolly in a window, searching for validation.

Her name was Patricia.

"Look at me," she'd say, staring at me in the mirror. Granting her request proved more difficult by the day because I didn't see the woman I tasted and felt and sometimes made love to. No, I saw nothing but my deceptions reflected back. That was why I looked away, almost always. Patricia would exhale, applying another layer of lipstick and say, "You make me feel so small."

When she died in our bathroom after swallowing my sleeping pills, all the shit that kept me ticking blinked out too. With nobody around to betray, the lie ceased to exist. Now all I've got is the three-storey house by the Hawkesbury River in Long Swamp Bay. That, and memories. She loved this place. We'd sit in the parlour and listen to the radio, the two of us sipping sloe gin fizzes, me smoking Lucky Strikes. I've moved the radio upstairs, which is where I live now. Nothing but static on the tune-box these days.

The house is almost empty.

No photos of us, no trace of the half-read book she left on the bedside table, *A Woman Called Fancy*. I trashed it. Sure, I could've kept it and the other memory triggers around, substituting them for the rungs on the ladder people use to climb themselves out of their grief, but no. That didn't seem right.

The house. All the things that brought the past back. And the scars in my brain where the doctor drove his ice picks.

"I've a steady hand," he'd said.

There are empty picture hooks around the upstairs rooms, little upturned fingers beckoning. The wall-to-wall carpet. It's pink.

Carpet.

I'll get to that. There's a lot to tell before I die. Like the alleyway in Sydney, stinking of piss and wet dog. The man who changed everything with a whistle from the public restroom. He wore a thin moustache. Flittering eyes. This man, in his yellow raincoat and battered fedora, led me into one of the stalls. Fluorescents threw sporadic light. Redback spiders covered the walls, but they only moved when the room went dark. Webs quivered as the man closed the door behind me. Behind us. He slipped the lock into the latch and put his lips to mine. Fear tastes like alcohol, only sweeter.

"What brings you to the city?" he said.

"Came to watch the greyhounds."

"Pick a winner?"

"Not this time." My throat was dry. "You ever done this before?"

"Yeah, mate. I guess I have."

Shaking as he held my cock in his hand. Stubble against my skin. And through the panting, the inevitable gasp, redback spiders watched. Our writhing reflected in tiny eyes. Perhaps I should have offered my wrist and let them seek a vein.

I deserved it.

The man took me to a bar afterwards. He bought the first round, sloe gin fizzes—watered down but heavy on the guilt. Before we left, I went to the men's room, relieved myself for what felt like forever. A splash of dried cum on my trousers. I cried a little.

We went to his place, a shoebox he rented on George Street.

There, I noticed the handmade quilt on the bed, something he'd brought with him, debris from another domesticity. The stitching. Patchwork beauty. It struck me as feminine.

"Tell me your name," I said.

"No names."

"Well, tell me *a* name."

"Call me Raymond. That as good as any." His voice was wax, dripping, burning, moulding me into something that looked and sounded like him. "We're safe here. Ain't nobody gonna come burstin' in, screamin' queer, screamin' Commie, drag us off to the fruitcake factory. Just you and me. *A Lovely Way to Spend an Evening*, as ole Blue Eyes sings."

Only it wasn't an evening. It was many. Memories stacked back-to-back, wedged between then and now. It went by fast, days tick-tocking closer to the moment when there's tick-tocking no more. Looking back, it feels like I haven't lived, just watched my life flash past.

In that blur, I learned a lesson or two.

Nothing in life is free. When you lose something important, something that makes you who you are, expect a whole basket of goodies you didn't bargain for in lieu. I'm not talking about the casseroles and sympathy cards, all the shit that flows in from folks you don't know once the casket's in the pit. No, the goodies I'm talking about arrive later.

Something gets taken from you, something slips in. That's the deal.

2

The sheets were our ally for a year-and-a-half. I cried my weight, hating every part of me he found attractive. When Raymond wasn't around, and Patricia was at her brother's place upstate, I drank too much. Cussing, punching myself.

The week before Raymond was slated to visit Long Swamp Bay for what would end up being the last time (our Sydney rendezvous dictated by the ebb and flow of the greyhound season), I wrote out my confession with a ballpoint pen. Coming clean stripped me bare, left me empty but no less afraid. And my spelling ain't worth a dime.

I tore the confession to shreds. Ate the pieces.

Raymond and I were in bed that night, sweating sin, when Patricia and her brother came home. We didn't hear the car pull into the drive, or the front door, those creaking steps. Her brother slugged me across the face. Patricia screamed.

We were undone.

Raymond left no forwarding address at his apartment. The city laughed at me with its honking horns, shattering glass. I moved out and rented my own shoebox on Elizabeth Street above a butcher's shop. Patricia had the house to herself. Nothing was on paper regarding the property yet, but I figured it would be soon. On nights when I missed her and the river at the end of the drive, I went back to that bar, ordered a sloe gin fizz and didn't bother to ask the poison dealer if he'd seen a tall fella in a yellow overcoat and a battered fedora.

Sometimes there was only the dark throat of the alleyway and the public restroom at the end. Others lurked there now. Nicotine kisses, shared cigarettes. Redback spiders.

A Lovely Way to Spend an Evening.

The police came knocking at my door a week later. They told me Patricia was dead, found face down in a pool of candy-coloured vomit.

3

"Will it hurt?"

"You won't feel a thing, sir. You'll be out like a light."

"What happens in the dark?"

"You'll be attached to this electro-convulsive shock machine." The doctor gestured to the suitcase-sized box on a gurney. A chill ran through me. It looked like a face, watching me. Dials for eyes. Its nose an energy meter. An unlit, emotionless mouth of bulbs. "Electricity will flow through your body until you are in a deep state. Enforced sleep, if you will. During that window of time, which will total, say seven or eight minutes give-or-take, I'll conduct the surgery."

"How dangerous is it? Break it down for me, doc."

"Trans-orbital lobotomy is invasive, and success varies. There are some who walk away from it cured of the homosexual ailment."

"Only some?"

"Well, to be frank, there are those who don't walk away at all. There are risks with every procedure, sir. This is no different."

"Goddamn."

"It all comes down to a matter of priority. And choice. See, you've got to ask yourself: Where do your loyalties lie? Man has little choice over the hand he's dealt, the diseases the Lord bestows on him. But in some cases, like the one we're facing now, man does have the choice to risk curing it. I'm sure someone like you understands the value of a gamble."

"Only greyhounds, doc. Look, I don't know about this—"

"I've a steady hand, sir. I'm not in the business of malpractice. The same cannot be said to all surgeons on these streets. It's nothing short of providence that's brought you here."

"How does it work? No spin."

"I will use what you would commonly refer to as an ice-pick, no different to the one you would find in your home. Comforting, eh? A nurse will lay a towel over your face, even though there isn't much spillage. Your eyelids will be peeled back, the ice-pick inserted into the socket, and with a hammer, I'll drive the point through the skull and into the brain, thus severing the frontal lobe. Only that which is not needed will be excised. I'll steel your homosexual impulse. It shouldn't take longer than three to four minutes. Less time than it takes to hard-boil an egg!"

"Jesus."

"And then you walk right out of here. I'll dress you up in a pretty lookin' pair of black sunglasses to hide the bruising, and off you go. Easy as pie, that's what my wife says."

"Your wife, she uhh, approves of your line of work then?"

"Approve, sir? Why, she's the nurse."

The black and white floor of the surgery room, like something in a photograph of a Yankee diner. Only the kind of things they dished up you'd have to be mad to order. Yet I did. I hated myself that much. It occurred to me that I may die, and I regretted not letting the redback spiders come at me way back when.

The mouth of the machine glowed, bulb by bulb.

My pulse was a chugging locomotive carrying me to nowhere. The doctor and his pretty wife towered over me, sliding into silhouette. I felt the size of a needle's eye.

It wouldn't be the last time.

4

It began with pens.

I don't know how and I don't know why. I only knew that they had to go.

This happened a month to the day after my surgery, which had been (as the doctor said it would be) a success. However, the proof was in the pudding. I attempted to dust off memories of Raymond—his stubble over my neck, brushing my nipples, a bite, his chin buried in my inner thigh. But the nooks where I'd tucked the echoes of him fucking me were empty. I walked there alone. And to be doubly sure, I bought some queer funny-pages and took them to the Long Swamp house I'd moved into now that Patricia was gone. Muscled men pushed their chests together, phalluses intertwined—drawings that would have brought a flush to my face months before and set my hand wandering. Now, though? Nada.

By day, I told myself I was free. Night-time was a different story.

I woke that morning, swimming through my usual pre-coffee cloud to settle into a life without my wife. She was never my 'Honey Bunch' or 'Sugar Dumpling' or any of those other diabetic love-a-boos, just plain simple Babe. It suited her. I'm old fashioned in many ways, and maybe that was why she loved me. For a while, at least.

I sat there, chewing my cereal, surrounded by the bare walls and the smell of my unwashed skin. And saw it glimmering in the sun.

It.

Your average ballpoint pen is just under six inches long. Inside, viscous ink waits. There is the tungsten carbide sphere, the pen point. It peered like Patricia when I smoked in her presence. Her eyes above the nimbus, the rest hidden by black waters.

Fear starts in your loins. It is cruel other pleasures spring from the same place.

I woke that October morning terrified of ballpoint pens.

Touching them with my bare hands wasn't going to happen, so I used a pair of yellow rubber cleaning gloves. Once the pens—all eleven I could find—had been thrown into a plastic drawstring bag, my fingers smelled of chlorine and rubber. I sat the bag on the kitchen counter and watched them writhe beneath the shiny black sheath. Listened to them mewl. Throwing the bag into the drive beside my bird shit-covered LaSalle Coupe was the best I could manage. A ballpoint speared the plastic, spitting an orgasmic stream of blue ink onto the concrete.

Dizzy. Fingernails nibbled down to the quick. I spat out the remains, not caring where the clippings landed. I felt like dying but would settle for a drink. Pacing. My steps echoed through the empty upper floor.

I tried to impose rationality upon the irrational (I may have been dumb enough to let a carrion-cook jab an ice-pick in my brain, but generally speaking I'm no Silly Sally) asking myself, over and over: Why did I find pens, of all things, so goddamned scary? Was I worried I'd trip and land on a pointed tip? That was a stretch. Maybe it was the ink. Could it be absorbed into my system when smudged on my fingertips?

And once the source of fear had been removed, like the homosexual disease that had destroyed my life, there was nothing but dread left. I went to the window overlooking the water—so far down below—until I calmed. My breath fogged the plate glass. I had a mean case of the shivers.

The following days were a haze of unanswered phone calls and white noise from the broken radio. Nothing felt solid, as though I were a ghost, my hands passing through coffee cups, unable to flick light switches. I couldn't eat, became drained. There was daylight and moonlight—heat and cold. I slipped in and out of sleep, but there were no dreams, only the sensation of

143

shifting from one kind of silence into another.

5

Linen.

It wrapped around my limbs, strangling me. Sucking at my skin. Breathless, I threw off the sheets. A thudding ache in my jaw from grinding my teeth in my sleep. Nearly choked when I attempted to swallow. A headache bloomed behind my eyes, in the places where the ice-picks had been hammered. All this agony—and agony was what it was—funnelled into those two little holes in my skull. It was colossal. I fought the urge to throw up.

I snaked to the end of the bed, hands clutching the bare mattress. Peered over the edge. The linen looked like a coil of entrails, stinking and putrid in the semi-dark. I didn't know what to do, or how to digest this new anxiety. Morning had never seemed so far away. I backed up and drew my knees against my chest. I must have drifted off at some point because I remember bolting awake, thinking to myself, *what's that sound?*

A delicate scratching.

I pulled the gloves back on, their smell my saviour, and left the sheets in the driveway.

In the bathroom I stared at the mirrored stranger. The same logic—which implied that pens were harmless, that linen didn't want to strangle me—told me that the sick man in the mirror couldn't be me. No, the reflection was the instigator of lies; he was They. And I knew this because they cry crocodile tears. Watch as their tongues slither out to lick the salt.

Slu-uuuurrrp.

I smoked my last Lucky Strike. It had no taste.

6

Next came clothing.

I didn't want to pull my shirt up over my face, just in case the fabric scratched at my eyes, so I slit the shirt off my chest with a pair of scissors, too frightened to think about nicks and cuts. Their eventual stings were small compared to the headache, which I had, with resignation, come to think would be with me forever.

Naked and kneeling on the floor. Screamed into a pillow.

There was no reason to fear my clothes, and yet I did. It seemed so simple, really. Fear can make logic out of anything.

I ran to the bathroom and cut the shirt into ribbons. Fed the shreds into the toilet. The water rose to the lip of the bowl when I flushed, a single matted sleeve waving at me. I duct-taped the lid shut. Clothes banged against it.

Slammed the door. Backed away. I didn't know what to do, so I crossed the room and plugged in the radio. The soft hum of electricity reached my ears and I broke out in a sweat. All I could find was static.

At first, I thought propping a chair against the door handle of my wardrobe would be enough to trap my attire inside. I laughed.

A goddamned chair? Who was I kidding?

I could hear Patricia's voice telling me to wise up, that a job half done is a job undone. She was always like that, with her little sayings masquerading as big disciplines. It used to make me mad enough to spit—but now, looking back, all I can hear are the wonderful things she told me to do that I never did, all the advice I never took. Yeah, that's happiness for you.

The chair just wouldn't do. No way.

I taped the handles together and stuffed rolled-up tissue paper under the door. The clothes were trapped.

I ended up pissing in cups, shitting into toilet paper. I was too afraid to go outside. Sometimes I heard the telephone ringing downstairs. I no longer went below. Not anymore. My boss at the mill must've thought I was dead.

Cold came with the night. The venetian blinds shivered in the breeze, as did I. Something scurried in the dark, louder now than ever before.

7

My breath was ragged, the fever strong. The only heat in the room radiated off my flesh in waves. It was sometime after midnight. The scratching had woken me again.

I felt the crust of sleep in my eyes when I blinked. There didn't seem to be any water in me anymore. Icy blue moonlight caught flakes of skin peeling from my arms as I climbed to my feet and reached for the cabinet beside the dead radio. That's where the scratching sound was coming from.

Sudden rapping at the window. I spun on my heels, almost in tears, and saw the glimmer of small eyes and a shiny beak through the glass. The moon highlighted the bird's charcoal-black wings. It was a crow, lost in the night, not a vulture, which had been my first thought. Strangely, that didn't make its presence any less hair-raising. I had to turn away, focussing instead on the cabinet again.

On the scratching coming from within.

A hand that couldn't be my hand grasped the handle. It couldn't be *my* hand because *my* hands, as I remembered them, were not so skeletal, so yellow, with the fingernails almost completely bitten off and scabbed over.

My stomach rolled. Bile climbed my throat.

The cabinet door swung open and the scratching stopped.

There was only one thing on the shelf and it was covered in a thin layer of dust: a three-inch cylindrical vial. As soon as I saw it I had a sense of having put it there, but couldn't remember when. Time no longer existed in the apartment. Knuckles crunched as my hand—

(yes, *my* hand)

—gripped the little glass to see what it kept. I pursed my lips together and blew. A thin whistling sound. Dust coiled.

The milky liquid within the vial settled and I saw the chunk of brain. It was bobbing, maybe even pulsating with blood-filled vessels and thoughts. My little souvenir.

This sickness of mine.

The sound of a thousand ice-picks thundering through bone— shattering skull, piercing sinew. Disease bubbling out like blood, clots and all. Everything went white, and then black. I thought someone was in the room with me, flicking the ceiling lights on and off. But no. The strobe was in my head. And the flashes were only growing brighter, just as the darkness was getting deeper. I could feel myself being torn between the two, jolted back and forth, until something in me ripped.

The vial slipped from between my fingers and hit the carpet, the lid bouncing free. A cold splash across my toes. I stumbled back a few steps and my calf muscles pressed against the bed — my safe place. I allowed myself to fall, arcing down, down, onto the mattress, just as my mouth filled with coppery heat and those thousand ice-picks withdrew all at once. The sound of wings on the other side, fading.

I woke to daylight. A moment passed. I took a couple of deep breaths and studied the ceiling. Delicate tree shadows.

The memory of her fingers, tickling my arms. His tongue in my mouth.

I have nothing.

Babe.

A word I'd shared between two people, and which now belonged to nobody.

I swung off the mattress and my feet touched the floor. The pink carpet slipped between my toes.

Burning coals.

My yell echoed across the almost empty room. Knees gave out. A forest of synthetic fibres and wool piles rushed at me. My outstretched hands landed first, followed by my knees, my balls. Bolts of white-hot pain — like the electricity that had flowed through the face of the shock machine once they'd put the leather strap between my teeth and attached electrodes to either side of my head. I squeezed my eyes shut as my face hit the carpet. I inhaled dirt. Coughed once, twice. And then nothing.

The room was gone.

If I concentrated hard enough, I could distinguish the ceiling, but looking for it was like stargazing in the mid-afternoon. Thick pillars of material swayed around me: the great stalks of carpet yarns. Pickled nylon binding and winding strands of hair underfoot. Some were mine, some belonged to her. I don't know if Raymond's hair had fallen here, too. It probably had.

I dropped to my knees, muffling a scream. "Help me!"

There came the beating of wings. Stilled. Crows perched in the tall piles. They had ballpoint pen talons.

I ran, passing keg-sized dust balls. It was humid. Dirt turned to sludge beneath me. I wove through the piles, experiencing what I imagine is the pure fear a newborn feels: the unconsented terror of being forced into a new world.

I told myself that this wasn't real, that it was a dream. I knew better. I almost always did. The doc had taken away my sickness, not the part of my brain that made me lie to myself. No, that part of my brain still worked fine.

Things that had once belonged to my wife, objects I had thrown away when I moved back in, towered over me. Her copy of *A Woman Called Fancy* was the size of an upended above ground swimming pool. A gigantic makeup case.

These were tokens of her independence from me, her betrayals—only amplified, as everything now was. They frightened me as they had frightened me then.

"Babe!"

My voice woke something in the dark beyond my vision. Something big.

It had been sleeping, and like most things born to eat and drink and breed, it woke knowing only one thing. Hunger. I could hear it scurrying.

The creature in the dark must have smelled my stink. It drew closer, stampeding, snapping the woollen spires. The patchwork crows took flight. Their inkblot scat landed on my shoulders. Burned.

I ran. My tiny strides nothing compared to those of the monster. And hold no delusion—that's what it was. A monster. It had my scent and I knew it would never give up.

My screams vibrated through my body. I felt pain. Real pain.

I slammed against a dripping wall of meat, cursing myself for not looking at where I was going. I bounced backwards and watched the great mass rear up on gigantic segments. From the gnarled knots of its hair, eight black legs stretched and cracked to life. It turned, the great abdomen swinging past, a red hourglass etched across its hide. It rose up, the head towering half the height of the piles. A slit opened along its girth, revealing pinched teeth.

It bellowed radio static.

I dove beneath it as it arched its back, escaping. There were other rows of carpet on the other side, and somewhere there was light.

Running.

The spider bleated behind me as the first, still unseen monster, intercepted it. I glanced over my shoulder. Another redback scurried on a series of unstable legs, as one joint buckled and the next carried the weight. Its face was ornamented with many eyes.

The giant spiders fought, territorial and defensive, before the smaller of the two rolled onto its stomach and curled into a ball. Clouds of dust through the twilight.

My pursuer pointed its head skyward, revealing a soupy, wet mouth and long incisors. It continued its march. I lurched through the forest, passing more remains of my former life. More magnified landmines.

I crawled over hills of grime and purple crumbs. Despite the unreal landscape around me, it was these random objects from our past that disturbed me the most.

I tripped, my ankle flaming with pain. Sweat dripped into my eyes. Blood hung thick in the air—my blood. The wound was deep, bone through the cut. My heart skipped a beat when I saw what I'd tripped over.

A crescent moon. Or at least that was what I thought at first. Curved as a scythe, it gave off the rich stench of spoiled cheese.

A giant fingernail.

I ignored the bleeding gash and limped on. There was

brightness ahead. Warmth through semaphore flashes of dark-white-dark-white.

(A broken fluorescent. Flickering. Dead. Alive. Dead. Alive.)

Sunlight, strong and warm and kind against my face.

I fell again, landing hard. Winded. Carpet rot, salts and dank liquid splashed into my mouth, making my stomach lurch. I spun my head so quick the bones in my neck cracked. The spider scurried behind me, so close. It stopped short, its stench, like shit and dishwater, crashing down on me.

It reared up on its hindquarters again, only this time convulsed, exposing its flexing abdomen. I knew that what I was seeing was impossible, insane—yet no more insane than living in a world without Patricia.

The veins in my arms pushed up through my skin as though my blood were offering itself as sacrifice to the monster. *Don't give up. You haven't come this far to give up now.*

The spider's mouth parted and belched, splattering me with a scorching film of bile. Its many legs twitched, playing with its own filth and past meals, some fresher than others.

Steaming gastric juices. Ticking chewed-up clocks. Human flesh.

A broken head—still spilling brains—rolled in my direction, thumpedy-thumpedy-thump, and landed face up between my legs. The beaten-in features dripped acidic green, its boiled eyes pierced by twin ice-picks.

"I've a steady hand," the doctor gurgled through a wet, red smile.

I pushed away, gagging. I wiped the spider vomit from my face as my legs carried me off.

The creature roared behind me, but no longer chased. I dared a glance over my shoulder and saw it watching me, as the spiders had always watched, cold and neutral and without a trace of judgement. It lowered its head, as though in reverence.

8

A loud crashing sound. Bursting glass. I don't think there was any pain. It's hard to tell. The light took it all away. It was so bright. It illuminated the shadowed cabinet and the contents of my keepsake, the empty apartment, the doctor's office, the public restroom where the spiders spun their webs and truths were told for the first time.

All burned away.

Now there is just the tinkering sound of broken window shards, the rushing wind as I fall.

Silhouetted against the brightness is a shape, like a flick of charcoal on empty canvas. It's Patricia, or at least I hope it's her. Unlike happiness, there comes a time when the cost of hoping is free. Now with the tick-tocking over and done with, I figure this moment of gratis is well earned, if nothing else.

I never thought it was possible to miss someone who hated you so much.

And then she—it—is gone.

Grief for what is lost fills me like venom. The haunt of a taste on my tongue.

Sloe gin fizz.

Shadow Debt

1

Ian and Nanette caught *Cactus Flower*, starring Walter Matthau and a young Goldie Hawn at the Rialto in 1969 for $1.40. A difficult year for Nanette to forget. Boot prints on the moon, there seemed to be more copies of *The Godfather* than people, Judy Garland died of a drug overdose—a million hearts breaking at once—and Saint Catherine's wedding bells rang just for them. The reception followed at Nanette's parents' house on The Hill.

Forty-eight people attended, cars lining the road overlooking the coast. They took photos during a break in the rain on the cliff that would change Nanette's life half a century later. Her uncle drank too much and broke an ankle falling off a chair he'd been dancing on. "Between this and the bloody weather," said one guest, "it's good luck, for sure."

Cars peeled away. Waves buffered the rocks below. That night's party became the following day's floor to clean. Ian and Nanette wouldn't be able to afford a honeymoon for another three years, but that was fine. Good things to those who wait was how Nanette figured it. So, they waited, and when the time was right, when finances aligned, memories that money couldn't buy were made.

Ian gripped the quilt his wife of fifty-odd years had crocheted for him.

Drool spindled from his mouth. Rainwater shadows traced their faces in the nursing home common area as a movie Nanette would sooner forget played out on the television. *Cactus Flower*, starring Walter Matthau and a young Goldie Hawn.

"A buck forty," Nanette said. Hers was the voice of someone who couldn't be surprised anymore. Someone who had poured herself into the lives of others for years, with little left behind for herself. She'd celebrated (not that it was much of a celebration) her seventy-second birthday the month before. Her words stretched thin, warbled. "And Goldie won the Oscar in '69, too. Remember that, Ian?"

Almost sarcasm there, even if she hadn't intended it. Of course, her husband didn't remember. People used to know her for her humour.

The Rialto—like Truman Place Nursing Home—had been an irrelevance to them prior to spending time there together, the meaningless turned meaningful. Memories tied from one place and time to the other, strings which when plucked, chimed hurts that wouldn't stop singing. Nothing lasted, except her memory. It haunted her. On those days when her husband shit his pants and didn't know how to care anymore (let alone ask for help), when he nodded off with his mouth open and she had to shoo flies from crawling in between his lips, Nanette wished Dementia would come prowling for her, too. It didn't seem natural that everything that once defined their lives together only existed in her head now.

Side by side in the common area. Together alone.

Lauralee joked about Nanette's steel-trap recall. "Nothing slips you by, Mum." This, their daughter said all the time, like it was a good thing. Maybe Lauralee said it as an atonement of sorts. A backwards acknowledgement of the shit she put them through.

Nanette turned from the television. "Time for me to choof-off, Tin-Tin."

He used to call her 'Snowy.' Now, he didn't call her anything.

Cataract eyes, drawn to the ping of her voice, searched for recognition. Today, Ian found it, and smiled. All gums, no teeth. A grunt. Nanette slipped inside her jacket, rain lashing the windows again, and picked up her handbag. Squeezed her husband's knee to let him know she still loved him. Doctor Tomislav told her this was good to do. He'd also said there would come a time when Ian would no longer remember her at all. Sensory echoes linger. Sometimes. If you're lucky.

Every day was a goodbye, tiny deaths lined back-to-back.

"Love you," she said.

Nanette wove through Truman Place, thanking the carers she passed. Stopped at the doors to the carpark. Braced for the cold. She would feel that chill in her marrow all night. Nanette drew a scarf about her neck—a picture of composure on the outside, a destroyed church filled with screams and broken glass within. Her smiles to the admin staff were well rehearsed, that wave almost regal. She walked into a day that hurt to exist in.

And you deserve to hurt. This is what you get for remembering.

Lauralee and her husband, Roy, were always bugging Nanette to trade in the VW Beetle, but she couldn't bear the thought of parting with it. Letting go had always been hard for her, and harder yet later in life. Those gears—like her bones—ground on, a couple of old great dames who weren't what they used to be. But the heating still worked, and her mechanic serviced the engine well enough. Nanette was determined to drive the car into the ground. 'Stubborn' was another word her daughter described her with.

That one, she agreed with.

Nanette drove at a deliberate pace on account of the wet roads. At least the rain had stopped. A granite day with tug-of-war winds. Newcastle's suburbs shrank to nothing in the rear-vision mirror. Fourth gear clanked back to third as Nanette took Scenic Road Drive up The Hill towards the house she'd inherited. Only it wasn't the road she saw, but Goldie Hawn and Walter Matthau instead. 1969. Puzo paperbacks and a starlet's painkillers laid out on the rim of a bathtub. The Rialto's overstuffed seats and its enormous screen as it bled Technicolor. Nanette may have smiled as she drove, but if she did, it was an unconscious smile. The cinema still stood in the city's heart, fifteen minutes from here, though it had been years since she'd been—well before Ian took his turn. *Those slightly sticky carpets. The thrill as the lights dimmed to black.* It was all so clear to her.

155

I'll go there soon, Nanette said to herself. *Just for me this time. Only me.*

A barricade separated the bluff from its drop, shark-belly oceans beyond. Being a June baby, she loved winter but longed for change. The cold huddled within her in ways it never used to. Ian never was one for the damp, having battled pneumonia in '86, the year their granddaughter, Frances, came into the world (with a slap on the bum—gosh, the lungs on her!). And while her husband did get better, he never shook that cough. You heard it when he laughed. Ian hadn't laughed in a long time.

Three months until spring, Nanette reminded herself, gripping the wheel, her wedding band glowing in the silvery light. *And by then, Frances's bub will be here, too—*

All thoughts froze.

A mud-splattered car was parked on her right. The figure stood at the cliff's edge on the other side of the barricade, directly across from Nanette's house. There weren't many properties left this far up The Hill as the majority of her neighbours had moved away, bought out by developers looking to erect an enormous hotel on the spot. Prime real estate, they said. Postcards just waiting to be printed. Nanette, despite their handsome offers, refused to give up her land. "You'll just have to build around me," she said. And as if to call her bluff, they were already in the process of doing so. The Hill was a mess of half knocked-down buildings draped in fluttering tarps, trucks and DO NOT CROSS tape. But it was a Sunday and the construction sites were unattended now. No wonder the figure at the cliff's edge assumed they were alone.

They had been. Until now.

"Oh, good lord, no," Nannette said, skidding to a halt behind the car in a cloud of exhaust. Her heartbeat leapt from its arrhythmic slouch as she fumbled for the handle. The door buckled outwards. Wind razors. "Be careful!" Nanette called, slopping through grass to the barricade. "Don't do it." These words knuckled free, leaving holes in her chest shock soon filled. "I'm here with you," she said.

The woman on the edge of the seventy-foot drop wore an orange sports jersey with a tiger's face on the back. Curly black hair whipped in the wind. Leggings. No shoes. Nanette could just make out her profile. A sliver of cheek, an upturned nose. Thin blue lips.

Nanette glanced over her shoulder, back to the road below. No cars—for now at least. Just a sheet of rain in pursuit. "I know you can hear me."

"Leave me alone, lady," said the girl.

"Tell me your name."

"You can't be here."

Adrenalin and fear coerced Nanette's senses into overdrive, and even though her eyesight wasn't what it used to be, details bubbled to the surface. She saw every cloud in the sky. Every ocean wave shaved with froth. The eyes—threatening and sporting—of that tiger, stared back at her. Cartoon teeth and the little rips in the fabric.

"You're right. I can't be here," Nanette said. "But I am."

The young woman dropped her arms, making the mop of hair fling harder, tugged by invisible hands that might push too hard and send her flying. "Go away."

Nannette, dentures clattering, blinked back tears. "Something awful has happened to you, sweetheart. Tell me. I want to hear you say it. It's so important you do."

"Too late."

"Too late for what?"

"For him to change," said the girl. "And for me. I took it. I took it all and he knows."

"Are you hurting, sweetheart?"

The young woman shook her head. "Not anymore."

"I guess that's what makes jumping easier," Nanette said. "You're numb. It sounds terrible. You must've been through Hell, and all because he wouldn't budge."

"Th-th-th-they never d-do."

A beat.

"What's your name?" Nanette said. "I want to hear you say it. I want to hear you."

Silence from the woman. Wintery hands made a noose of Nanette's scarf. Pain flared, a skeleton without cartilage rattling under loose skin. "Tell me, sweetheart."

"Toni. Toni Payover."

"It's not your fault, Toni."

"W-what?"

"It's never been your fault," Nanette said.

"But he knows what I did. You don't get it. Nobody does!"

The young woman turned. Pigeon-toed feet twisted in grass by the cliff's edge. The saturated ground could give way without warning. Others had died at this spot. Nanette recalled a family coming up here to picnic in the mid-70s. One of the children, a boy, climbed the barricade when their backs were turned. Nanette read about it in the papers and had stored the article away in a scrapbook in Ian's study.

Toni's eyes were railroad spikes, irony and wet. Tears froze on her cheeks. "What did you say?"

"I said, it's not your fault, Toni."

Nanette lifted her hand. The rain came down. Waves crashed, a thousand sighs at once, sighs of relief as the young woman stepped toward the barricade. The orange jersey fluttered on her frame as she hunched. Nanette expected the earth to crumble at any second, or maybe lightning would strike them down. Because everything that could go wrong would go wrong. And usually did.

Only, no.

The young woman—hardly more than a girl—took Nanette's hand and let herself be drawn into a hug. They shivered together. Something warm fluttered at the middle of them where breast met breast, two women at opposite ends of time brought together under the same sky.

2

"**A**nd *then* what happened?" Lauralee gripped her tea, her husband, Roy, by her side at the kitchen table. They clung off every word. "She climbed over the railing to you?"

"Yeah," Nannette said, still buzzing. "She didn't say anything, just kind of glared at me, into me, not in a kind way, but not in a mean way, either. Just shocked, I guess. Then she shook me off, got into her car—and poof—gone."

Roy placed his hands on the table. "Holy smokes."

"That's actually insane, Mum."

Nanette sipped her coffee. A few years before, she never would have consumed caffeine so late in the day for fear it would keep her up. That didn't bother her so much anymore. Insomnia was a given now, and no amount of bartering with the dark changed that. Tonight, she might treat herself to a brandy. "Thank you for letting me come over and stay," Nanette said. "I don't mean to impose."

"You're fine," said Roy. "You're never imposing."

"Of course, Mum," her daughter said. A bit abrupt. "Don't be silly."

"I've got the jitters something shocking. Look at my hands. Look!"

Lauralee came around the table and sat by her mother's side, shoulder-to-shoulder. "You've done a great thing. You've saved someone's life. You get that, right?"

"Just wait 'til Frances hears about this," Roy said, beaming his handsome smile.

"What time will she be back?" Nannette asked, taking another gulp. The coffee was too milky for her liking, bland, almost without taste. It was hot, though. And hot was enough.

"Around six," Lauralee said, pushing a lock of auburn hair behind an ear. "She's doing her Lamaze classes with Faheem."

Nannette nodded. "Such a good egg. Is he joining us for dinner, or is he back at his parent's tonight?"

"I'm sure he'll stay," Roy said. "Boy eats like a horse."

Lauralee laughed, so like her father's—minus the cough. "So is Frances right now."

"Well, she's eating for two," Nanette said. "Let me make dinner for us. A thank you for letting me spend the night. I'm so shaky. What a goose, I am."

Roy and Lauralee tried to hug the self-doubt out of her. Soon, Frances and Faheem came home on a burst of frigid air that made the fireplace logs glow. The story was shared again, shocked oh-my-gods echoing through the house in the old part of Mayfield, not far from the nursing home where Ian slept even when he was awake. Nanette suggested they go visit him the following day, and everyone agreed.

With unspoken reluctance.

Of course, Nanette didn't blame them. Better to remember great people as they were at their best. Nanette's family had already said goodbye in ways she couldn't herself. Yet. Maybe she envied them that.

Shadow filled the kitchen window. The scents of meat, gravy, and vegetables crept from room to room. Faheem left his studies to offer help that Nanette shushed away. "Off you trot, you silly boob," she said. He laughed. Roy and Lauralee came for wine. Frances shuffled over to put her head on her grandmother's shoulder, each taking turns to rub her enormous tummy.

"We should call the newspaper and get them to write a story about you, Gran," Frances said. "Or get you a YouTube channel." Frances pulled out her phone and set to swiping. "Toni Payover, did you say?"

"I believe so."

"Well, with a name like that, this shouldn't be hard."

"Oh, Frances, don't pry," Nanette said.

"Just try and stop her," Faheem said with a laugh that got him a kick in the shins from his wife. "Once she's on a mission, it's impossible to stop."

"Boom," Frances said, lifting her phone. "Antonia Payover from right here in not-so-sunny Newcastle. This is her, yeah?"

Nanette leaned in, pulling on her readers which were suspended from her neck on a chain. The young girl with the curly hair smiled coyly up at the camera, eyes rimmed with dark mascara that bleached her face by comparison. "That's her."

Arms outstretched. Tiger jersey billowing.

"Well, that was easy," Frances said.

An electronic clicking sound dinged from the phone in the pregnant woman's hands. "What did you do just then?" Nanette asked.

"Took a screenshot, Gran. I'll send it to your mobile."

"Oh, no, don't—"

"Too late! Look, I don't think it'll hurt to have, like, a record of this. Just in case."

"In case of what?" Faheem said, stretching.

His young wife shrugged. "Crazy, Gran. Absolutely crazy."

Nanette went to the cupboard to make a cake, seeking distraction. It helped, as did that nip of brandy. Sifted flower in a bowl. Scooped butter with a wooden spoon. Nanette took two eggs from the carton and cracked them with her hands. Not a shard of shell made its way into the mix, either. The smooth dance of someone who knew their way around a kitchen. She smiled again, thinking of her VW Beetle. Like it, she thought there was still a bit of mileage in her. Perhaps there was pride, too.

Neither egg had a yolk.

3

Nanette, pins and needles in one leg, limped into the bathroom off the nursing home common area and pushed the door open with a balled fist. She found her daughter bent over the basin with the tap running. Nurse gown green tiles covered the walls around them and the floor beneath their feet. A cracked dispenser dripped long slimes of pink soap in the corner.

"Are you okay?" Nanette said, adjusting the shawl around her shoulders.

"No, I am not okay, Mum," Lauralee said. She chortled. The overhead fluorescents stammered like neon moths' wings in the corner of Nanette's eyes.

"I'm not sure what you expected—"

Lauralee yanked paper towels from the stack on the vanity and padded her face. "Can't you just let me be upset? It isn't easy seeing Dad like that."

"I know it isn't," Nanette said, stepping closer. She caught her reflection in the mirror over her daughter's shoulder. It had been a month since she'd saved Toni's life, and the days had worn her thin. Insomnia was worse than ever, too. "But this is what getting old is like, Lauralee. Good luck ignoring it. It's our duty not to ignore it. What if this happens to me? Are you going to run off on me, too? That'd break my heart."

"Don't say that." Lauralee threw matted towels into a push-peddle trashcan, a gasp of faecal breath escaping from the garbage. She turned, hands on hips, flipping hair out of her eyes. "Mum, I'm not sure coming here every weekend is helping me much. Or Dad. I know it's important to you—"

"Oh, Lauralee—"

"It's too much," she said. "Work is kicking me in the guts, too. We've got this new manager and he's watching us like a goddamn hawk. Roy's under a lot of pressure, as well. His knees are giving him grief and we got word that the waiting list for surgery isn't moving like it should be. But more than anything, Mum, we're trying to keep things on track with Frances. You know how friggin' hard having your first bub is."

"I do know," Nannette said, almost defensive. "A mother never forgets."

"Coming here is hurting me."

"Your father needs us," Nanette said.

Lauralee's hands came together before her lips and she closed her eyes. A crossbow of memory pierced Nanette's chest: her daughter, a snug-as-a-bug in her crib looking up at her, desperate for cradling and to know she was loved. Nanette bending to scoop her up, the baby's eyes easing shut.

The time between then and now was a lifetime and a day.

"Dad doesn't know who I am," Lauralee said, breathing the words out nice and slow. Those beautiful green eyes opened once again to glare at her mother. "We just watched him spew on himself. It was like something from *The Fly*, for Christ sakes."

Nanette assumed her daughter was talking about the 1986 film with Jeff Goldblum, who she normally liked, and Geena Davis, who she'd always liked, but which she didn't see on account of its grisliness as reported in all the papers. The 1958 film, though, that one she'd watched at the drive-in with her father. He loved fright films. Patricia Owens up there on the screen next to Vincent Price, unnerving and charming as always. Nanette swallowed, her throat dry. She hated that her mind worked this way, firework memories that burned and blinded.

Buttery popcorn. Her father's car seats and how the leather squeaked when she shied away from the horror. There was no flinching today. Nor was there anyone around to comfort her and say this all was make-believe. Her father was the memory of a memory now.

"This is happening," Nanette said to her daughter in the cramped bathroom. "There's no cheating it."

"It wasn't vomit, you know that, right? The nurse told me he hasn't had a bowel movement for days. Shit has got to get out of you one way or the other. That's why it smelled that way. Why it, it—"

Nanette rushed forward and embraced her daughter, squeezing the resistance from her, the crib not so far away after all. She smelled of expensive shampoo and cigarettes—the latter Nanette would have commented on in any other circumstances, but let it slide this time. And even then, she would have only commented out of jealousy. Nanette hadn't smoked in over thirty-five years, but she craved it every day. "It's hard, so hard, sweetheart. I can see that you're hurting."

Lauralee exhaled and slinked free. "I'm not some girl on a cliff looking to be saved," she said, bitter. "All I want is to be upset for a minute or two, okay? Let me be upset, and don't underestimate my ability to rough it. I'm no help to you, or him, here, right now. So, look, you take as long as you need but I'm going back to the car. I'm letting him go, Mum. And you should, too."

It was the beginning of Spring, but the house on The Hill was yet to unshackle itself from the cold. Door snakes under the jamb. Electric blankets on the beds. Hot water bottles at Nanette's feet. She boiled water on the stove kettle, listened to its hum and the flicker of burning gas. The day at Truman Place had left her weak. Nanette's hand rested on the old, wooden counter. Ian, who used to be so good with his hands, had laid it after tearing up the old Formica. A draft spidered through the kitchen, making the pots and pans tinkle-tinkle on the ends of their hooks. Her body tensed when the landline rang.

"Hello?" Nannette said into the receiver.

She had a mobile phone but didn't use it, fearful of relying on it too much, or not having it work when she needed it most, or of winding the battery down by accident. Frances had scolded her over this multiple times, saying she was old school to a fault. Faheem scribbled instructions in a notepad for her. He worked for a telecommunications company in the Wallsend mall, and was patient with Nanette's flubbing and repeated questions. The man, she suspected, would make a fine father. However, that didn't mean Nanette would be snapping photos of her great-grandchild-to-be on the phone they'd wrestled her into accepting. So long as there were still Kodak stores in the city—not far from the Rialto, come to think of it—her Nikon in the tallboy upstairs would suit her fine. "But it's important you're, like, connected," Faheem had said. To which Nanette reminded him that she had her desktop computer connected to the internet (mostly used to sieve for recipes and movie trivia), which would serve her fine should she need it.

The receiver was cold under Nanette's grip.

"It's me, Mum," came Lauralee's voice down the line. A sigh. "Look, I was being a bitch earlier, and I'm sorry for putting you through that. We all know you've got enough on your plate. I wasn't being fair."

The screaming kettle drowned those acceptances, all the promises to do better.

They spoke for a short while and then parted ways, promising each other to do better. Nanette shuffled the mail—bills, mostly— and tore up two envelopes marked with the hotel developer's insignia. Afterwards, she climbed the stairs with a hot toddy, passing—without the need to look at it—photographs lining the wall on her right. The mix of alcohol, lemon, and honey left her lightheaded. Old boards creaked under her slippers, a spare hand skirting the well-worn balustrade her daughter used to ride when she was a kid, which Frances had ridden in her overalls when visiting, and which their great-grandchild would buffer with the seat of his or her pants long after Gran and Poppy were gone. Assuming, of course, that Lauralee didn't sell the place, which she very well may. Nanette turned at the top of the stairs and reminded herself that it wasn't a bad time to start believing in God again.

She sipped from her drink and changed into her nightgown, drew the collar to her neck. Tomorrow morning she'd have a long bath and thaw. The mattress squawked, almost gull-like, when she eased against it and rolled onto her side to reach for the novel on the bedside table that she'd been reading for the past few weeks. Fingers clawed at the dustjacket as she swung the hardcover over her stomach, slipping on her readers. Something as simple as turning in for the night with a book left her breathless these days. Another sip. Another gasp for oxygen. Arthritis knuckled through her joints. She soon settled, and with a rattling exhale, slipped a finger into the novel.

The pages were blank.

Nanette sat upright. She flipped from cover to cover, quite certain she was going mad. Swung her legs around. Feet brushed the slippers she'd kicked off.

"What?"

Wind made the house groan

Her eyes shot to the dresser in the corner of the room where Nanette sat to put on her face of a morning (she never left home without doing her eyebrows, at the very least). There, among the artificial pearls she never felt comfortable in, the decoupage jewellery boxes Frances made for her when she was young, and all the bottles of cheap perfume, was the picture frame where her wedding photo should have been.

The front door swung open, snagged on a gust and thrown against the wall so hard the plaster cracked. Not that Nanette cared. She was happy to see her son-in-law and daughter on the threshold in their puffer jackets.

"Show me what's going on before we call the police," Roy said, stepping inside without taking off his shoes as he would on any other normal day. But that was just it. This was, Nanette knew without hesitation, no normal day. Not anymore.

Lauralee took her mother by the hand and asked if she was okay.

"It's given me a fright, sweetheart," she said. "It really has."

Roy backhanded his runny nose as he turned to face them. Lauralee eased the door shut, the hush of the house revealed in the wind's absence, not that it left them, not really. It was everywhere, a kinetic stain that tingled their skins and made the windows rattle in their wall cages. Roy cleared his throat. "It's in your room, right?"

"Not just there," Nanette said, lifting an arm to point. She rattled, too. "Look."

Lauralee walked by her mother's side, the two of them following Roy as he crossed the large living room to the staircase with its shiny, smooth balustrade. They watched him lace his hands behind his neck, head tilting in an almost confused puppy-manner.

"Why would someone break in and do this?" he said, turning back to face them. "It makes no sense."

Every photograph on the wall—a hopscotch of events, reunions, and birthdays—had been removed. Only the frames remained, milky white as cataracts in a dying man's face.

4

"You don't suppose this has all got something to do with the lady you saved, do you?" Frances said, leaning in to devour the sandwich Nanette prepared in anticipation of her visit. Her enormous stomach bulged beneath an out of season Christmas sweater, breasts swathed in a curtain-sized cardigan.

Nanette pinched her lips as though the proposition itself were sour and searched the view outside the window for distraction. Spring had pounced over the past two days and bees were out on the side lawn. Nanette pitied them. Any day now, the frost would come for one last hurrah and send them back into hibernation. It always did.

"Well, I can't see how it could," Nanette said, fussing about the kitchen to settle her nerves. Cupboards opened and closed, the refrigerator checked twice, shifting rolling pins and a meat tenderiser in the top drawer by the sink. "Frances, it's far more likely that I'm losing my marbles. Maybe I'm getting rid of all this stuff in my sleep."

"Nope," the young woman said. "You're too sharp for that. Besides what are you doing? Digging holes by the cover of night? Yeah, right."

"Queer, the whole thing is," Nanette said.

Frances chortled, spitting crumbs. "Just say weird, Super Gran." She managed to get the food down. "I'm serious though. Maybe there's some sort of correlation, or something." She made it sound a little like an unanswered question, even though it wasn't. Nanette didn't take the bait. Frances shrugged, but not in a dismissive way. It was the shrug of someone who believed things that others didn't, someone who wouldn't push their theories or agendas on those who weren't ready to listen.

Everything about Frances was an invitation. It was in the welcome of her face, the earthy warmth she brought with her into a room. Qualities she inherited from her father. Lauralee had been a challenging child to raise, especially during her late teen years. The smashed plates. The runaway attempts. Coming home with bruises. A stint in rehab. There had been many nights when Nanette and Ian sat on the edge of their bed upstairs, speaking but not looking at each other, turning their anger at a daughter they couldn't understand on themselves instead. Over time, they drove each other apart in unfair ways. The fighting over nothing yet everything. The affairs they indulged in (Ian admitted to his, while Nanette did not). Dignity became a myth.

But swift as Lauralee's angst arrived it evaporated, leaving behind an edge of inappropriate honesty that didn't blunt until she met Roy and settled down. Ian and Nanette healed, mostly. It took time to sort through the vacuum of what was left behind. Who were Ian and Nanette when they weren't upset at each other anymore? Over the years, they didn't speak of those rough patches, even if Nanette felt them stirring, as no doubt did he. It just wasn't worth indulging in—even when she needed the ammunition. They resigned to keeping those forgotten but not really forgotten rooms closed in the big house of their marriage. No wonder she didn't want to let people tear her home down. No wonder it was so hard to let go.

Nanette sat at the table across from her granddaughter, hands in her lap and toying with her fingernails—not that there was much of them left. She'd nibbled them down to the quick. Music lilted from the living room where Frances put an old record on the turntable earlier. They sat, swaying to Dusty Springfield's *I Only Want to be With You.*

"Gosh, this song," Nanette said. "It came out in 1965, if memory serves. No, wait. 1964, that's right. Takes me back, I tell you. Your grandfather and I played it at our wedding. My uncle, who you never met, lovely fella but a drinker with gout that used to give my aunt all sorts of grief when he got to shouting at night, dancing to Dusty on a table at the reception. Right here in the backyard is where we had it. Drunk as a skunk, he was, a shock to nobody on God's green earth. And, oh Frances, you should've seen him. Doing the twist like nobody's business. Let's call it enthusiastic, shall we? Well, poppet went topsy-turvy and came down like a sack of potatoes. What's a wedding without a broken leg, they said. Good old-fashioned luck, right? Aunt Meg was fit to be tied."

It was Frances's turn to smile now, but the smile was short-lived.

"Oh, our little karate expert is kicking!" she said.

"May I?" Nanette had made a promise to herself that she would hold her urges in check and ask before reaching in to grab Frances by the stomach. Lauralee had scolded her many times over for doing this when she was pregnant. "Guess you're never too old to learn a lesson," Nanette, reflecting on her daughter's reaction, had said to Ian at the time. "But that's what kids do, even when they're grown. They keep on teaching you every day. Well, consider myself schooled."

"Go ahead," grandchild said to grandmother with an easy smile that made Nanette almost want to cry. "You don't need to ask."

"Still." Nanette placed a liver-spotted hand on Frances's stomach and waited for a jolt that didn't come.

"Gun shy," the pregnant woman said, reaching for the second half of her sandwich. "Worry not, there'll be a round two. I think we're going to be welcoming a boy into the family. I can feel it in my waters. Like, there's almost a taste in my mouth. Isn't that nuts?"

Nanette leaned back in her chair. "Not mad at all. When your mum was sick as a kid, I swear I could smell it on her. Your grandfather would say, 'Oh, you're being daft,' but I wasn't. A mum knows these things. Well, snips and snails and puppy dog tails, or sugar and spice and everything nice. Either way, that bub of yours will be cherished through and through," she said.

"Aw, thanks, Gran."

"And I appreciate you and Faheem staying with me for few days until things settle 'round here. I know how silly this sounds, but I can't shake the feeling that I'm, well, being watched or something. Do you know what I mean? I'd actually say that to you, not your mother. I trust you. It's awful, to be honest."

"It's no trouble at all, Gran. And yeah, you've got to trust those feelings." They reclined into a moment of wordlessness, which Nanette could tell Frances was not comfortable in. It wasn't surprising when the young woman shifted gears, a hop in her step. "I will say, though, if I go into labour between now and Thursday, you'll have to fetch the mop and bucket if my water breaks. I hope you're prepared."

"Hardwood floors, sweetheart. A wipe or two, and Bob's your uncle."

Frances laughed, fanning her face as she tried to get the last of the bread down. "Stop, you'll make me choke and—"

Music gave way to a needle screech in the adjoining room. The sound left behind was almost feline, or like a Theremin in an old science-fiction film from the 1950s, something Nanette's father would have watched at the drive-in and enjoyed. A gasp dragged from the two women at the sound. Nanette stood, drawing in pointy shards of air. Her chest tightened, pulse thundering like the footfalls of children in a room where they shouldn't be running.

"Don't go in there," Frances said, eyes wide. "Don't you feel it?"

Nanette nodded. Yes, she could.

The air thickened. It reminded her of going on summer walks

and how the bush roared with cicada song, until, for reasons she would never know, they silenced in unison. That chasm of slimy non-silence she found herself in. Or the warning bells that rang when she saw men she didn't know coming her way on the street, which made her lock the VW's doors at the traffic lights in town even when nobody was around.

An ozone of threat.

Nanette crossed the tiled kitchen floor to the archway leading into the living room and touched the architrave, which was marked with Lauralee and Frances's height scrawls. Her granddaughter joined her side, leaving behind a trail of breadcrumbs. Together, they peered at the turntable under the far window by the front door. A curtain stirred. Nanette whisked across the shag rug Ian bought in the early '80s from a long-closed dealership and stood over the player. She breathed. In. Out. The trilling continued. And with good reason. Bending forward, Nanette saw that the record had been robbed of its grooves.

Frances snatched the old woman's arm. "SHIT, Gran!"

Nanette turned and watched the wet patch blooming at the crotch of Frances's stretchy pants. "Sweetheart, you've broken—"

"But I'm at thirty-six weeks," Frances said, gripping her stomach. She paled. "My phone's in my handbag under the table. Call Faheem."

"Sit down." Nanette guided her granddaughter to the overstuffed living room couch by the architrave and shuffled to the kitchen to retrieve the phone. Rifled through the bag. Knees popped. "I don't know how to work this thing."

"Jesus, Gran. Just give it here!"

The baby, a boy, was born twelve hours later at the John Hunter Hospital where the midwives wore pink and had their own TikTok channel, which Lauralee showed Nanette around hour five of the labour. She watched them dance, impressed but not caring. Her body was at war with itself and was offered relief only when an exhausted Faheem slinked into the waiting room to parse out updates. Later, Nanette buckled under fatigue and dipped to sleep. She woke at the prod of an old ulcer flaring, chewing her dentures to realign them, glancing to see someone turning from the waiting room. A flicker of movement, someone in an orange jersey with a tiger stretched from shoulder to shoulder. Only when Nanette limped over to confirm what she'd seen—or who—there was nobody there. The long, empty hospital corridor, windows inked by night, stretched to zero, a vanishing point like a needle stick puncture. Frances and Faheem named their child Nasir Ian, and they buried him four days later. He'd been born without eyes, nose, ears, and mouth. A writhing, asphyxiating child on a gurney, tethered to his mother by a slimy cord that Frances begged the midwives in their pink scrubs to leave be and never cut. No Tik Toks were recorded that night.

5

Nanette's knees pressed against the railing, dehydrated bee corpses rolling across her hiking boots. She tried to look down. Imagining Toni standing there and how she must have felt. Guillotine horizon. Death kiss rocks. Her head spun, and she clutched her jacket. The past two weeks had hollowed her out. She was the Tin Man from *The Wizard of Oz* rusting in a winter that didn't know how to move on.

Knock my chest and hear the echo. That space is where the best of me used to be.

Anger boiled the tears out of her. She was dry. Nobody—let alone anyone in her family—deserved this. Nanette hadn't grown up with enemies, but even if she had, she wouldn't wish this crushing throb upon them. There were moments when it seemed too much to take, that this weight might crush her after all. The thing with mourning, Nanette long ago learned, was that you never got over the bad stuff. You just got better at dealing with it. Over time, agonies just stack higher and higher, like those beetles that have to carry around the corpses of those they've killed. Forever, until you die.

There must have been a decision to turn away and head back for the house, but Nanette wasn't conscious of it. Her boots—having shaken off the dead bees Spring had fooled into life only to cut them down within days—might have been in charge. She trudged through the mud, subservient, up the driveway to her door. Tarps from the construction sites flapped in the wind. A seagull cawed.

The funk of dead flowers inside. *Enough*, she thought. Nanette bundled up the dead flowers and carried them to the garbage bins out back where they crunched into dust, minus a thorn or two. She didn't bother keeping the sympathy cards, either. Everything had to go. *It has to hurt if it's to heal*, as her mother used to say. And this hurt beyond compare.

Later, Nanette called Frances who talked to her in slow, medicated staccato. "I guess—today is a bit—better. Faheem? He's—he's okay. But not—really. We're fighting."

"You know you're welcome here any time, sweetheart," Nanette said.

"I—know, Gran. I always feel—safe—at your place."

"Call me day or night. I'm here for you. Or just come over. You're never not welcome. Ever. You hear me, Frances? Ever."

"…Super Gran."

Kiss-kiss sounds down the line. Nanette sat in a chair in the living room, staring at the turntable and the LP records without their grooves. Another empty photograph on the mantle. The rectangle of unbleached wallpaper where a painting had hung for years. Too much. It was all too much. The absences had slowed, maybe, but were still occurring. Chomps out of her life, taken without clemency. The bites of a wild animal.

Toni's tiger.

Nanette, who had been drinking a coffee with a tiny splash of Irish Crème in the bottom, tossed her cup at the hardboard floor. It shattered into a dozen pieces, liquid splashing. The rug wasn't there anymore, either.

"Bloody fool," she announced to the empty room.

Yet her feet were already doing the thinking again, and the answering, too, whisking her up the stairs in a daze. The buffered balustrade to her left. The house that the private developers hungered for groaned in the wind, like someone shouting from far away for her to stop, don't do it, it's not worth it.

Late afternoon light bled into the study, illuminating her computer and Ian's old encyclopedias (which she'd assumed could be sold off someday at a decent price until Roy informed her of how valueless they were now that everyone used the Internet). Her hand—though it could have been anyone's hand—reached for the top drawer of her husband's desk, yanking it out, revealing the phone Faheem had tried to talk her into using. Beneath it were the instructions he'd scribbled in a patient, neat hand. She flicked a nearby lamp and read. Tried to turn the device on. Dead. Found the charger, plugged it in. Settled behind the desktop. It was a laptop her daughter bought and attached to a monitor scored from work at the blood bank. The clicks and whirrs of a machine she didn't understand or trust yet had to understand and trust, as it came to life. Checked the connection. The wi-fi was on, which led her to think it was always on, always with her even when she had no need for it, like other things in her life that swam in her presence without announcing themselves.

You were right to lock your doors, she thought. *To hold your handbag. Something wants to do you harm. You were never alone. It's here now.*

It. A thing of real weight, which if given the opportunity, may prove heavy enough to leave prints in the dusty floors Nanette hadn't bothered to sweep since the night at the hospital. Dust. Dust everywhere. It hadn't taken long for the elements to try and bury her, erosion in reverse. Instead of wearing away it crept closer.

The lamp flickered. Nanette watched the bulb dim and brighten, the filament in its ochre eye stammering. Arthritis blazed too, and she couldn't catch her moan in time. The lamp settled, though Nanette could have sworn it buzzed at a higher frequency than before.

She cupped the mouse and steered the little arrow on the screen. No, it hadn't been something 'other' directing her. This was her doing. Her need. A quick Google search told her how to make the Facebook account. Instructions were followed. It was easy, really.

Not bad for an old great dame who ain't what she used to be.

These were the actions of a woman who had torn up her blouse to fashion a tourniquet when her daughter came off her bike and busted open her knee as a kid. The woman who accepted that her husband wasn't perfect and slapped him across the face when he confessed—not because he'd cheated but because she hadn't wanted it confirmed. This was the woman who, in Greece a decade ago with Ian, had almost been mugged at gunpoint and negotiated her way out of dodge by turning her back on the would-be thief, stripping him of his power. Had she been afraid at the time? Of course. But if it had to be done, it had to be done. When Doctor Tomislav sat her and Ian down to lay out the bones of his diagnosis, she told her husband, to his face, that she wasn't strong enough to do whatever came next on her own. Spades were spades. Rome wasn't built in a day. And if something had to be done, Nanette would see it through, whether she liked it or not.

Her first Facebook profile tile was blank as the frames downstairs.

A vibration through the floor that she felt in her shins. The phone was charged now.

She took Faheem's note and let those dot-points guide her through the process of unlocking the screen. Messages she'd had no reason—or the means—to acknowledge until now buzzed-buzzed-buzzed. The one she needed came through after ten minutes. It was a screenshot of Antonia Payover's Facebook account attached to the SMS Frances sent her.

That deliberate pose. Mascara eyes. Dirty eyes. Those almost trashy eyes.

Nanette watched a video on how to search for people on YouTube, and within nine minutes sent Toni a friend request and private message.

Seven minutes later, a reply came through. Nanette hadn't realised the laptop volume was on high, and the chime reminded her of a single wedding bell ringing. Outside, the sky flooded with purples and reds as the sun exploded on the guillotine's edge. Stars winked to life, distant allies. Or maybe just burning gas.

"**I** dreamed of you," Toni said.

Six grey chicken nuggets sat on the table between them like fleshy, over-salted runes. They were at the King Street McDonald's and the smell of grease hung in the air. There were no shadows in the large dining area where they sat, just depthless neon light. Drunk teenagers fought the touchscreen nearby, and a toddler screamed in its highchair—a broken winged bird sound.

"You did?" Nanette said, hands in her lap. She flicked her nails. Click-click-click. Her breath came in stutters. Nothing about this was easy. She could see them embracing on The Hill months before, that raw and honest moment. Everything was different here. This was miserable, and more miserable yet because it didn't have to be. Not if they didn't want it so. Not if they could drop the awkwardness act and stop pretending like they each hadn't been consumed with the other since that day in the rain.

"Uh-huh," Toni said. Her voice verged on something real. Nanette leaned forward to let her know that she should continue. "Lady, it's like you're a ghost, almost. These aren't bad dreams I've had. But I'm having them every night, and that freaks me out." Toni extended a long pale finger to one of the nuggets and prodded it. Nope, no life there. "I felt like I knew you'd find me."

"You did?" Nanette said. A flicker of hope.

"Uh-huh." Toni laughed into her hand, a laugh of disbelief. "I can't believe this is happening. It's fucking nuts, you know."

"Toni?"

The young woman looked at the old woman.

"Toni, I want to ask you something that's going to sound quite, quite weird." Nanette held firm and thought again of her granddaughter and the invitations she presented by just being herself, which Nanette hadn't been comfortable enough to accept. Until now. In that moment. Within the King's Street McDonald's under the neon glare where there were no shadows. "Have things you cherish disappeared on you?"

"Huh? What you mean?"

"Like, um, ph-ph-photos," Nanette said, a little flummoxed. *Keep going, don't back out now.* "Trinkets. Special things. Treasures that are special to you. Things that maybe remind you of someone you loved."

Teenagers dropped a tray on the other side of the restaurant, cups pinwheeling on the floor. Both women jolted against the hard, plastic booth. They stilled, their time together scored by music through unseen speakers, a voice singing about memories and dust. Toni shook her head. Scratched her upper arm through her jumper. No tiger jersey this time.

"Please, Toni. Please tell me what you're thinking. I'm worried I'm going crazy—"

"I don't know what to say, lady."

"Then why'd you come to me meet me?"

Toni pressed a thumb to her forehead. "Because you asked."

"And you said you wanted to come," Nanette said. "Not tomorrow. Not in a week from now. Right now. This night. To this place. You gave me the directions."

The unforgiving lights in the McDonald's made the tear beading down Toni's cheek glow. She shoved a hand under the collar of her turtleneck to scratch at the skin, granting Nanette a glimpse at bruises.

"You don't have to go back to him, Toni. You can come home with me. I'll take you to a refuge or something."

Toni ground her jaw. "You don't know me," she said.

Nanette reached across the table, pushing aside the food they bought and ignored, and grabbed Toni by the wrists. She felt the young woman's flesh under her fingers, the chicken-like bones of her all picked at and thin. "I feel close to you," Nanette said. "Close to you in ways I can't explain."

"Let. Me. Go."

And Nanette listened, hands slinking back across the table, curling inwards like broken witch's legs under a house. She breathed out her oxygen to make space for self-consciousness, which crawled right in and nestled on cue, whisker tickles and the occasional bite. Nanette watched Toni watch her reach into the handbag on the seat and withdraw a handkerchief. It surprised her when Toni accepted it when offered.

"It's my husband's," Nanette said. "He's not well."

Toni dabbed her eyes, giggled. "Only old people use hankies." She seemed to steel herself and dropped the bud of fabric on the table by the overturned nugget box, its underside transparent with grease. "Smells nice though. What is that?"

"Eucalyptus oil," Nanette said. "That's how Ian likes it. Liked it. Kind of a gentlemanly smell, don't you think? Handsome, in a way."

Nanette tripped into a smile that didn't last long.

Because the handkerchief faded away to nothing in front of them. It was a special effect from an old movie. Something cheap, something honest. A Superman X-Ray vision cross-fade. Ian's handkerchief was gone. Nanette glanced at Toni to ensure that she, too, had seen it, and found the young woman's eyes wide and wet. Twice, Nanette had been wed on The Hill overlooking the ocean. First to her husband in 1967, the year of *Cactus Flower* and Puzo and the overdosed starlet, and then again to Antonia Payover earlier that year. Some vows spoken and others not, yet every bit as binding. Memories and dust.

Toni clenched her jaw and spoke through gritted teeth. "I'm supposed to be dead, aren't I?"

Nanette knuckled the bridge of her nose. She had no reply because she didn't have anything to say. Sometimes a question is its own answer, the snake devouring its tail.

"I'm scared, lady," Toni said, and Nanette believed her. "I caught the bus here. Will, will, you, um, drive me home?" They looked at the space on the table where the handkerchief — monographed and scented — had been. "Please?"

Talkback radio on the AM station as they wove along Beach Road in the Beetle, the announcer's words bleeding into a song Nanette knew was from 1971 because that was the year of Lauralee's birth. *I Don't Know How to Love Him* by Helen Reddy. Speckles of rain on the windshield caught the glow of passing headlights.

"Take a right," Toni said.

Nanette steered them into the Meriwether suburbs where the

streets seemed so wide at that time of the night at that time of the year without surfers and families heading to the shore. "Drop me here, thanks."

"Are you sure?" Nanette said, easing on the brake pedal.

"I don't want him to see you dropping me off."

They stopped. Rain fists against the roof.

Nanette reached for the glove compartment where she kept a pen, where there were old envelopes. She wanted to write her address down for Toni in case she needed somewhere to stay when whatever trouble she was in became too asphyxiating. If the bruises she tried to hide deepened and spread. Only the woman was gone, the door open, a mouth of night chewing her to black.

6

Lauralee and Roy stood in the nursing home kitchenette with the activity nurse, laughing as the three of them mummified leftovers with clingwrap. Their voices carried across the open area to where Nanette sat in her chair, turning to face her husband.

Ian was a hermit crab within a wheelie-recliner shell, mandible fingers under a blanket, his beak of a mouth biting at ghost sandwiches as news played out on the television. His feet kicked. A twitch. Nanette touched his ankle, so thin she could put her hand around it without trying.

"Tin-Tin?" she said. "Are you in there?"

The crab didn't answer.

"It's me. Your Snowy. Please, speak to me. I need to hear your voice."

Another kick.

Nanette lowered her head, unable to stand losing any more of him, knowing that it might actually kill her. To think there had been days when she didn't feel the weight of this responsibility seemed a fiction. "I know you can hear me," Nanette said. "Even if you don't understand what I'm saying. But listen if you can, because if I don't speak it out aloud, I don't know if I'll get through this."

She wrestled the urge to cry, and won. This time.

Her words were a whisper within the great room.

"There's a debt on us, Tin-Tin," she said. "And I know it's coming for you next. Why wouldn't it? Makes perfect sense, really. I'm afraid for you. I don't know where these things go. Not Heaven, that's for sure. You know I don't believe in God. People are the only creatures on Earth smart enough to fear their own death, and smart enough to develop religion to reconcile that fear. God is just our pleas echoing back. So, where will this debt take you, my darling? I don't know. I wish I did, but I don't."

Nanette clenched her fists. Arthritis flared, the old pains.

"I'm not going to let this happen to you. I'd sooner kill myself. We—I—can pay up. If we're clever," she said. Paused. Collected her thoughts. "If we're cruel."

I can't believe I'm about to say this.

Only that was a lie. She could and would believe it because if she didn't, then the vanishings would close in on the man in front of her. And whatever remained of Nanette once all was said and done, wouldn't amount to much.

"If this girl was dead…"

Nanette touched her husband's face and noticed that her wedding ring had vanished from her finger.

7

Clouds feathered by the moon cast shadows over the ocean like the continents of a big black atlas. An oil tanker or two out there, little red lights blinking, blinking. Waves crashed at the bottom of the cliff, a sound that pulled Nanette towards soothing and dread at the same time, catching her in the numbness between.

And numb was good for now, considering the wheels she'd already set in motion.

She sat on the metal barrier, her back to the road, and heard the approaching car climbing the hill before she saw it. Arthritis chewed from her hands and into her elbows and shoulders, the small of her back and knees—like her body was trying to weaken and cripple her from the inside out, stopping Nanette from being able to do what she'd come here to do.

Headlights crested the road and the familiar car drew to a stop a few metres away. Darkness swooped over them once again and there was only the stars and moon. The way Nanette needed it. A door clunked open, clunked shut. Footsteps over gravel, over grass.

Nanette lifted her chin, the coolish evening air swishing about them.

"It's gorgeous, isn't it?" she said to the young woman standing behind her.

"You can't message me like that again, okay?" Toni said. "He checks my phone and computer. It could really screw things up for me."

"I'm sorry," Nanette said. The barricade was hard and uncomfortable. "I won't do it again, I promise." A quiver in her voice.

"Well, I did what you asked and I'm here, lady," Toni said. "What do you want?"

"Sit with me, Antonia."

Nanette heard the young woman's sigh over the crash of the ocean—a considerable achievement. Toni climbed the barricade and sat as requested. Close, but not too close. Nanette smelled bubble-gum and perfume, the sickly stink of that flesh beneath the heavy Tiger jersey, chemicals and sweat. The smell of dependencies people don't want to talk about. Dependencies on a drug, a system, on a need to do good.

They looked at the ocean together.

"This is where my husband and I had our wedding photographs taken," Nanette said. "Handsome devil, he was. Not anymore, though. Dementia. It's awful, Toni."

"Getting old scares me," she said. "Sorry. Shouldn't say that, I guess."

"It scared me, too, when I was your age. But what are you going to do? There's no fighting it. I'm older now than I was when you and I met up here, and older now than I was when I sent you the message to come and see me tonight. That's just how it goes."

"You said it was an emergency."

"It is," Nanette said, trying to keep strong and struggling.

Looking at the young woman next to her wasn't an option. She kept her focus on the cloud shadows from coast to coast instead, where there wasn't all the guilt. "And you're older now, too, Toni. Every damn moment chips away at what we've been given."

Toni let loose another one of her monumental sighs, only it was different this time. There was compassion on her breath, as well as the rubbery scents of bubble-gum. "Are you okay, lady? Can I help, or something?"

"Would you have jumped, Toni, if I hadn't stopped you?"

Silence between them that wasn't really silence, just a chomp of time filled with beach sounds and the blare of a car alarm somewhere. The alarm ended and the moment grew too heavy between them to remain still any longer.

"Yeah," Toni said, hunching over. "That actually feels good to say. Yes. I know I would've."

The arthritic pain of bones fighting bones reached into the base of Nanette's neck. "You still can, if you want," she said. "Jump, I mean." She looked at Toni then.

The young woman's eyes shimmered in the dark. "What?"

"I'm not one of those people who think suicide is selfish," Nanette said, not wanting to speak this way but speaking this way because the purge had taken control. "Not anymore. Maybe when I was younger, yes. It's shocking how much you can change, Toni. But it's not a terrible thing, ending it all because it's too much. Why would we do this to ourselves? If there's nothing after this, and things won't get better, and you're in absolute torture, why not opt out? That's not selfish, Toni. Selfishness is what I did to you. And for that, I'm so sorry."

"Don't talk like this, Nanette—"

"It's true and you know it. What I did is criminal, I tell you. Downright criminal."

Toni reached to take Nanette by the hand, cold skin against cold skin with a soft sprinkle of rain pitter-pattering their faces. "Is that why you're up here tonight?" Toni said. "To—"

Nanette stood, the uneven ground beneath her. There was nothing between her and the cliff's edge now. Toni leapt into action, gripping her chest. "Don't do it, lady!"

"Why not?" Nanette said, bitterness in her voice now. She may have brought Anotnia here under false pretences, but the emotion flowing out of her was genuine. "My husband is almost dead. My great-granddaughter died. She—she had no eyes, Toni. No mouth. She suffocated. I don't think my daughter loves me, not really. The pain of it all, it's too much." It felt good to bleed the hurt out, and as the tears spilled, Nanette knew she'd been a fool to keep them in so long. "I don't want to be alone anymore. I don't know *how* to be alone. I don't know how to let him go."

Antonia began to cry too, emotions coming in waves. "Please, come back with me," she said, yanking on the old woman's arm. "You're scaring me. Please, don't do this. PLEASE!"

Nanette turned to face the woman she'd lured in. Everything had gone to plan up to this point, mostly. Now was when Nanette was supposed to grab Toni by the shoulders and twist her to the left, swinging her off balance and into the air. There would be a long scream as Toni plummeted, a thud on the rocks that she wouldn't be able to hear, Nanette then stumbling away from the edge in case the earth gave way and took her with it, climbing over the barricade and calling for emergency services on the mobile phone in her pocket.

Come quick! Something terrible has happened. Yes, yes, I brought her up here, and yes, I think I was going to maybe do something terrible to myself. But she saved me, only she slipped and I couldn't catch her. Not in time. I'm sorry, so sorry, so—

"Sorry," Nanette said. The wind thieved the word from her lips and carried it away. She wasn't sure if Toni heard it, and in the end, it didn't matter. If the young woman couldn't see the apology in Nanette's face, then she was sure the girl was blind. Sorry to Toni for drawing her here. Sorry to her husband for letting him down. Sorry to herself for allowing this fear to warp her beyond recognition.

"Come with me," Toni said, leading Nanette away from the edge and over the barricade. The tiger jersey fluttered on her frame, sounding like plastic bags caught on a barbed wire fence. Their hair whipped. Nanette cried into Toni's shoulder, the heaves coming thick and fast. Behind them, the horizon hazed as rain carved its way across the ocean. "Into the car, quick," Toni said. "Or you'll catch your death." Nanette clung to the thin arm beside her and let herself be led as the skies opened, wondering if that expression, 'or you'll catch your death' was something Toni's own mother had said to her, a maternal hand-me-down from person to person to Nanette, a woman within a stranger's car who was crushed by the guilt of what she'd almost done. Someone in terrible need of parenting.

Toni jumped into the driver's seat next to her, dripping wet.

"I'm freezing," Nanette said.

"There's not many houses up here. Is that yours over there?" She started up the car and gestured to the square peepers of homely light hovering in the dark. Nanette said yes and continued to shake, images of dead babies and old men and empty picture frames and missing wedding rings carouselling through her head.

They stumbled over the threshold. Memories pounced on Nanette from all sides.

Her husband thumping mud off his boots before entering. Her daughter slinking in, a disciplinary note from school tucked into her backpack. Her granddaughter, so excited she threw the door open too hard and the mirror on the nearby wall popped off its hook and shattered on the floor, wailing at the thought of seven years bad luck.

Toni helped Nanette into a house that hardly felt her own any more. The bank owned it once. Now, a new collector had muscled in to ensure debts were anted up. As if to prove this, Nanette made note of another missing artefact as she closed the door, heavy against the wood, all dizzy. A stool in the corner was gone, the one given to her husband when he was a child, handed to him in pieces through a broken bit of fence by a kid in a temporary refugee camp in the Hunter Valley, its underside inscribed with a message. *Grateful to you for friendships, beloved Ian.* One of her husband's most cherished belongings, Bo Bo's shoeshine step, the boy he spoke with through the fence for months until the boy said it was time for him and his family to leave. Lauralee loved it, too. Used to lay wax paper over it for charcoal rubbings that she set in Paddle Pop stick frames. She would compose poems about Bo Bo and the life she wanted for him and his family. But the stool—and the history attached to it—had been plucked away while Nanette was out there on the cliff. Another penny in the jar for a collector who knew no compassion.

"Sit," Toni said, helping her onto the couch in the living room opposite the record player, the hard flowery upholstery that had little give to it. Nanette felt so silly at having taken a turn, requiring the help of someone she'd intended to kill. "I'll make tea, or something."

"I'm fine," Nanette said, head in hands, watching Toni's shadow on the floor slinking from view. Pottering sounds from the kitchen. Cupboard doors opening, closing. A running tap. Cutlery in the top drawer. The click of the kettle and its hum. Nanette focused on her breathing. In, out. In, out. Not enough in, too much seeping out. Would she really have gone through with it? Her guilt over the crime that hadn't happened hardly compared to her determination to commit the crime in the first place. Burns either way. *What a mess*, she thought. *Goes to show you're never too old to learn what a terrible person you can be.*

Her insides twisted, shivers that had nothing to do with the rain. Nanette studied her hands—hands that would have pushed the tea-maker to her death had she not waivered—and tried to recognise them as her own. Only the pains in their joints were familiar. These weren't the hands that cupped Ian's cheek after he set his boots down and kissed her, or the hands of the woman who held that disciplinary slip after coaxing it from her daughter, who sat with Frances to make a mosaic of the shards to counter bad luck with a hot glue gun and paint. These hands were different. Liver-spotted. Weak and blue. And deserving of their aches.

A scream cut the air.

"JESUS CHRIST," Toni shouted from the kitchen. "Someone's out back—"

The front door—which Nanette hadn't locked—crashed open

and she watched a broad-shouldered man step inside, marching the mud in, rain churning around him like a billion gnats. Wind caught the curtains and made them writhe as though desperate to escape their railings, yet unable to do so. Trapped, as was she. The man brandished an axe. Its scuffed blade dripped water onto the floorboards.

Nanette shot up off the couch, gripping her throat. Her turn to scream this time, drawing the patter of feet as Toni ran into the living room behind her, followed then by the sound of the back door being jimmied. She heard it rattling in the kitchen. Nanette was almost positive that it—unlike the front door—had been dead-bolted before leaving. The rattle stopped.

"HENRY, NO!" Toni said. Her pitch equalled that of the kettle.

Nanette saw the yearning in the intruder before her, a feral need to correct and beat his definition of sense into those he saw as senseless. You didn't get to her age without clocking the type. A Neanderthal in white sneakers. Knuckle-happy and low on apologies. A wife beater in a sloppy old wife beater.

"Don't move," he said. "Neither of youse." Tattoos moved when he moved.

A breathless offsider entered behind him and slammed the door shut. The curtains dropped in defeat. This one, thickset and elfish, held a short-bladed steak knife. "The back way was locked," he said between pants. He wore a backwards hat, a gold tooth glimmering in his mouth.

"Johnny, no," Toni said to the second man. "Make him stop."

"Don't play with us," Henry said. "Pony up, show us where it is and we're fuckin' off." He glared at Toni. "And you're coming with us."

Nanette begged them to leave, not that they listened. The twisting in her guts worsened, ulcers flaring. A voice pierced through her thoughts: *This is how you die.*

Henry was scratchy eyed and jittery, long-limbed and round of chest, like a pre-schooler's crayon drawing come to life. Spittle flew when he barked. Toni grabbed Nanette by the elbow and almost pulled her off her feet in an attempt to back them into the kitchen again. The kettle's cry steamed out behind them.

Henry dove forward, thumping so hard the whole house shuddered. "I'll do it, bitch! I'll fuckin' do it. Where'd she stash the money?"

Righting herself, Nanette looked into the intruder's face. He'd directed that comment at *her*. "She, she hasn't given me anything—"

It didn't matter what she said, nothing would satisfy him. He came at them like a storm, his offsider, Johnny, jabbing the knife in their direction. Toni forced herself between them. Her partner raised the axe and broke her face open with the hilt. Nanette tried to catch the young woman as she fell, and failed. Toni landed on her knees. A splatter of blood. Shock rippled through them.

"Hen—ry," Toni said, coughing up broken teeth.

Johnny snapped forward again, knife first. The blade jabbed Nanette's arm, the papery skin beneath her cardigan slicing open. There was no pain, though she imagined that would come later. If she survived. "GIVE IT TO US," the offsider boomed.

Rain pummelled the tin roof and beat at the windows. Nanette stumbled, kicking a side table by the architrave between the two rooms, the architrave marked with her family's heights. A lamp overturned and shadows swung around the room as Toni folded in on herself on the floor and rolled onto her side. Nanette tried to thrash at her attacker, but only managed to rip her wound open in the attempt.

Indecision flickered across Henry's face as he towered over his girlfriend. "Look what you did. It didn't have to go this way. You fucked it, Toni. You always fuckin' fuck it over. You never should have taken it!"

Toni tried to speak but her nose slid off her face. She blinked in blood.

Nanette raised a knee into Johnny's groin and kicked the wind right out of him. It made her want to roar—but gloating would only slow her down. She turned and ran into the kitchen, trailing red as she went, and dove for the top drawer by the sink. Yanked it open. She gripped the meat tenderiser and yanked it out, the familiar old weight, swung around, eyes skimming the mugs Toni set out for them, their normalcy an offence. Hefted the utensil high and fast. But not high enough. Not fast enough. Johnny was right there, bearing down on her, knocking her against the counter. The landline fell off the wall and dangled on its coil.

Her mobile phone, though, was still in her pocket.

Johnny's knife shot up, its tip under her chin. "Don't fight us, lady," he said. Doggish breath on her lips. "He's not playin' around. Give us the money and we'll ghost. Pinky swear. We know she has you hiding it. Henry's known for ages."

Screams from the living room. Thumps. Voices both masculine and feminine, hard and full, solid but hollow—like dead, dry wood clashing together. It was awful.

The offsider knocked the tenderiser from Nanette's hand, which cracked tiles as it skidded to the floor underneath the architrave separating the two rooms. She watched it glimmer in the sconce light. The bulb blinked, once, twice, a conspiratorial eye to let her know that none of them were ever as alone as they thought they were. Soon, Johnny's face blocked her view and all Nanette could see were the splotches of his skin, acne scars. The eyes boring into her leapt about their sockets in pinball jolts.

"Look at me," Nanette said. "Look!" And he did. He did look.

Search the face you're holding a knife to and tell me I'm who you think I am. That I'm capable of doing what you think I've done. Do I look like someone who would hide money here for this young woman? Hide it nice and good in a place you'd never find it?

Her thought fizzled and turned inwards.

Maybe I do.

Nanette almost murdered someone, after all. Had she ever looked in the mirror and seen someone capable of that staring back at her? Perhaps. The man with the knife was doing the one thing so many men, including the husband she loved even when loving him was hard, had done to her over the years. He refused to underestimate her.

The knifepoint pierced the skin—just. A ripple of liquid coursed her throat.

"Is the key in your cunt?" Johnny said, smiling now. That glimmering tooth. A dollar at the bottom of a wishing fountain.

His eyes shifted downwards.

A thump from behind them as Toni landed on the tiles, chest first. Her hand bumped the tenderiser and she grabbed it, rolling onto her back despite the agony she must be feeling. Swung it when Henry huddled close. The metal struck his left leg. Over the offsider's shoulder, and even though Henry wore grubby old jeans, Nanette saw the bastard's kneecap clock off its counter. Henry let loose an almost cartoonish howl and buckled, drawing Johnny's attention for a moment—but a moment was all she needed. Nanette backhanded the knife away and grabbed the kettle Toni had boiled for them. Heaved it. The lid opened. Water scalded her attacker's neck and face.

The room thickened with screams.

Sconces flickered once again.

Nanette dove to the girl, who was almost on her feet. Their arms intertwined in monkey grips, blood on blood.

"Fuck you!" Toni shouted at her partner—not that Nanette suspected they had ever been equals—and brought the mallet down on his head. Nanette winced. She felt herself pulled into the living room, almost tripping over Henry as he dropped to his knees again, bloodied face in his hands. The axe thumped to the floor. Nanette wanted to grab it, but Toni was already tearing her in the opposite direction. Toward the front door.

The *open* front door.

Nanette sensed the shifting of air and the thrum of rain and saw the billowing curtains before noticing the figure in the slicker running into the room to meet them. The shock of this third person snatched the breath from the old woman's throat. Caught between fronts, an attack from behind, and now, up ahead.

Henry was on his feet again. The thud of his footfalls.

An avalanche of man.

Toni pushed Nanette, who tumbled back onto the couch she would often snuggle on with a book in the days before everything went to Hell. The sigh of cushions. Lucky. An unbroken fall like that killed people Nanette's age, snapped their hips, hospitalised the elderly long enough to catch pneumonia on the wards. Her head bounced—a vision of the ceiling, the flickering lights, and then of Henry swinging the axe in a gore-blind arc. Toni spun aside as all around them books blinked into nothingness on the shelves, the height markings on the architrave vanishing one by one, shifting the pressure in the room and making Nanette's ears pop. She watched the axe clomp down on the third stranger, right between the neck and the shoulder, stapling rubber into flesh.

Roaring, Henry yanked the axe free. Blood hazed the air.

The figure landed on their back, hood thrown aside to reveal their profile. Shock punched through Nanette. Her granddaughter's wide eyes. Her granddaughter's nose. Her granddaughter's mouth issuing a goldfish gasp. The old woman, no longer thinking, rolled off the couch and rushed to her kin on the floor, the person she'd said could come here whenever she needed to feel safe. Nanette's joints creaked as she swooped low, arthritis bolting up her spine, skin peeling from her open wound to reveal all the wet red. She must have been howling, too. Not that she knew it. Chaos turned black to white, up to down. Something to conquer that couldn't be conquered. His avalanche was too heavy. And maybe it was heavy for Henry, too. Because he stepped backwards now, the axe by his side, a spent thing. Disbelief etched his face. He may not have known what he was doing but that didn't change the fact that he'd done it. Frances's blood gushed up between her fingers, proving that.

Johnny stumbled from the kitchen. Steam curled from his head and shoulders. "Burn! BURN!" he growled, less a threat than an admission. Boiling water had made webs of his face, black widow eyes blinking and stupid. He ran to the front door and left.

"Look what you did," Toni shouted to Henry. She was on her haunches. Next to her, the remaining LP records in the rack vanished. Pop-pop-pop. She choked, gripping her hair. Looked up and said what she needed to say. "I have it," Toni said. It may have been a whisper, but they all heard it. "I'll take you there."

The lights flickered again.

"YOU WILL LEAVE THIS HOUSE," Nanette screamed at them. Her body throbbed. She pushed against her granddaughter's wound, only it wasn't enough. How could it be? Will, love, wishes, or fairness had no place here—and neither did these people.

Henry grabbed Toni by the hair and hurled her—thrashing—to the front door. A car roared to life outside, headlights turning the rain into a glowing silver curtain. They ran through it. The curtains were flying again.

Nanette might have heard Toni calling for her, but she couldn't be sure. At this point, she didn't care. Her focus was on Frances. The old woman wept as she dragged her mobile phone from her saturated trousers.

"I'm sorry," she said to the mother who wasn't a mother on the floor. Without meaning to, Nanette had conscripted her family into this war, a fight that couldn't be won. Because everyone fades. She'd long ago learned that memories aren't as steely as you need them to be. Nobody escapes the vanishing. And when it comes for you, you wonder why you spent so much time trying to please those you never respected, and in the face of death realise your efforts to be remembered mean nothing. All of Nanette's energy to guide and care for her family were crumbs for the crows to pick at. Those black beaks can't be cheated. Ever.

"Wait, sweetheart," Nanette said to her granddaughter, who tried to cling to her but couldn't maintain the hold. Frances convulsed. Her Wellingtons squelched against the floorboards where the rug used to be. Blood pooled around her head. A scream drowned on gurgles like someone pulled underwater. Nanette limped to the front door, swiping her phone as she went. The dial tone in her ear.

She watched Henry throw Toni into the backseat of an old Hyundai across the street from the driveway where her granddaughter's car was bumper-to-bumper with the Beetle. Henry crab-crawled into the front passenger seat, the car taking off before he had a chance to close the door. Johnny steered them into a sharp U-turn, kicking fans of soil and gravel. Wheels screeched. Headlights swirled.

Nanette thought it before she saw it.

Fight them, Toni. Don't let them win.

The car jolted off course—as though someone within had heard her thoughts and was yanking the steering wheel off-kilter. The engine rev of an accelerator stamped in panic. Burning rubber. The nose of the car swiped to the left—too far to the left, across the soft grass and through the barricade where Toni had tried to suicide, and failed. Because of her. Nanette the hero. Super Gran.

Arcs of light caught the rain, the car a silhouette against the horizon as metal buckled and the car skidded to the cliff's edge. Nanette pounded down the steps, arms outstretched in the rain, as though she could catch the vehicle in her fingers. A useless, pathetic gesture. She watched the ground yield, the car roaring as wheels spun in open air. Earth turned to sludge and the Hyundai tumbled from view.

Only the ocean out there now. Clouds full of lightning above.

A distant crash, enormous in the night.

8

Ian gripped the quilt his wife of fifty-odd years crocheted for him. It was grubby with potato mash and Sustagen-thickened milk. Nanette would take the blanket with her when she left. It could do with a patch or two, as well. Her husband had worn it thin over the past months now that he'd taken to rocking in spot and trying to massage warmth out of it.

Neurological ticks, Doctor Tomislav called them. One of many. Leg jerks. How his eyes sometimes filled with tears. *He's not really sad. It's dryness.*

She sat by Ian's side, hand on his knee, not looking at him but at the television in the nursing home common room. Residents in wheelie recliners positioned in front of the glowing screen, churchgoers before an altar. It was late in the afternoon and staff had dimmed the overhead lights. The summer air was still and tinged with urine and bleach. It followed her home, those smells. She had to wash it from her clothes and hair. Nanette hated it, as did Lauralee, who had come with her today (under protest), and was waiting in the courtyard outside.

Staff had put on *Cactus Flower* again, only the DVD must have gained a scratch or two since last time and it skipped every now and then, not that anyone noticed but Nanette. Employees hunched over computers, typing notes in that awkward, almost dread-infused lull between tea rounds and preparing residents for evening toileting and showers.

A buzz from Nanette's pocket.

She drew out her mobile phone and saw the message from Frances. Now that Nanette was a pro at using it, her granddaughter bombarded her with texts and photographs. It was something she'd never tire of. There was no such thing as too much love in her life. The days she didn't hear from a member of her family left her palsied with anxiety.

Thankfully, Nanette had Sandy now, a terrier mix named after the dog in *Annie*. She'd been scrolling through the stations one night—her chest seizing every time the wind rattled the shutters of her home or calling the police when a possum pounced on the roof—and came across the film version from 1982. Albert Finney and Carol Burnett were marvellous in it. She remembered dragging Ian to see it with her at the Rialto, and while he'd conceded that Finney was great as always, it just wasn't his thing. It was then, that night at home, terrified and sad, Nanette decided to get a pet.

Sandy was hardly the pit-bull guard her daughter thought she needed, but the poppet made her feel loved and safe. Faheem drove her to a breeder in Broadmeadow, even offered to pay for the deposit. "I love you," she said to him. "But don't be a boob."

Nanette studied her granddaughter's selfie, taken in the rehabilitation ward at John Hunter hospital, Faheem in the background on his phone. Frances's smile didn't sit right on her face. It rarely did these days. Still, Nanette appreciated the gesture, small as it was. Texts and pictures were easier for Frances than visiting the house on The Hill. Nobody could blame her for that. Though Nanette hadn't told anyone yet, she'd made the decision to sell the property to the developers after all. Get herself a ground-floor townhouse by a bus route, a place with no steps in case her arthritis worsened and she couldn't walk anymore. Nanette tucked the phone away. No, not 'in case her arthritis worsened'. When it worsened.

Carers emerged from behind their computers, sniffing out a waft of faeces. Nanette's cue to head home. She tried to lift the rug out of her husband's hands.

"Come on, let it go, Ian," she said. He didn't. "Ian, please."

Those claw-like fingers clung to the lattice weave.

A rabbit bounce of anger. She could have screamed at him then, threatening to leave and never come back because she was too tired and hurt. But Nanette didn't scream this, or say it. She let the blanket go.

I'm not going to fight you anymore.

If she were going to love someone, she would have to love the whole of him. Front to back. Down and up. Reconcile that he hadn't always been a good person, and neither was she. If you loved someone in their prime then you had to love them on the way out, she supposed. Those lips she used to rub in bed now sat on an old man's face like a wrinkled Band Aid on the bottom of a foot. He used to have a manly smell, an almost savoury stink from working hard and crawling onto the mattress without washing because he was too damn tired, and she'd roll over in the middle of the night and breathe him in and it wasn't just homely, but erotic. Now, he smelled like antiseptic and rot. And she had to be okay with that. She would have to love him, still. Even if his eyes were not his eyes anymore. They used to see her as she really was, and to his credit, Ian rarely questioned what he saw. Now, nothing. Those eyes might as well be toenail clippings trapped in a sink plug. A brain of sawdust. She had gone stretches of her life fawning over him, almost to an embarrassing degree. But she'd despised him at times, too. Now, at the end, all she had to do was tolerate him, and let him have the blanket, even though it was filthy. Anger, she could park with her betrayals. This, Nanette knew, was what it was like to die with someone. It was marriage. Would she kill to keep this, so little as it was, from the vanishings, from it all?

To some degree, she had.

Nanette may not have been the bullet, but she was the gun that night Toni died. She could handle not sleeping. Insomniacs live with guilt all the time.

She squeezed his knee to let him know she was there and kissed his brow. He was cold and clammy. Nanette gave him an opportunity to remember her. The glow from the screen reflected in his waxy skin, lending animation where there was none. She leaned in close. "It's me, Ian." Just a whisper so nobody else could hear. "Me. Your Snowy."

No response.

Nanette slid the paperback she'd placed on the floor into her handbag and straightened her cardigan. She didn't look back on her way to the courtyard where Lauralee sat in a chair in the sun, watching chickens pick at feed one of the staff had sprinkled on the garden. A lit cigarette dangled from her left hand.

Caught, Lauralee rolled her eyes as Nanette slid open the glass door and joined her. "Don't have a go at me, Mum. I told you I'd quit when I'm ready and—"

But Nanette didn't have a go at her daughter. She sidled beside her and extended her shaking index and middle fingers, the universal 'give me a drag' sign. Lauralee gave her mother the once over, likely wondering if this was a trick, and maybe seeing the hunger in Nanette's expression, extended the cigarette butt-first.

The inhale. The burn.

"Tastes just like I remember," Nanette said, handing it back.

After dropping her daughter off at home, declining the offer to hang around until Roy returned and join them for dinner, Nanette drove away but parked around the corner for a while. She cried in her stuffy VW Beetle on the almost empty Mayfield avenue, watched over by big redbrick houses and churches with the windows boarded up. It took a while to settle, but she got there. Or, at least Nanette convinced herself that she was settled. Like the chill, unease had its hooks in her and wouldn't let go. She dabbed her eyes with a handkerchief—

("only old people use hankies," she remembered Toni saying)

—and started up the engine.

It would be good to be greeted by Sandy at the side fence, but going home didn't sit right with her. Not yet. Maybe it was that the days felt longer now, and she didn't want to see the new safety railing the council erected by the cliff's edge on The Hill where Toni, Henry, and Johnny died. The metal glimmered like a cut that never healed.

Nanette drove into the city. It had been years since she'd been down some of those streets. Heritage listed sandstone buildings. Glimmers of ocean between cafés. She parked off Hunter Street and walked, rounding a corner to the Rialto. It didn't matter what was playing, if it had started already or if she had to sit in the foyer to wait for another session, if it was something romantic or frightful or foreign. Being there without Ian was what mattered. Doing so, she believed, would be like letting go. But the cinema was gone.

Afterword:
Little Notes On Little Hurts

This collection opens with a quote from Damien Angelica Walters, cribbed (with permission) from her terrific short story, *S is for Soliloquy*. For those of you who have come this far and would like to journey with me one step further, I now present a soliloquy of my own.

What follows is hardly academic. Hell, I'm not certain half of it makes sense. But it's all real. All raw. These are the little truths behind the little cuts contained in this volume.

"Here is where all the lies end and everything else begins…"

Damage, Inc.

This story was written during a time of intense burnout at my day job where I worked with vulnerable people living with complex mental health needs and a variety of comorbidities.

I knew something wasn't right.

Sleep had become this long-rumoured thing, and when it did eventuate, I'd wake up in the middle of the night trapped by thoughts of clients. I foolishly thought I was impervious to vicarious trauma. Wrong. Something had to change. But like most change—you know, the big stuff—I avoided it for as long as possible. Or maybe I was just afraid. Soul erosion ensued. Exhausted, the boundaries I'd put in place between work and home blurred by the day. I didn't feel like writing much at the time (fatigue was a killer)—but I'd accepted an invite to contribute a story to a Jack Ketchum tribute anthology, and having known the man (this volume of stories is co-dedicated to him), the honour was too great to pass up. *Damage, Inc.* (a reference to the Metallica song of the same name) emerged over a month.

"Write from the wound," Jack, or Dallas as we knew him, often said.

The words purged out of me. Maybe the closest thing I've come to a literary fever.

Once the story was complete, I re-read what I hardly recalled writing, and broke down. There I was on the page, asking for help. Nobody was going to save me but myself. I didn't resign, but I certainly made overdue adaptations in my life. I've since moved on from that job, though I still work with vulnerable cohorts. The tribute anthology didn't eventuate, and that's okay. Maybe it was too soon. Jack hadn't been gone that long. The good folks at Shock Totem released *Damage, Inc.* instead. I dedicated the story to Jack/Dallas. How could I not? It was like he'd guided me through the process in some way, the greatest, and sweetest of all hauntings.

Write from the wound.

I did just that.

For those wondering, the wound is still tender. But at least it's healing.

Cut to Care

This little story—a comic splatter parable of sorts—stemmed from questions that continue to plague me, especially as someone who has worked at the frontline for several years: What if helping others makes *us* feel good about ourselves? What if you became addicted to that validation? Does the super objective make a vampire of us, rendering the good deed invalid to some degree? Does that even matter? Should it matter? If a tree falls in an empty forest, does it make any sound? I just don't know. I honestly don't.

Tallow-Maker, Tallow Made

Ideas are funny things. They sometimes float about, half-formed for years.

One memory: going home to visit my family and being taken out to a graveyard by my aunt who showed us where some of our relatives were buried. There were headstones beyond the boundaries of the consecrated ground. My aunt said these plots belonged to bushrangers.

Another memory: I moved into a new apartment. It was old. Cracks in the ceiling. Loose tiles. The tub wouldn't drain after my first bath. I sloshed in the water, plunging the plug hole. The water turned an ochre colour, like the hue of a smoker's fingertips. I unscrewed the plug and watched my bathtub vomit up a long knot of auburn hair, semi-sealed in a putty of soap scum.

A final memory: remembering hearing how fingernails and hair continues to grow for a while after a person dies. This struck me as a fitting metaphor for grief.

Yeah, ideas are funny things. The way they float about. But not half as funny—or rewarding—as those special moments when these disparate blobs come together and congeal.

Boom.

Nona Doesn't Dance

I worked in nursing homes to fund myself through university.

There were family members who would only visit our residents—their loved ones—on special occasions.

We carers knew who these strangers were from conversations we'd had with residents after showering them, talk that was sometimes triggered by seeing photographs on the mantlepieces in their little rooms as we picked their incontinence pads off the floor. We would watch from the nurses' station as our residents, propped up in wheelie recliners in the common area, pretended to *not* be in pain on Christmas Day, to *not* be hurt that they had been abandoned, to *not* resent that their sons and daughters and nieces and nephews only came to see them out of obligation. Our residents would smile. They would hug these strangers, the ones from the photographs. They would offer sweets from tin boxes (the lids always made a loud noise when dropped on the floor). And this, all this, the whole performance, our residents did for the benefit of these strangers once a year, on the only day they were allowed to be remembered.

This story stems from those feelings. The feelings are sad, and maybe more than a little angry.

Little Balloons

I don't have a story about where this one came from. How about I dedicate it to someone instead?

When I was in my early twenties, a friend and I were walking up Oxford Street towards Taylor Square in Sydney. It was the dim hours of a Saturday morning. We had been hopping from one gay bar to another and had decided to call it a night. It was summer and we were doused in sweat, sticky with spilled alcohol. There was a pub on the corner with wide open windows flanked with rainbow flags. The window was crammed with men and women, a jigsaw of smiling faces. Thudding music. A car pulled up at the curb not three or four strides ahead of us. Two large men jumped out of the car, ran across the footpath, and reached through the window to stab a young guy in the neck with a broken beer bottle.

Little Balloons is for him. I hope he's alive.

Eels

Versions of this story had been swirling about in my head for years in various incarnations. One such version was a short film I made at university called *White on Grey and Flower Print*, which was about a young photographer on a country road who is approached by a bloodied woman who has obviously been in a car accident. Instead of helping this woman, our photographer gets click-happy. This short film, shot on video and edited between two VHS machines, ended up winning multiple awards and screened at festivals around Australia. I'd never been fully happy with it. There was more to that story, I just knew it.

I often dream that there is an eel in my bed. I think the eel is guilt. I'm not sure what I've done, but I know I deserve the panic it evokes.

The film. The eel. These two mental projects—one healthy, the other strangely condemning—congealed in 2020. And the rest, as they say, is (literary) history. Except for the eel in my bed in the middle of the night. It still comes to wriggle against my legs, snapping at my toes.

The Acknowledged

I couldn't make it home for Christmas one year because of the pandemic. I booked myself into a hotel outside of Bowral, New South Wales, instead. If I was going to be alone for the silly season, I might as well be alone on a nice comfy bed with air conditioning and a bottle of wine. It was nice, actually. Despite being quite social by nature, solitude fuels me. And I needed fuelling after the year that had just passed.

On Boxing Day, I loaded up the car and headed back to Canberra. I stopped off at a National Park for a bush walk along the way. I didn't have enough water, but assumed I'd be okay because I had no real intention of staying out too long. I didn't notify anyone where I was because nothing would go wrong. Not to someone like me, right? I didn't take a map with me, either. I was only going to go on the short route. There were signs. Easy! I'd be back in twenty minutes, snug in my car in no time at all, ready to get back on the road, having exercised off some of my Christmas indulgence.

Well, I got lost in the National Park.

This fact rendered me immobile for ten minutes. I stood there, baking in my fuckupery. The route I'd selected was signposted, sure. But the harsh Australian sun had bleached the colour-coded arrows a uniform white. I was going in circles, burning up, thirsty. There's a misapprehension that everything in the bush wants to kill you. Nothing kills more people in the bush than human error.

As to how I got back to my car, I'll never know.

But I did. Luck had a lot to do with it.

I remember turning a corner, the trees peeling back, and seeing my blue Mazda 3 in the lot. Heatwaves made the car look like it was at the bottom of a lake. Semi-crazed with exhaustion, I got into the car, stripped down to my underwear and blasted the air conditioning as hard as it would go, crying as I plastered my body in wet wipes I kept in the backseat, drinking water so quickly it rolled down my chin, looking in the rear-view mirror and calling myself an idiot over and over again. I guess writing *The Acknowledged* was my way of acknowledging that. A kind of promise to myself to never be that stupid again.

Too Old for Ice Cream

This story stemmed from two core memories.

Our old childhood house was situated across from a train track—the way the house shook when the freights rolled by in the night, us boys listening to them rumbling on and on from our bunk beds. In these recollections, it's always summer.

The other memory was of the pub in town. The way it smelled. How it felt welcoming but adult, a glimpse of a maybe future where grownups had the authority to come and go wherever and whenever they wanted, and how that world—boozy and sloppy around the edges—seemed attractive and frightening.

I've learned that many people I've met since then, spent their youth facing terror, wishing days away so they could grow up quickly and battle evil head-on. But then, once older and still haunted by that terror, they do nothing but wish for the years to reverse so they can climb back into the snug naïvety of their childhoods where at least there existed (if only for a short while) the hope that things get better.

Love Amongst the Red Back Spiders

Growing up gay hasn't always been easy. There have been times when it's been astronomically hard. But then I remember that people like me stand on the shoulders of giants. When I remember this, my little problems in my little life start to shrink. And shrink.

Love Amongst the Red Back Spiders was always my way of honouring those giants.

I—we—owe them a lot.

Shadow Debt

I was in my early twenties, backpacking around the world, and found myself in Santorini, Greece. It was the offseason. I was driving my rental around a mountain and was waved down by a woman in a black dress. The woman was screaming. There were men in the field across the street looking for something—or someone.

The woman didn't speak a lick of English and I spoke about as much Greek. But somehow, through a combination of hand signals and the motherly desperation beaming off her like heat, I ascertained that she was asking me to help her find a child.

A couple of cars sped around the blind corner, kicking dust. If there was a kid on that road anytime soon, it would be mowed down. Of that, there was no doubt.

I took to the field with the others.

The distant sound of vehicles reached my ears. I glanced at the corner that I, myself, had peeled around at too great a speed only minutes before. The child was there. He marched towards the road with his yo-yo, towards the sound. I've never run so fast.

I swooped the boy up, his mother and the other adults rushing to me, pulling him out of my arms. Cars zoomed by behind us. The family, bowing, kissing my hands, returned to the house (every inch of it was white) and drew the door shut. I stood beside my rental. Dead silence everywhere. The winter air was cool on my face. It dawned on me that I hadn't just helped someone in need, but I had quite likely saved that young boy's life.

Shadow Debt stemmed from this day in Santorini. It percolated for years, emerging fully formed after talking to my old personal carer friends who were still working in the nursing homes during the pandemic. They wept when they told me about their residents, how alone they were (and as I knew only too well, those residents had been alone to begin with). I knew then that I wanted the hero of *Shadow Debt* (if a hero she is) to emerge from that world. I wanted to make visible someone younger people had forced into invisibility, someone that someone else deemed irrelevant. Because of their age.

To that hero, to all the heroes like her, I just want to say, *I see you*.

The debt is ours. Not yours.

Aaron Dries
Canberra, Australia
February 2022

Story Publishing History

Horror Hurts: An introduction to CUT TO CARE by Mick Garris (original to this collection)

Damage, Inc. (First published in *Shock Totem 11: Curious Tales of the Macabre and Twisted*, Shock Totem Publications, 2019)

Cut to Care (original to this collection)

Tallow-Maker, Tallow Made (original to this collection)

Nona Doesn't Dance (original to this collection)

Little Balloons (original to this collection)

Eels (First published electronically as *The Woman with Eels in her Mouth* at the Does the Dog Die In This? Blog, 2020)

The Acknowledged (written for *Pink Triangle: Rhapsody*, LVP Publications, 2022, but first published in *Cut to Care: A Collection of Little Hurts*, IFWG Publishing, 2022)

Too Old for Ice-cream (original to this collection)

Love Amongst the Redback Spiders (First published in *Tales from the Lake Vol. 2*, Crystal Lake Publishing, 2016)

Shadow Debt (original to this collection)